I0680787

Finch Books by Jennifer Walker

Single Books
Within the Folds of a Swan's Wing
Finding Aloha

FINDING ALOHA

JENNIFER WALKER

Finding Aloha
ISBN # 978-1-83943-759-5
©Copyright Jennifer Walker 2022
Cover Art by Fiona Jayde ©Copyright February 2022
Interior text design by Claire Siemaszkiewicz
Finch Books

Published in 2022 by Finch Books, United Kingdom.

Finch Books is an imprint of Totally Entwined Group Limited.

FINDING
ALOHA

Dedication

To Mom and Dad,
who introduced me to the magic of Maui.

To the Hawaiian people, for your graciousness in
sharing your home, in acknowledgment that the
island — and all of its beauty — belongs to you.

Chapter One

The garlic from Dad's Caesar salad clings to my breath and burns my eyes as I hide away under this stifling blanket.

Crap. I should've brushed my teeth. *Why didn't I think about brushing my teeth?*

I rack my brain trying to remember where I might have put a pack of gum or a Tic Tac, or God, even one of those disgusting cough drops. But my mind comes up blank.

My chest burns, forcing me to do some of those short, panicky breaths dogs do when they first show up at the vet. It's been forever since I've taken a fresh breath of air. All I want to do is toss these suffocating blankets off me and smooth the frizzy mane my hair has become. But I'm paralyzed, terrified someone will barge in without knocking and my nightly rendezvous with Marcus won't be able to continue.

In one desperate move, I pop my face out of the covers and gulp in air like it's water from an oasis.

Sweet, sweet oxygen!

My brain starts functioning again and has a chance to fantasize about what's about to take place. How thrilling it's going to be to see his face again...to kiss those lips, press my body against his. The deceit... The sneaking out... I'm not going to lie. It makes this all feel so...so...*badass*. And lately, well lately, I've enjoyed a bit of badass.

As if he knows right this second that I'm thinking about him, there's a buzz in the pocket of my jeans, and it sends a deeper buzz through the rest of my body.

Without rustling the covers, I carefully slide my hand under my butt and pry my phone out without allowing my bed to creak and groan. The screen lights up and buzzes again, making me smile with what's written. It's from Marcus.

You coming? I'm already here. Can't wait to see you. Brought a little treat for us too.

He sends an emoji of two people kissing, followed by a leaf emoji. Meaning he's brought a joint, but I giggle because it looks like he's brought us a salad. *Is there a weed emoji?* Probably better he didn't use that anyway, just in case Mom and Dad ever creep on my phone. No one can get in trouble for sneaking out to eat a salad.

I expertly navigate the screen with my thumb as I text him back underneath the covers.

Yeah, I think they're both asleep. Coming now. Can't wait to see you too – and eat salad with you lol.

In one swift movement, I throw the covers off and roll over to sit up. As I stand, I reach around to return my phone to the back pocket of my jeans, but it slips through my hand and lands with a crash on the hardwood floor.

Shit.

I'm not sure whether it's loud enough for my parents to hear. I still my body and hold my breath one more time, listening for any sign of footsteps through the hall.

I'm sleepwalking. That's what I'll tell them. *Yeah, if they ask, I'll just mumble something incoherent about algebra, then wander back to bed, pretending not to remember in the morning.* I might have a tough time explaining why I'm sleeping in jeans and a T-shirt, but whatever. It's not like I can get in trouble for sleepwalking. I mean, how could I get in trouble for something I don't even remember?

I wait for a few more seconds, then exhale a slow and relieved breath, because all is silent other than the faint *sh...sh...sh...*of my dad's CPAP machine in the other room. *Alleluia for sleep apnea!* It has made this whole sneaking out thing way easier. The only downside is that Mom has recently made the spare bedroom on the main floor her own personal refuge. She claimed Dad was just too noisy to sleep beside, which was weird at first. He used to snore louder than a train whistle before the machine, and she didn't seem to have a problem with it then.

But when I started questioning why they were sleeping in separate rooms, it got me thinking about Tamara Lindsay. Poor Tamara Lindsay, who accidentally walked in on her parents in a very compromising position—*position number 69* if we want to get real about it. And now Tamara is damaged for life. Seriously. The details Tamara gave? No one needs to see their parents doing that.

So, I figured *whatever*. If Mom and Dad no longer want to sleep together, it just means that at least I won't ever have to worry about walking in on things Moms and Dads should *not* be allowed to do. What it does mean is that I have to be a little more careful about creeping past Mom's bedroom downstairs.

I crane my head toward my bedroom door and don't hear any footsteps coming up the stairs. I'm positive Mom is asleep by now.

I peer at the clock as I reach down to retrieve my phone.

Twelve-fourteen a.m.

Yeah, they've both got to be asleep for sure.

My jacket is draped over one arm, and I hold my pair of red Converse with my other hand as I inch my way across my room. I open the door soundlessly, grateful that I convinced Dad to fix the creak in it last weekend. After a quick glance across the hall and into the front room, I gently close the door behind me and tiptoe all the way down the stairs, making sure to skip the step third from the bottom because of the groan it makes. My heart gallops like a racehorse the whole way. I'm convinced Mom and Dad are going to barge out of their rooms any second to pounce on me.

But somehow I slide past Mom's bedroom without incident and make it to the back patio door. I don't dare creep out through the garage or the front door. That would basically be suicide. But the patio door is quiet, discreet and leads to a perfect escape route just left of the house. There's a large pine tree there, wedged between the fence and the shed. It creates cover and forms a darkened shadow, despite the glare of the porch light that is always left on. All I need to do is inch my way down the length of the shadow, all the way to the far corner of the yard. The fence is old and needs to be rebuilt, and sharp slivers dig into my bare arms as I slide along it. But I'm eternally thankful for my parents' procrastination in fixing it so my nightly escapades can continue.

Once I reach the end of the yard, I pry loose the third board from the left, the one I wedged back in last night. I lean it against the neighboring boards and squeeze myself through the ten-inch gap in the fence.

Crap, my T-shirt snags on a rough edge of wood as I squeeze through, and I swear under my breath. I just paid full price for it at H&M. *Oh well, this is worth it — totally worth it.*

The entire world belongs to me as I race through the back alley, the glow of streetlights chasing me as I run. There's a crispness in the air — a sure sign of autumn's impending arrival — but that's not the reason for the outbreak of goosebumps all over my arms. Every inch of my skin tingles, and my heart races from exertion and anticipation. I don't slow until I reach the chain link fence enclosing the park of the elementary school down the street.

It's here that I slow to a walk, because, well, it's not like I want *him* thinking I'm this excited. *No, I've got to play it cool.* I let my breathing slow, slip my jacket on as an attempt at camouflaging all those goosebumps and make my way through the gate of the playground.

He sways gently on the tire swing, a beautiful human pendulum with ripped jeans and scruffy blond hair. His sneakers brush the sand with each pass and the chain croaks with his weight. He doesn't see me. He doesn't sense that I'm there. And I love the element of surprise, my growing sense of urgency. I quicken to a run the last few steps, kicking sand up as I go. I reach my arms around him from behind, his delicious boy-smell filling my nostrils as I press my face into his neck.

"Guess who?" I whisper into his ear.

"I hope it's who I think it is or this is gonna be super-awkward." He doesn't turn as he says it, causing me to doubt my confidence just a bit. Then he reaches around smoothly, pulling me onto his lap and swiveling me around so our faces are just inches apart. "Oh, good, just the person I was hoping it would be." And that mischievous smile of his is irresistible once again. I can't help but reach up to pull his lips down to mine, our bodies a jumble of arms and legs jutting from the hanging tire.

Eventually, we untangle our entwined bodies and trade the tire swing for a picnic table. We stretch out and light a joint, the glowing embers twinkling like one of the distant stars hanging in the night sky.

"I remember when I first saw you at the mall that day, at the beginning of summer. You were all shy and quiet, like you didn't even want to be noticed. How could you ever think you'd just blend in?" He nudges my shoulder playfully as he takes a long toke, then passes the joint to me.

I inhale deeply, then roll over onto my back, tilting my face up to the black, velvety canopy of sky. "I don't know, Marcus. I just thought you were into Maggie. Everyone is—and that's fine by me. I mean, she's my best friend for a reason. It's because she's awesome. If I were into girls, I think I'd be after Maggie too." I giggle and pass the joint back to him.

"Yeah, Maggie's great, but...I don't know. You were the one who caught my attention. It's like you don't need to try so hard, like you have a quiet confidence that she doesn't. Not everything needs to revolve around you all the time. What you show the world is the real you. And I, for one, really like it." Marcus leans over to give me a soft kiss on the lips.

"I just can't believe we've only been together for a little over a month. I never thought when I saw you that day, that it would actually turn into something. You were all—I don't know—cute and cool… It just sucks we don't go to the same school. I mean, what's going to happen in a couple of weeks when school starts? How are we going to keep this going?"

"Trust me. We'll find a way…" The words drip off his tongue, slow and sticky like honey, and he leans in to start nibbling my neck. He drapes his right leg over mine and scoots in closer, so our bodies are flush. Then he inches his fingers just under the hem of my T-shirt, so his palm lies flat on my stomach. It sends an electric buzz through my entire body, but nagging thoughts in the back of my mind dull the feeling.

"But seriously, what's our plan? It's our senior year. I'll be super-swamped with the swim club, and you said you're hoping to be captain of your school's hockey team this year. Plus, my parents are totally going to be on top of me when it comes to my grades. They're really pushing for me to get into a good college. I don't know… I just worry that we're going to fizzle out, that this is just a *summer* thing." The word 'summer' comes out sharp and thorny, scratching the back of my throat.

"Relax, Jess. Things have a way of working out. Let's just enjoy the time we have together now and think about the future tomorrow." He continues his trail of kisses, his fingers creeping up to my ribcage. "This has been the best part of summer, and summer's not over yet."

My skin melts wherever his fingers touch, turning me into a swirling palette of watercolor, the tones becoming more vibrant with each of his breaths on my neck, each of his kisses on my lips. I push the nagging feeling of summer's end to the back of my mind and enjoy the pleasures of right now.

Eventually I nudge Marcus away, realizing I've been gone way too long. Sneaking back into the house is always the worst part of the night, and the closer we are to morning, the more likely it is my parents will wake up with the tiniest of noises. Dealing with an intense grilling session about my whereabouts is not how I want this night to end.

"So, I'll see you this week sometime? Maybe you can come by when my parents are at work?" I ask.

"Uh, yeah, sure. Sounds good. I've got nothing going on this week." The indifference in his words stings. He obviously doesn't feel my same sense of urgency. He tugs on his sweatshirt, then tilts his face down to give me one more quick kiss on the mouth. "I know how you get all up in your head about stuff, but let's just try to enjoy the end of the summer, okay? We'll worry about the rest when we need to."

I give him a slight nod and a weak smile, but I don't feel his confidence. The uncertainty of the changing seasons sparks an uncertainty about us. The phrase 'summer fling' flits around in my brain like a frightened sparrow, and I can't seem to catch it and tuck it away.

"Okay, so I'll text you later in the week then." He squeezes my hand as he takes a step backward. "I promise, things will work out. Stop stressing!" he calls, readjusting his cap and shuffling back the opposite way through the field. I feel a stab of hurt about the casualness of his goodbye, but I force my mind to replay every delicious moment prior to that, until the tingling in my body convinces me all's right with the world.

My solo walks home after my secret rendezvous with Marcus always have me feeling giddy and lightheaded, but today's race home feels extra wobbly, due to the slight buzz I got from the joint. I'm lost in my thoughts as I slide the patio door open and have almost made it past the kitchen island when my name slices through the silence.

"Jess, sit down. We need to talk."

Crap, crap, crap! I glance at the clock on the microwave.

Two forty-three a.m.

My brain races through a thousand lies I could come up with to try to squirm out of this situation.

"Uh, sorry, Mom. I had a coffee after dinner last night and I think it caused insomnia. I thought taking a walk in the brisk air might help me to fall back — "

"No, Jess, this isn't about you out in the middle of the night, although we'll get to that. I've had insomnia myself over the last little while, and I just can't take it anymore. I know this isn't the best time for either of us to talk, but I'm not sure I'll have the same confidence if I wait until morning."

I avoid Mom's heavy gaze and brace myself for the lecture of a lifetime. But it doesn't come.

"Jess, please sit down." Her words come out soft and hesitant, almost apologetic.

I double-check the time on the clock in case I've got things all wrong and it's much earlier than I think. But no, it is clearly the middle of the night, and my sly attempt at sneaking back in seems to be the last thing on my mother's mind.

I steal a glance at her and notice, for the first time, her red-rimmed and puffy eyes, and how her ragged robe, cinched tight at the waist, makes her look gaunt, almost child-like. *When did Mom lose so much weight?*

Her hands, pale and thin, tremble so badly that she keeps pressing them together, almost as if in prayer.

I reluctantly shuffle over to the kitchen table and plunk down on one of the chairs, my head swimming, my eyes probably bloodshot. Suddenly, I'm very confused, remnants of the weed pulsing through my veins and making my thoughts patchy, disconnected. The only other time I've seen Mom looking this lost and broken was years ago, when my grandfather died. A flurry of names and faces fly through my head. *Who in my life could have possibly met with a terrible fate? Is it Dad? Is it Gran?*

There's electricity in the air like right before a violent summer storm. I can't help but wonder what kind of damage it's going to cause. I reach my hand out to hers, trying to anchor the two of us to the kitchen table to calm her fraying nerves. Anxiety and trepidation swirl around us.

"Mom, what's going on? You're scaring me."

"Jess…" She breathes my name out with an exhausted sigh. The red rims of her eyes glisten with tears that are ready to spill. She pulls her hand away from mine, immediately creating a space between us.

Oh my God, it's my mom. *My mom.* She's the one who's sick or dying, or whatever this is about. That explains the trembling, the loss of weight, the fact that she's so rail-thin right now that her left hand is even devoid of her wedding ring.

"Mom, what happened? Are you sick? Is it cancer? How long have you known?" I close my eyes tight and hold in a breath, like shuttering a home right before the first surge of a hurricane. It seems that by locking myself down for a moment, I'm better able to brace myself for this impending doom.

"No, Jess, I'm not sick. It's not that. God, no, I'm fine."

The air starts escaping my lungs like a slow leak in a tire. I snap my eyes open because it's going to be okay. *Mom is fine. She's okay.* There's still a question of what the hell is going on, but it can't be worse than that. It surely can't be worse than that.

Mom breathes in like she's about to dive to the bottom of the pool, then spews poison through her mouth, her words burning me to the ground. "I've met someone else—another man." She pauses, looking down at her hands that are folded in her lap, as if they give her the cues for what to say next. Then she looks back up at me. And with her eyes and her words, she causes a black hole to implode my insides. "He and I...well...we're expecting a baby. I'm leaving your father."

The storm finally surges, a tornado of feelings threatening to carry me away.

"What the hell are you talking about?" is all I manage. My throat starts closing up as if the moisture from it has been sponged dry and I've been left with a pasty scum covering the inside of my mouth.

I don't know what she's talking about. *Did I hear things right?* I thought something bad had happened to *someone else*, not to *me*. I was just *consoling* my mother, for God's sake! I'm having a hard time comprehending how the last five minutes have unraveled so disastrously that I find myself begging to go back to the simple horror of being caught sneaking out with a boy.

"I'm sorry, Mom. I know I shouldn't have lied about where I was. I wasn't out for a brisk walk. I was meeting a friend—my boyfriend, actually. His name is Marcus, and you'll really like him, I think. I can bring him by the house so you and Dad can meet him and—"

"Jess, I don't care about your lies or being with a boy. Well, not right now at least. We need to talk. What I'm telling you is real, and it's important. Please listen to me."

But the words coming out of her mouth are flat and tinny, like they're being broadcast from an old-fashioned radio. I work to grasp the meaning of what she's saying, but I only catch random phrases, and it's like I'm trying to put together a puzzle without being able to look at the picture on the box.

"We've worked together for a long time and have grown very close over the years."

"Your dad and I have been leading separate lives for a while now, and we both knew this was coming. It would have ended years ago if it weren't for you holding us together."

"The baby wasn't planned, but Robert and I see now what a gift it'll be. It'll allow us all a new start. You'll be a big sister, just like you've always dreamed!"

And that's when the fireballs start spewing from my mouth, like when I get the stomach flu and can't stop puking. Swear words, accusations, questions—they all just shoot out of me faster and louder, until I can't even keep track of what I'm saying.

"What the hell do you mean, Mom? This doesn't make any sense. You're having a *baby*? You've been having an *affair*? Like, with another man? What about Dad? What about *me*?"

"I didn't plan for this, Jess. Your dad and me? Well, we've just sort of drifted apart. It has nothing to do with you. We just want different things out of our marriage right now."

When she mentions Dad, I suddenly remember that he's the other person in this messed-up family. *Where's Dad?* I suddenly need him urgently, as if his presence might dampen the blow that just hit me.

"Dad? Dad?" I scream at the top of my lungs. Immediately, I see movement on the stairs, like he's been waiting in the wings to be called in. He rushes over to me, dressed in his plaid pajamas and a robe identical to my mother's—a present from me two Christmases ago, when I thought it would be cute for them to be the same, to be a matching pair. I catch a whiff of whiskey on his breath as he tries to embrace me in a hug, and for some reason, this only heightens the anger inside me.

"How long have you known about this?" I push away from him and scowl.

"Jess, calm down and we'll talk this through." He takes a deep breath. "I found out about the affair around a month and a half ago, near the start of the summer. And I was angry…so angry." He wipes the palms of his hands down his face, pulling at the sagging skin as he does. "But your mother and I have been together for almost twenty years, so at first we tried to work things out. We really did try." He meets my gaze with pleading eyes. "But, ultimately, it's not what either of us wants anymore.

"Then last week, when your mother told me about the pregnancy, well…" He takes a deep breath and swallows hard, his face suddenly turning steely. "Obviously, that means we're done for good." It's only now that my dad's voice takes on a razor-sharp edge.

"Your mother wasn't supposed to tell you until tomorrow. She was going to take you out to lunch, where you'd be able to talk things through in a little more detail. But apparently"—he glares at her with an icy stare—"she couldn't wait and decided to spring this on you in the middle of the night. Your mother always did have a knack for the dramatic." Bitter sarcasm drips off every word. "But, now that you know, I suppose it's best if we all sit down and discuss this as a family."

I find his choice of the word *family* a bit sardonic, and I glare angrily at him. He ignores my rigid body language and comes close to me again, attempting to hold me, hug me…but I feel like I'm suffocating in the velvety folds of his robe, and I thrash him away once more.

That's when he moves away from me and goes to stand with *her*.

"Jess, I know this is a lot to take in, especially all of a sudden, in the middle of the night. Your mom and I haven't been happy for a long time. We've grown apart. Did I want this to happen? No. Did I know she'd fallen in love with Robert from payroll? No. But I've also had time to reflect on the fact that I'm not blameless in all of this. And I guess I should've fought a little harder a whole lot earlier on.

"But in truth, neither one of us really wants this anymore. So…yes. Your mom is moving out to be with Robert. And we all need to discuss some options with you. Things are going to change. We think for the better, although we know this initial shock is going to be really hard for you. But you need to know how much we love you. Both of us."

I can't believe my ears. *How on earth can he defend her right now, after what she's just admitted?*

I don't dare glance over at my mother or I run the risk of poking her eyes out. In the back of my mind, I keep thinking that God is punishing me. I knew all the lying and sneaking around would catch up to me, and somehow, I would be punished. I just didn't think it would be like this.

I stand paralyzed in the middle of the kitchen for a few more moments, because really, I don't know where to go. The clock on the microwave now reads nearly three a.m. and I have a hard time believing that my life has completely turned upside-down in less than a half-hour. Less than the equivalent of one single episode of *The Simpsons* has erased the entire world I live in.

I push past my parents and through the front door. I'm so eager to get away from the house that I stumble over my own feet as I race down the driveway and catch myself before completely falling on my face. Then I run. I run and I run and I don't feel my legs reaching or my arms pumping, but I have this crazy idea that if I move fast enough, I'll break away from the nightmare my life has just become.

Several minutes later, I become vaguely aware that the pavement beneath my feet has transformed to silky sand, and I find myself flopping into the rusty tire swing that held so much excitement just a few hours before.

Divorce? A new baby? I plant the toes of my right sneaker in the dimple of wet sand directly beneath the swinging tire and use the rest of my body weight to twist the chain around and around. The tension grows and the tire creeps higher and higher until my toe can't anchor my body any further, spinning me recklessly out of control as the heavy night air whips by around me.

Chapter Two

"So, she was, like, screwing some guy from work this whole time? How long has this been going on for? And your dad had no idea?" Maggie and I are draped on our stomachs across her pale pink bedspread, her flip-sequin pillow providing me with a welcome distraction from having to look at her head on.

After spending a half an hour or so at the park clearing my head in the early morning hours, I reluctantly went back home. Mom and Dad were sitting at the kitchen table, exactly where I'd left them, as if we were going to jump right back into conversation. They had been calling me repeatedly, but after I refused to answer the first fifteen calls, I think they decided it was better to give me some space. After walking through the front door, I bolted straight for my bedroom without saying a word to them. My body ached with exhaustion, and I felt utterly drained. I lay in bed for a long time, my anger toward my mother coming and going in waves. I just couldn't imagine my mother—the same mom who'd volunteered at every one of my swim meets, the same mom who'd made Dad and me crepes every Sunday morning, despite her revulsion for eggs — was having an *affair*. The word was dirty and cheap, something that belonged in a sleazy daytime talk show, not a word to describe the dismantling of my family.

I woke early this morning to a quiet house. Mom was downstairs sipping a coffee, waiting for me to appear.

"Where's Dad?" I asked her coldly, feeling resentment for having to speak to her at all.

"He needed to get a few errands done this morning. Here… Let me grab you a coffee or some breakfast. Are you ready to talk?"

There were many things I wanted to say to my mom, but none of them were what she wanted to hear.

"No, not to you." I said sharply. "I'm going to Maggie's." I'd turned my back on her before the words were even out of my mouth, and I slammed the door behind me.

Maggie… Maggie would know what to do. Maggie would be able to take some of the hurt and weight and anger that suffocated me, and she would show me how to breathe again.

And, sure enough, when she'd opened her front door eating a heaping bowl of Frosted Flakes, wearing pajama pants and an old T-shirt, all she had to do was look into my tear-stained eyes and I could tell she understood that something monumental, something life-altering, had just gone down in my world. She put her cereal bowl down on the front table in her foyer, wrapped me in a giant, boob-squishing hug and breathed into my hair, "Damn, girl. What the hell happened?"

Right there on her front door mat, I collapsed like a crushed soda can, and I sobbed. I cried and I screamed, and I rambled on incoherently for a long time — a really long time. She sat there beside me with her arm wrapped around my back, her face pressed against my hair, a soothing shushing sound whispering into my ear.

And that was all I needed at that moment. The thing about best friends? It's like they see into your soul and give you exactly what you need without you having to ask.

I lay here in her bedroom now, avoiding the inevitable fact that at some point I'll have to make my way back home. *Home...* The word wobbles in the back of my throat as if its meaning has been forever altered — a crumpled-up piece of paper that's been folded and refolded a thousand times and is now only a remnant of what it once was. Thinking about home makes me think about family, and that makes me think about moms. *My* mom. The same mom who has broken up my family, smashing my world to pieces for some dork named Robert. In my head I say 'Robert' with a slight French accent just to make him sound even sleazier, and it conjures up images of a scrawny, weasel-like man with a half-grown mustache, pale skin and way too many raised moles all over his body.

"She's seriously having a baby with this guy? No offense, but that's so gross. I mean, isn't your mom in her forties?"

Maggie's right. My mom just celebrated her forty-third birthday a few months before. Dad and I took her out to Olive Garden because she begged us to, saying that she had been refraining from eating carbs for an entire week, just so she could capitalize on the never-ending pasta bowl for one perfect night.

Dad is a restaurant snob and protested the whole week before her birthday. He convinced her that we would all have a much better meal at one of the fancy restaurants downtown. In the end, Mom won the argument, like she always does. So, Olive Garden it was. I remember thinking the restaurant smelled vaguely like vomit because of the parmesan cheese, and Dad grumbled and steamed as the pimply-faced hostess announced that it would be a forty-minute wait for us to get in. He complained that any restaurant not taking reservations wasn't a restaurant a sane human being should bother going to.

"Why would anyone bother waiting for forty minutes to get pre-packaged salad and greasy breadsticks?"

He plunked down on the sticky vinyl waiting bench in his Italian leather loafers and Hugo Boss suit, and he stewed.

I should have known right then and there that things between them were sagging, that the love for me, and for our life together, was just not enough anymore.

My mom spent the meal exaggerating the deliciousness of every bite, eager to enjoy her birthday night out, despite my dad's grumpiness. But at the same time, there was a distance between her and us, like she was sitting in a bubble on her own on the other side of the booth — like she was putting on a show.

My dad wasn't much better. He didn't even touch his food, saying he would rather stop for take-out on the way home. So instead, he ordered a double rye and ginger and stared stone-faced into his phone.

The evening went on in an awkward sphere of silence until the Olive Garden staff came over to sing *Happy Birthday* to Mom. She clapped her hands and pretended that it was a total surprise, that she didn't know it was coming, and Dad…? Well, Dad said he had to take an important call and he just stomped out to the car.

Come to think of it, that was the night Mom started sleeping downstairs. *"Because of Dad's snoring,"* they'd said. *"Because it would be better for both of us,"* they'd said.

Right.

So, yeah, I guess I should have known. But no one wants to admit their family is internally combusting.

With this thought, I roll over onto my back and throw the pillow into the air, punching it on the way down so that it smacks back into Maggie's quilted headboard. Then I sit up to try to clear my head for a moment, flames of anger starting to flicker in the base of my belly.

"Maggie, I'm just so pissed—mostly at my mom, but at everything really. It just sucks. It's just not fair!"

"I know, Jess. But honestly, things'll work out. I mean, sure, your parents may not be together anymore, and it'll be tough having your mom move out, but everything else will be the same. You'll still live at home with your dad, you'll still go to Mount Pleasant High School, you'll still be on the swim team, you'll still be best friends with the coolest girl at school…" She giggles and swats at me, and I pick up the sequin pillow one more time, this time throwing it at her shoulder.

"God, I love you, Maggie. You always know what I need to feel better." In this moment, I'm overwhelmed with feelings of gratitude for her—for my best friend, who seems to be the only one in the world I can count on right now.

We enjoy a moment of quiet contentedness, then Maggie raises her eyebrows and gives a knowing smirk. "So, how are things going with, um...Marcus? Are you guys still, like, hanging out?"

"Yeah, that's how this whole thing about my parents came out in the end. Mom was up when I was sneaking back in, although she hasn't even given me any trouble about it yet. I'm sure that's on the horizon, though. But now, it's not exactly like she can ground me for meeting up secretly with a guy when she herself *has spent the last year meeting up secretly with a guy*." The irony baffles me.

"And so, are you guys a couple then? Like, for real? Or is this just a summer thing?"

"Well, I don't really know. He says it's for real and I want it to work, but sometimes I get this weird vibe from him. But maybe it's just in my head. You know how I can get sometimes."

Instead of saying anything, she gets up off the bed and walks to her dresser across the room. She opens the small wooden jewelry box sitting on top and picks out various rings to try on each of her fingers. Then she lifts her French lavender perfume spray and begins spritzing it on her neck and wrists. Her silence speaks more than words.

"Mags, what's up? Why aren't you saying anything? Do you not like him or something?"

She's fighting to get a silver infinity ring off her left thumb when she spins to face me.

"I don't know, Jess. Maybe it's not meant to be a serious thing. And that's okay too. I mean, do you really want to start your senior year with a boyfriend? You guys had a great summer together, and maybe you need to just see it as it is—a fun and carefree summer. Maybe you just need to let it go."

She lifts her wrist to her nose to take a sniff, then looks down, her attention refocused on twisting the silver thumb ring.

I'm completely caught off-guard by her comments. They are definitely not what I'm wanting to hear at this moment. Her words are an icy stab in my chest, and I shoot her a fierce look as I peel myself off the bed to gather my belongings.

"You know what, Maggie? You're just jealous. You're jealous because for once...for once in your life, a guy isn't all after you. Is it so hard for you to believe that a guy can be into *me*? What? Am I not pretty enough or cool enough or whatever? God... I thought you were the one person who had my back!"

"Jess, you know I didn't mean that. You know how much I love you. You're my BFF. I'm just looking out for you. And if he's a cool guy, then great. Maybe things will stay strong all through the school year and you'll end up marrying the guy. Who knows? I'm just saying, as of right now, I would be cautious. I don't want you to think that it's more than it is."

I turn to give her a pleading look. "I really want this, Mags, and I need you on my side. God, I really need you on my side right now." I tear up again, even though I thought I had rid my body of all the tears it could ever possibly make.

My mind races back to my mom—my mom and the loser she's been sleeping with. Suddenly, out of nowhere, I feel such a sharp fury of anger toward her that it makes me physically sick.

"Maggie, I just can't believe she did this to me—to us—to my dad." As quickly as they came, the tears subside and are replaced with a rage so violent that it causes my hands to shake and my face to burn hot.

"What the hell does my mom think she's doing? She's such a freaking hypocrite. How can she ban me from dating, from sneaking out, from doing anything, when she's been sneaking out for more than a year herself?" As I admit the words out loud, it gives me a sense of power over her. She has no jurisdiction over me. Whatever she wants to say about Marcus and me, or any boy I want to date, doesn't matter. She has no legitimacy at all. She's a two-faced cheater and I'm ready to call her out. I'm ready to let her know that from now on, I make my own choices and I'll date whoever I want. From now on, I don't give a rat's ass what she thinks about anything.

"Maggie, I've gotta go. It's time I face my mom and tell her what I think. I'm choosing how to live my life from now on."

I jump off her bed with a newfound sense of hope and enthusiasm. Things are going to turn out okay after all.

Except that they're not. Everything is definitely *not* okay—because as I round the corner from Maggie's house, I find my dad on the front lawn with some woman in an ugly gray pantsuit, hair-sprayed bangs and three-inch stilettos that are aerating the lawn. They're laughing and chatting while Dad swings a rubber mallet two more times on top of a For Sale sign that is glinting in the sun.

"Dad?" is all I manage as I race, full force, down the cul-de-sac. The smell of fresh-cut grass wafts through the air, mingling with the scent of Asiatic lilies coming from a patch in front of Mrs. Creston's front walkway. The Dayton girls I babysit every couple of weeks are drawing with chalk on their driveway—a deluge of rainbows, hearts and happy faces that swirl together as I pass. They call out for me to see their latest creation, but I don't even turn my head their way. I hear Mr. Grenshaw's three-month-old German Shepherd puppy barking through the front window of the house, and for a split second it pulls my attention away as I admonish the old man for locking that poor dog up day and night.

Then I slow and the burning sensation in my chest lifts just a little. I'm left standing in front of the lady with the terrible bangs, the sign and my dad.

"What the hell, Dad?" I glance at the sign up close, and for the first time realize that 'Bad Bang lady' herself is pictured on it, appearing in the exact same ugly pantsuit she's wearing now, attempting to exude a sense of relaxed confidence by tilting a bit to the left, so it looks like she's actually leaning on the words For Sale. All it does is make her look even more smug and arrogant, causing me to want to scribble four-letter words all over her plastered smile.

I step directly in front of her and turn to face Dad square on.

"What the hell is going on, Dad?"

"Why don't we go inside, and we can chat for a bit, Jess? We'll let Sheila be on her way for the day."

"I don't give a crap about Sheila. What is going on? Are you putting the house up for sale? *Why* are you putting the house up for sale?"

He sidesteps me so he can address Sheila again in all of her teased-bang glory.

"So, I guess we'll see how offers go and we'll touch base later in the week? I know the market isn't great right now, but like you said, we've priced reasonably enough that I think we have a shot at things going pretty quickly. Jess'll have to start school in the next couple of weeks. It would be nice for things to be wrapped up by then so we can get her settled in. And I don't want to have to be flying back and forth all the time, so the quicker things are finalized, the better."

He reaches past me to shake Sheila's hand while I stand there, numb with shock and horror. *What does he mean by 'getting me settled in'? Where does he not want to fly back from?*

I'm vaguely aware that Sheila is walking back down the driveway to her car, mostly because her sickly sweet, fake peach perfume follows her, and suddenly breathing freely becomes a little more manageable. I'm in such disbelief about what's going on that I don't even know what to say.

"Are…we…moving?" I force it out in tiny bursts, like the last remnants of a tube of toothpaste.

"Jess, let's talk about this inside. Come on," he says, as if he's coaxing a dog. "Come on in."

In a last-ditch attempt at showing him I make my own decisions, I stomp right past him to the front walk and barge into the house on my own.

"Mom! Mom, you need to come here, quick!" My mom is the last person I want to be talking with right now, but I'm afraid she's the only one who can make some meaning of what's happening.

"Jess, you rushed out so quickly earlier this morning. We've been worried about you. You haven't been answering our texts. Honey, I know this is hard for you and it will take some time for it all to sink in, but there are a bunch of things we still need to discuss. Here… Let me make us all a pot of tea, and we'll sit down."

She bustles around the kitchen for a few minutes, and it seems to me I have no choice but to plop down at the kitchen table. Bolting out of the house again is not going to give me the answers I need right now, and there are obviously things going on that I'm not yet privy to. Dad quietly takes a spot at his chair beside me, patiently waiting for Mom to join us before starting to explain anything.

I notice for the first time how much older my dad looks. He's in his mid-forties, and he's never really been someone in peak physical condition. He drinks too much and he used to smoke, although — thank God — he at least gave that up a few years back. He doesn't eat great, especially since he works late at the office most nights. All this has contributed to him developing one of those thick, round middles that makes his pants sit way below his actual waistline, causing the appearance of a saggy, nonexistent-looking butt and spindly legs.

And now, adding to his pitiful body shape, I notice that his hair is receding quite a bit on the top and at the back, and the hair that remains is streaked with wisps of silver and gray. Even the grown-out stubble on his neck and cheeks has a silver glint, the skin sagging loose and droopy like a cold piece of Kentucky Fried Chicken.

And his eyes… His eyes are so tired-looking and empty. It makes me realize how hard this whole break-up has been on him, too. Mom can try to convince me as much as she wants that this divorce is a two-way street, that Dad has been absent and unhappy too, that somehow, it's *his* fault she's running off with another man, but it's all bullshit. She's the one to blame here, no matter what's been going on between the two of them. She's the one pulling the plug on their marriage.

I glower as she hands me my cup of tea and takes the seat across the table.

"Jess, your dad and I have been discussing this over the last several days, and we think it's best to sell the house. Robert has asked that you and I come to live with him, and I think with the new baby coming, that's the best situation right now. He's got a great little bungalow on the north side of town. You'll have your own room, of course, and it's just a ten-minute walk from your new school—"

"Excuse me? *New* school? No one told me about going to a different school. No way! No freaking way! It's my *last* year of high school. I'm not switching schools now. All my friends are here. The swim team's here! Why can't I just stay here with Dad? It doesn't make any sense. I don't want anything to do with you anyway. Who said I would want to live with you and Robert? I'm seventeen years old, and I can choose to live wherever *I* want to live. Right now, I don't want anything to do with you, with the new baby or with your stupid-ass boyfriend!"

At Maggie's house, I was ready to be so confident, so strong through all of this. But now, everything has changed. My hands start shaking so badly that I ball them up and shove them under my thighs. My heartbeat thrums near my throat and I know tears are soon going to spill out of my eyes with this sudden burst of anger. I will them off long enough for me to finish this dismal conversation, so that I can hole myself up in my bedroom.

"Dad, why aren't you saying anything? Why aren't you fighting for me? Don't you want me to stay here with you?"

"Honey, you know I want you to stay with me. But we can't stay here. We've got to sell the house, and it has to be ASAP. At this point, moving in with your mother might really be your best option."

"I just don't get it. Why do we have to move at all? I love this house. I love this neighborhood, my school. I know you feel the same. Just because *she* has messed this up, doesn't mean our lives have to change too. Please, Dad…"

I look pleadingly at him, begging him to see things from my point of view. I reach across the table to grab his hand, thinking that the physical connection will somehow bridge us together.

But it stays limp on the table. His eyes flick rapidly down to his lap, then up to my mom, and finally they land on me. His voice is hoarse, but his words ring out clear and certain.

"Jess, my company is transferring me to Hawaii. I'm moving out of Canada."

Chapter Three

I roll over in bed and notice dust particles dancing and swirling in the orange haze of late afternoon light that slants in through my bedroom window. I must have cried myself to sleep after locking myself in my room all afternoon. I think back to the conversation with Mom and Dad this morning.

Selling the house...moving to Hawaii? It all seems like an impossibly horrible bad dream. When I heard the news, all I wanted to do was meet up with Marcus and have his kisses erase everything, if just for a moment. I tentatively pick up my phone to check for any new texts, but just see the half-dozen unanswered ones I'd already sent to him earlier today.

11:18am: *I need to see you. Something huge is going on.*

11:25am: *Marcus, are you there?*

12:23 pm: *Marcus, I'm dying here. Call me.*

12:40pm: *SOS. Hello???*

1:15pm: *Please call me. It's an emergency.*

2:03pm: *I need you.*

I dance my thumb around the screen one more time, simmering with frustration that he still hasn't replied.

5:09pm: *Forget it. I'm coming to your place. See you soon.*

5:09pm: *...*

Finally! I've been waiting all day for those three little dots to appear on my screen.

5:10pm: *Sorry, wasn't checking my phone. Meet me at the park in 15*

I don't dwell on the fact that it took *six* texts to get Marcus to respond, or the unbelievability of him not checking his phone. It doesn't make any sense, but right now, I just need him. I need him to help me figure out what to do with the ragged remnants my life has become.

When I get to the park, I find a spot on the swings to wait for him. I start drifting back and forth, enjoying the gentle breeze in my hair. Shifting my weight with each pendulum, I surge upward. My legs pump rhythmically, and it feels invigorating to put my excess energy to good use, to push myself higher and higher up. As I alternate between swinging up and back, I find my thoughts flit back and forth with an impossible dilemma and no easy answer in sight.

Do I move in with Mom and start this new life as a third wheel in her mid-life-crisis love affair?

Or do I leave everything I know and love in order to cross the ocean and be by Dad's side?

How am I expected to make such a critical decision?

As I reach the crest of my swing forward, I see Marcus loping up through the walkway in front of the park, a plain white T-shirt stretched taut against his chest and his faded jeans sitting low on his hips.

In one giant leap, I push off the chains I'm holding so tightly to, and feel myself flying free in the air, not knowing where I'm going to land.

"God, Marcus, it's so good to see you. You won't believe what's happened." I wrap my arms around his strong back and bury my face into his chest.

"Geez, Jess, what's going on? I was literally just with you last night. How could anything *drastic* have happened since then?"

"You have no idea!" It's like I'm a balloon that's been untied, and the air rushes out of me. I ramble nonstop into the soft hollow of his collarbone about the turn of events my life has taken, one catastrophe after another. I go on and on, and it feels therapeutic to just let it all out. After a few moments, I lift my chin slightly away from his chest so I can take a much-needed breath of fresh air. As I do, a rush of French lavender fills my nostrils.

I pull back to look at him and notice a dark purple hickey peeking out at the base of his neck, underneath the scruff of his blond hair—a dark purple hickey that was definitely not made by me during our stolen time together last night.

Suddenly, it all comes together, like a dissolving fog that has been previously clouding my vision. The weight of it all crashes on top of me with the force of an avalanche—how the last two people on earth I could trust and hold on to have just shredded my last threads of hope.

"You…and Maggie? You've been together? For how long?"

"Huh, what?" He catches me glaring at the hickey and reflectively raises his hand to his neck. "Jess, it's not like that. It's not what you think. We just, you know, hang out sometimes. She's a cool chick, that's all."

"How long? How long have you been secretly *dating* my best friend?"

"Like I said, we're not dating. It's just casual…like you and me." He takes a step away from me and drops his arms to his sides. "Jess, you're great and all. I like that we hang out sometimes. But I've never said we're a couple or that we're exclusive, or anything like that. So, relax. It's no big deal."

"No big deal? But she's my best friend…" And as much as I want to scream this out so the entire world hears me, it catches in the back of my throat and ends up coming out weak and lifeless, a wilted flower.

"Jesus, Jess, you're making a way bigger deal about this than you need to. What you and I had together was great, super-fun. We had an awesome summer. But, you know, we didn't really intend on it going anywhere. You said yourself that it would be too difficult for us to stay together once school started." He runs his hands through his hair, then stuffs them into his pockets.

"I'm sorry, Jess. You're really cool, and I've liked hanging out with you. I didn't mean to hurt your feelings or anything, so I feel bad about that. But, you know, these things happen. Sometimes people just need to move on when things aren't quite right."

It takes me a moment to realize he's breaking up with me. Well, breaking up a relationship that apparently only I believed we were in. How could I have been so stupid? How did I get so wrapped up in this? I open my mouth to say something, to convince him that I'm worth staying for. I want to beg and plead with him. I want him to scoop me up in his arms so we can just be together again. But the sight of the dark purple hickey causes me to pause just a little too long. The doubt rises between us like an insurmountable wall, a challenge he's clearly not willing to tackle.

"So, yeah. Let's just call it quits, Jess, and leave it at that. We can still be friends or whatever. And I'm sorry about what's going on with your parents. That's totally gotta sting. I'm just maybe not the best person to, you know, help you through it, I guess. But honestly, I hope it all works out. And yeah, thanks for hanging out this summer. It was cool."

With that, he holds up his two peace fingers as he turns around, and he just walks away. He just strides back down the park pathway he came up minutes ago, when life was so full of promise and possibilities. No kiss goodbye, no look back.

He's just gone.

Chapter Four

My stomach lurches as the plane dips and curves farther south. I suppose we're lucky we were able to get a direct flight to Maui, as it has at least allowed me to catch up on a bit of sleep.

Sleep...something my body hasn't done much of in the last few days. After my heart-wrenching break-up with Marcus, I ran home to find solace in the quiet of my bedroom but sleep just wouldn't come. I desperately wanted to find comfort in Maggie, but now she was just one more pawn on the other side of the chess board. Marcus must have told her about our break-up, and how I now knew that he and Maggie had a thing going. She must have called me and shown up at my house at least a dozen times, but I just couldn't face her. At first, Mom and Dad were perplexed about why I didn't want to spend my last few days at home seeking comfort in my best friend, but even they caught on that something wasn't right and agreed to turn Maggie away when she showed up. *I mean, what am I supposed to say to a best friend who has betrayed me so savagely?*

My parents didn't provide much support, either. Mom immediately started packing up her things, taking one carload at a time to Robert's house, in order to make the move there permanent.

"Jess, I really would like you to come with me. I think you'll learn to love Robert, and it'll make so much more sense for you to simply move across town with me, rather than move across the globe with your father. You'll still be able to swim, just in a different club. You'll see your friends. You'll just be at a different school. Life will go on. It'll just be a slightly different normal."

They were all lies, though, because nothing would be normal again. I no longer had a family, a best friend or a boyfriend. Really, I had nothing to stay for. I decided it was better to just start fresh in a place not filled with hurtful memories.

Apparently, Dad did list the house at a steal of a deal because he got requests for showings the very next day. Within forty-eight hours, our house — the only home I had known for seventeen years — was being sold to a busy family of five, complete with a back yard playhouse and a dog. Dad handed the keys over to Sheila and bought two one-way tickets to Maui the same day.

Of course, he did his best to convince me *not* to come. He knew Mom would be distraught with the prospect of her only child moving two thousand miles away. But at the same time, I think he enjoyed the fact that he got to win. Mom may have pulled the rug from under him with regard to their marriage, but he was able to keep the consolation prize, which was me. And I guess I have to admit that *my* motives were more revenge than anything too. I just didn't want my mom to believe she could get away with this, that I condoned her actions. I don't. I still think she's selfish and undeserving, and I want to hurt her as much as she hurt me.

The plane continues to dip farther, allowing a blinding ray of sunshine to attack me through the small window. I shield my eyes and peer through the glass so I can get a better look at my new home.

The wide ocean splays in front of me, presenting an ombre of blues smeared beneath an endless horizon. Rich indigo out in the distance melts into shimmering turquoise right beneath me, then kisses up to endless golden beaches. I spot dark, shadowy blotches in the ocean filled with mysterious underwater creatures and tropical coral reefs. And farther inland, beyond the strips of sand and surf, beyond the imposing luxury hotels and tourist condominiums, stretch large areas of dry desert and barren grasslands. Towering above the entire island, like two sentinels guarding this little piece of paradise from threatening foreigners, are two lush, green, mountainous volcanoes, one on each side, with a deep valley between. Wisps of clouds encircle the middle of each, giving the entire island a mystical feel, like this is a world of its own, a world calling me to discover its hidden treasures.

I've always been obsessed with tropical rainforests — such a stark contrast from the evergreen firs and spruce trees abundant in my Canadian hometown. Since I've been a seventeen-year-old captive of seven-month-long winters, followed by disappointing summers of rain showers and mosquitos, the glimpse of a tropical expanse like this takes my breath away. Mom and Dad used to splurge every spring break for an all-inclusive trip to Mexico, but those trips typically included a private coach to and from a luxurious resort, sparkling man-made pools and immaculately tended gardens—hardly an untamed wilderness to explore.

Now, gazing out of the tiny window upon our final descent, the knot in my stomach starts releasing as I imagine the endless hours I'll spend exploring every inch of this island. Maybe a fresh start—a new world—is exactly what I need right now.

As if he knows I need a surge of reassurance, Dad turns from his seat located directly in front of me and reaches his hand through the armrest.

"So, honey, what do you think of our new home? Are you ready for an adventure?"

Even though I still carry many open wounds and the feelings of resentment burn heavy in my heart, for the first time I think maybe I am. I squeeze my dad's hand in return, feeling thankful that I have at least one teammate left in the game.

After deboarding the plane, we're herded through a simple airport to the luggage carousel on the main floor. I'm shocked by the warm, humid air, even more so when I realize the entire airport is open to the outdoors. A tropical breeze blows in through the unenclosed space, carrying with it the sweet smell of gardenia blossoms. As I reach down to retrieve my luggage, something gently grazes the back of my neck. I turn to see two small yellow birds, engrossed in an act of aerial gymnastics, diving and looping around each other, then finally resting to perch on one of the large TV monitors secured to the wall.

I can't get over how much the outdoors merge with the indoors in this strange place, to the point where I can't really detect the difference. There's definitely no indoor-outdoor living at home.

Home… I wonder how long someone needs to be in a place before they automatically think of it as home?

Dad and I attempt to distance ourselves from the crowd of tourists fumbling to retrieve their luggage, when we spot a barrel-chested, middle-aged man wearing flip flops and a baggy Hawaiian shirt, holding a sign with our names on it.

"Aloha!" he says with enthusiasm, the dimples on his cheeks deepening even farther with his warm smile.

"My name is Keanu. I've been hired to drive you to your new home and help you settle in here. We're excited you've come to join us!" He opens his arms wide, like a king who is presenting his kingdom. "Welcome to Maui…the Valley Isle!"

He reaches out to me, placing a strand of pale pink and white flowers around my neck. The scent coming from them is intoxicating and I can't help but be brought back to a memory of my childhood.

There was an indoor botanical garden located near the center of our hometown, a lush oasis that was open year-round, despite the bitter cold and snow blanketing the city. When I was a young girl, Dad used to take me there on weekends, allowing Mom a few more hours of precious sleep. We would dress quietly and slip through the front doors without waking her. Dad would always stop for a coffee on the way, ordering me a piece of warm banana bread as a treat. We'd arrive at the imposing, pyramid-shaped glass greenhouse, and I would anticipate that first rush of warm, humid air as we stepped through the front entrance. It felt like a different world in those gardens, a tropical microcosm in the middle of a dreary and frigid city, heavy with winter's grasp.

During those mornings, Dad would sit and sip his coffee on one of the many wooden benches lining the intricate garden pathways inside. I would run through those cobblestone paths, eager to get lost in the tropical magic. Dad had told me that fairies lived in those gardens, and that if I was quiet enough, patient enough, one might come out of hiding for me to catch a glimpse.

My favorite plant in the entire garden was a beautiful plumeria tree. Full and lush with bright green leaves, its flowers were dazzling when in bloom. I would crouch down beside it, entranced by the delicate blossoms, the way the pink edges of the petals gradually blended to white then exploded into a vibrant yellow sun in the middle. I was convinced those petals were actually fairy wings, and that the yellow center was the shiny, blonde hair of the fairy, her face tucked in, hiding so she wouldn't be found. I once nestled in the cool, moist shadow of that tree for what seemed like hours, waiting for the fairies to emerge. Dad had finished his wanderings of the garden and was starting to get impatient to leave. But I knew if I walked away, it might be the exact moment a fairy would appear, and I would miss my chance.

Finally, he'd called to me, dangling a small bag of freshly made sugar donuts from the garden bakery café. He knew me too well. The thought of the warm, sticky pastry melting in my mouth had been enough to pull me from my trance. As I stood and brushed the peat and moss from my legs, I caught a flicker of movement out of the corner of my eye. The very flower I had been staring at, that I had been unwilling to move from for the last hour, was suddenly turned away.

There was no wind in the indoor garden. In fact, there were barely any other guests wandering its pathways. But somehow, this flower, of its own volition, had turned so its petals faced away from me, and the yellow star in the middle had folded inward. I still can't explain it and would never admit it to anyone else, but I've always suspected there to be some truth in garden fairies.

The delicate scent of the plumeria lei around my neck brings me back to the present as I assess my new surroundings. We pile our luggage into Keanu's SUV, and I'm grateful for the ability to sit back and absorb the luscious scenery.

After a few minutes, we leave Kahului, the major city in Maui, and head south on the highway toward the coast. The West Maui Mountains tower over us on our right, and I see a trail of what look to be giant windmills spinning feverishly in the strong afternoon trade winds.

"See? Over there are the Maui wind turbines." Keanu explains. "A lot of people seem to think they're an eyesore, but they provide a good chunk of Maui's power. The winds here are crazy strong sometimes, so you know, it's smart to harness the power. Besides, anyone who comes to Maui is looking out over the ocean anyway, not up at the slope of the mountains." He chuckles to himself then continues.

"Are you into hiking, though?" His eyes meet mine in the rearview mirror. "There are some pretty epic hikes through those mountains. You'll think you're in a Jurassic Forest in there! Just remember to stay on the marked trails, because there can be flash floods at any time. With Maui, the weather changes in an instant and can be a different season within every square mile of the island."

I look at the fields of barren farmland on either side of the highway.

"So, what's with all this land then? It looks pretty dry to me. There are actually rainforests up there?"

"Many people are surprised to know that Maui has more micro-climates than almost anywhere on Earth. In one day, you can hike through lava fields, deserts, a tropical oasis or, on rare occasions, even the snow-capped peaks of a mountain. But tourists only see one — the beach!" He laughs and sticks his arm out of the window, making air waves with his hand. I rest my head back against the seat to stare out into this exotic island that I've chosen to be my home.

To my left lie the remnants of a once-prosperous sugarcane field, evidence of a long past, thriving sugar economy that is no longer in existence. Keanu points out the Puunene Sugar Mill, a rusty and dilapidated building looking more like a haunted house than the epicenter of a billion-dollar economy. He goes on to tell us how, for one hundred sixty-eight years, the sugar industry brought people from all over the world to Maui, weaving different histories together to create the rich culture of Maui today.

"Is sugar not grown in Maui anymore?" I ask, enjoying the way the tropical breeze makes the hair around my face dance in front of the open window.

"No, Maui has recently stopped growing sugarcane. It just isn't as viable in today's economy and has actually caused a lot of damage to the island. Naturally nutrient-rich, the repetitive planting of sugarcane has left much of the soil here dry and nutrient-deficient. Current efforts are underway to restore the fields to a favorable state for growing other types of vegetation and focus it on supporting small, local farms. Sustainability for local agriculture is what native Hawaiians are striving for. Out with the big corporations, local is best!"

He punctuates this statement by punching the steering wheel with the heel of his hand. A moment later, the highway veers left, and my breath catches in my throat. Gone are the dry, barren fields and the looming, mist-covered mountains. We are now snaking our way along a road that runs parallel to a sparkling azure sea, more beautiful than anything I've ever seen. Bright fuchsia and coral bushes dot the side of the road, and tall palm trees sway in the breeze, acting as perches for tropical birds of every color. Every few seconds, a grove of them opens up to expose wide stretches of golden beaches with clear, turquoise water lapping up onto the sand. Soft, wispy clouds float lazily across the sky and the vivid triangles of sailboats dot the horizon. Way out in the distance, I glimpse what look to be three separate islands emerging from the dark sea, and I make a note to myself to ask Dad about them. I have so many questions about this new world, and I'm eager to start exploring.

For about ten minutes we drive through the lazy beach neighborhood of Kihei, which seems to be made up mostly of middle-class homes and rental condos. The traffic almost comes to a standstill because there are so many people attempting to cross the road at any given moment. An older couple strolls hand in hand down the sidewalk, while a tan teenager races across the street right ahead of us, his longboard tucked up under his arm. A group of young kids throw a Frisbee in a lush green space bordering a wide, sandy beach.

This is what I imagined when I decided to move to Hawaii, I think to myself, *long, lazy days lounging on the beach, soaking up the tropical sun.*

The road curves again and it's obvious we've entered a different neighborhood once more. Rich, green foliage and brightly colored flower beds decorate perfectly manicured lawns. Sprawling homes perch on oceanfront property, secured behind massive iron gates. We glide past opulent five-star hotels, each seizing its place on a pristine shoreline. There must be at least five or six of these luxurious vacation retreats, the kind of place one might imagine for a once-in-a-lifetime, dream vacation. The tourists strutting out of these hotels, with their designer sunglasses and matching purses, provide a stark contrast to the working-class locals filling the streets of Kahului or the casual tourists of Kihei.

"Where are we now?" I wonder aloud.

"This is beautiful Wailea, Maui's iconic resort community for the rich and famous. Tourists who look for opulence, privilege, privacy and luxury all come to Wailea. The immaculate beaches, impeccable service and top-notch golf courses are irresistible to those with money. Aren't you lucky to be able to call this home!"

"Home? *This* is where we're staying? In Wailea, Dad?"

"I guess so, sweetheart. The company told me they'd put us up in a rental for now but didn't give me many details. I had assumed it would be a small condo of some sort. I really wasn't aware of the layout of Maui."

"So, do you live here in Wailea too then, Keanu? You seem to know so much."

"Me? Oh, no way. I grew up in Kahului and have stayed there my whole life. This place here? This is for people from the mainland who bring a load of money to Maui. Those of us who are local don't tend to live in communities like this…" His voice trails off, but there's an edge to it.

Despite the breeze flowing through the open window, I'm damp and sticky with sweat, eager to get to our new place so I can change out of my travel clothes. Either Keanu is against air conditioning or figures that as Canadians, we're craving some warm, tropical air, because he hasn't turned it on once during the entire half-hour drive. I start to feel carsick from the heat and the winding roads, and I worry that I'm going to have to ask him to pull over. But unexpectedly, we pull up to a keypad at the entrance of a gated community.

"Okay, Mr. Kennedy, we're here at your new home. You just punch this code in here," Keanu reaches through the window to punch in a four-digit number that I can't really see, then settles back into his seat, waiting for the heavy iron gates to open up.

"It's a beautiful community and it's very secure, so I think you're going to really enjoy your time here. I've stocked the fridge with some basic supplies to get you started, and of course, the house comes fully furnished. The pool gets cleaned on Tuesdays, the gardener comes on Wednesdays, and Jackie — the housekeeper — will be here to tidy up every Friday. Anything else you need while you get sorted out, you just call me anytime."

He passes a large manila envelope over to my dad, presumably containing further detailed information about our new home, then slowly continues along the smooth, newly paved road that snakes though the elite community.

Holy crap! is all I can think, scrutinizing this new neighborhood with elaborate homes and lush foliage. I mean, back in Canada, I know my parents did okay, moneywise. We weren't crazy rich, like a couple of kids I knew, who received fancy, brand new BMWs for their sixteenth birthdays or the latest Louis Vuitton for Christmas. But both my parents had good jobs, and I really never wanted for anything. We lived in a bit of a yuppie neighborhood just west of downtown, recently gentrified because it had the perfect balance of being a short commute from downtown but with the quaint character of turn-of-the-century homes. The streets were narrow and tree-lined, the homes lined up like full-sized ginger-bread houses decorated with wrap-around porches and painted gables. They were from an era before attached garages, so there were back lanes running parallel behind the main streets, leaving room for spacious front yards with neatly paved pathways and tidy gardens.

I sometimes asked my dad why we didn't move out to the suburbs, where a bunch of my friends lived. I knew roughly what our house was worth, and for that much money we could have purchased a brand-new home twice the size of ours on the outskirts of town. But being a land developer, Dad was always most concerned about property value and was certain our home's central location was its most appealing characteristic.

"Jess, oftentimes the land a home is built upon is worth far more than the home itself. So, you can't really judge property value by looking just at the house. Sometimes people will spend a million dollars on a home, just to tear it down and put something brand new up. It's all about the land."

I think of my dad's words as we slowly manage our way through this newly developed, gated community, where the elegance of the homes matches the upscale value of the ocean-view properties. There were definitely no teardowns in this community. Each estate we glide by seems to surpass the previous in size and grandeur, and I'm left wondering how many millions of dollars each one is worth. We follow the road around a few tight curves and up a sharp incline. Large stone walls have been placed all along the drive to block our view of the massive homes inside, but every so often I catch a glimpse of an expansive rooftop balcony or shimmering pool set back from the main house. I have a difficult time imagining that the house we're supposed to be moving into is located in such a prestigious area. We definitely can't afford this on my dad's salary. I keep thinking that the smaller, less extravagant homes must be located at the top of the drive, perhaps where parcels of land have been separated into quarters, or homes have been sublet into individual condominiums. Our middle-class home in Canada definitely does not match the worth of these elite mansions.

But we creep farther up the hill, making one more hairpin turn, when Keanu puts the car into park and announces that we're there.

My jaw drops at the sight before me. I climb out of the stuffy car and stand unmoving on a luxuriously spongy green lawn. A modern estate home sprawls before me, with stacked stone pillars and giant cedar crossbeams acting as anchors for floor-to-ceiling glass windows. The entire front of the house is a glass wall, like it's a super-fancy greenhouse. For a moment it reminds me of the botanical gardens with the fairy, and it's not lost on me that the architect probably designed the house to conjure up that feeling exactly — an indoor-outdoor oasis. *And it's for us? We're going to be living in a home designed by an actual architect?*

Perched above the two-story glass windows, the roof slants up at a low pitch, covered with built-in solar panels that mirror the late afternoon sun and bluebird sky. The sight of them brings my attention to the faint burning sensation at the back of my neck, where the sun's rays are scorching my pale Canadian skin.

I mindlessly step out of the sun into the shade of a lime tree to the right side of the property, affording me views of the side of the house and the back yard. At the back of the house, funneling from the rooftop patio, is a double-wide curved staircase descending to a gently sloped and meticulous, green lawn. There are so many windows in the house that I can practically look straight through them to the back yard and beyond. Halfway down the back lawn, an Olympic-sized swimming pool covers the entire width of the yard, the pristine water inviting me for an afternoon swim. It takes all my willpower not to just drop my backpack and race to greet the pool with a giant cannonball. I look over to the right and notice a small *ohana*, a guesthouse, nestled in among a handful of ripe fruit trees in one corner of the yard, beside a bright red hammock swaying listlessly in the tropical breeze.

Beyond that? Well, the entire world appears to be laid out before me. All the way around is an unobstructed, panoramic view of the Pacific Ocean, shimmering in the late afternoon sunshine. The property is so high up on the hill, so high above the other incredible homes we drove past on our way there, that it appears we are the only ones living on this little piece of paradise. I run to the edge of the back lawn, just to see where it ends. I see that at the back of the property there's a sharp drop-off about twenty feet down, made up of shiny, black lava rocks, then below that ridge, the road curves back and forth between homes and gardens, eventually turning into a thread of gray at the very bottom of the hill. Past that, there is nothing but the sprawling blue sea.

I'm the king of the castle, and you're the dirty rascal... The childhood rhyme fills my head and suddenly, none of this makes sense. My life is a shaken-up handful of dice, and I'm having a tough time believing that the Yahtzee I've just rolled belongs to me.

Unable to wait for my dad to awkwardly lumber his sweaty body all the way out to the far side of the yard, I walk back to the side of the pool and plop down into one of the cushioned pool loungers.

I take a moment to just absorb it all—the aromatic lemon trees lining the north side of the property, the twelve-person hot tub that bubbles discreetly under a pergola just south of the pool, the half-dozen cushioned pool chairs lined up along the stone pool deck, each draped in bright white linens and with a matching pool umbrella.

This is our new home?

Chapter Five

"Honestly, Dad, I just don't get it. Something's not clicking here. How are we actually *affording* this place?"

It's the morning after our arrival, and we're sitting at our elegant ebony dining table, enjoying fresh grapefruit and homemade cappuccinos. I've never made a cappuccino in my life because, well, who actually *owns* a cappuccino machine? But now I do. I am one of those mystical people who owns a cappuccino machine. I totally don't get it.

Dad pockets his phone and downs the remnants of his tiny cup in one last gulp.

"Well, honey, I told you. My company gave me a raise when I agreed to move here. Most people don't just up and drop everything for their job and, well, I've shown them loyalty by doing so. Plus, it's not like we own this house. We're just renting it from the company while we're here, however long that's going to be. Granted, they're renting it out to us for a ridiculously low price. They want us to like it here. They want us to stay.

"We're all really hoping this deal I'm in the middle of is going to take off in the next few months. If it does, that'll be huge for us. *Huge.* If we can solidify the purchase of this land we're looking to build on, there are going to be big things for us, for you and me, honey. They just might give me a promotion and enough money to buy a house like this for real."

"It's just so, so…different from what we're used to. I'm sorry, Dad, but we've never been rich. But this house? It makes me feel like we're stupid rich, like, *filthy* rich. Do you think we look like snobs, living up here on the hill?"

"Jess, we're in Maui. Half the people here are filthy rich. That's how this economy survives. The people who live here need to rely on foreigners like us to come and spend our money. It's all good. You're going to fit in just fine."

Something about his words doesn't sit well with me, especially after Keanu's talk about Maui's efforts to support 'local', to give control back to the people who live here. My dad makes it sound like by living *here*, in this place of extreme grandeur, that we're somehow doing *them* a favor. It sounds so entitled, so elitist. I think of Keanu and how he scoffed at even the notion of living in this community.

"It's just that I've never had to, you know, start fresh anywhere. What if I don't fit in? What if no one wants to hang with me? God, it's my last year of high school. I don't want to spend it alone, like a loser."

"Jess, take a look around. You're in paradise! How bad could things get? You're going to love it here. *We're* going to love it here. I promise."

He kisses the top of my head as he starts to walk away, then turns and pauses.

"By the way, your registration day at school is on Friday, then school officially starts Monday. If you want, I can come with you, but I don't know if showing up on the first day with your old man'll boost your reputation. It might actually cost you. I guess you can decide about that one." He laughs at his bad dad joke. "You better enjoy the next couple of days of lounging around, because you're going to be busy with school pretty quick.

"And just so you know, I'm probably not going to be around for dinner for the next few evenings, as I'll have to work late getting things all settled. Looks like Keanu stocked our fridge and pantry pretty good, but you can always order a pizza if you want. Oh, and he mentioned that there's even a couple of bikes here if you're wanting to do some exploring. This house really did come stocked with everything! Just keep your phone with you in case you need to get a hold of me. And have fun riding up and down the giant hill we're on. That'll give you the exercise you've been complaining about needing!"

He closes the massive oak doors behind him, and in an instant I'm alone—totally and utterly alone in this little piece of the world where nothing makes sense. My first instinct is to call Maggie and unload all this craziness onto her. Even if I video-chatted with her, she wouldn't believe the palace I'm living in. But when I go to dial her number, I hesitate, because well, calling her would mean I forgive her for being with Marcus—and I don't, not yet anyway. Although, from this far away, Marcus somehow doesn't have the magnetic hold on me that he did before.

But no, I'm not ready to face Maggie yet. *Better to let her suffer a little.* Besides, with the time change, it's only six in the morning back home, so she's likely not going to pick up anyway.

Thinking about Maggie causes me to also think about Mom. She insisted on coming with us to the airport, despite the awkwardness it caused my dad. Luckily, Robert had the sense to stay at home. My mom's eyes welled with tears every time she glanced at me slouching in the back seat of the car. She must have asked me a zillion times to stay with her instead, that life would be glorious with her and Robert.

"We all just need time to adjust," she'd said. I didn't even acknowledge her trembling voice with a rebuttal. I'd already decided whose side I was taking, and no matter what she said, I was *not* going to change my mind.

But then she gave me one last hug before I entered the security checkpoint, and as much as I tried to hold back from hugging her, willing my arms to hang rigidly at my sides, I just couldn't do it. As if operating from muscle memory, I reached around her back and let my cheek fall to her shoulder. The sobs burst out of me like tiny explosions, which only caused my mom to squeeze tighter. Then, through our loose-fitting T-shirts, I suddenly felt the hard bulge of her already protruding belly press against my flat stomach, and the realization came. Things would never be the same. It made it that much easier to drop my arms, blow one last kiss and walk away without turning back.

So now, sitting in this cavernous mansion I'm somehow supposed to think of as *home*, my body aches with loneliness. I try to use self-talk to get me out of this funk.

I'm in paradise.
This is the choice I made.
I should enjoy every moment.

I say the words so many times in my head that I hope I'll start to believe them.

I decide I may as well take advantage of the little free time I have left before the stress of acing my last year of high school eats me up. I change into the one bikini I've packed in my suitcase, seeing as the rest of our stuff isn't going to be shipped here until next week. I grab my Air Pods and the latest John Green book I'm halfway through and decide to lie by the pool before the sun gets too high in the sky and roasts me.

I'm only on the third song of my *Pool Chillin* playlist, when the sound of a chainsaw or machine gun or something obnoxious and annoying starts roaring at me from the side of the yard. I turn over from my stomach to my side and notice a strange man balancing precariously on a ten-foot ladder over by the fence. He's attempting to trim one of the palm trees with what seems to be a massive electric knife, the kind my dad uses to carve our Thanksgiving turkey. Nothing about the situation looks remotely safe, and I almost jump up to help him. But then I think better of it, figuring a bikini-clad teenager startling him might make the whole situation even worse.

I think about calling Dad to ask him if he knows why this guy is at our house, when I remember Keanu mentioning something about the gardener coming on Wednesdays. *So, I'm guessing, this must be the gardener?*

It's hard to believe he works outside all day long in this sweltering heat, what with the amount of gear he's wearing. I mean, he's covered head to toe in long pants and a long-sleeved T-shirt, even though it's already approaching eighty degrees. He's got thick Teflon gardening gloves on, and his face is almost totally concealed by a dark face mask and a ridiculous-looking sun hat. But he moves among the palm fronds with skill and precision, cutting the dead leaves off and letting them plop down on either side of the ladder.

I feel incredibly guilty sitting there on my ass while he's working so hard right in front of me, so I decide to go inside and grab him something cold to drink. I browse through the stocked fridge and settle on two ice-cold cans of sweet tea. As I pass back through the double-wide French doors leading from the kitchen to the patio, I catch the gardener tilting back his hat and pulling down his face mask. He wipes the sweat off his brow with the back of his hand, but it must be covered with dirt and dust because he stops immediately, and instead pulls up the front of his shirt to mop his face with the hem.

The glistening of a tan and rippling set of abs is not what I expect to see on who I assumed was a middle-aged gardener.

He drops the front of his shirt and instinctively looks my way, apparently sensing that he's being watched from afar. His handsome face is now uncovered, his smile wide and open as he lifts his right hand in a hesitant attempt at waving hello.

I'm suddenly super-flustered, not knowing whether to just turn back into the house, sit back on the patio lounger to pretend I don't notice him or walk on over to bring him the cold iced tea, like I'd intended.

Despite my awkwardness, I stride over to the side of the yard where he's working, the grass soft and cool on my bare feet. As I approach him, it's clear that he is *not* the middle-aged man I first thought but is a tall and lean teenager right around my age, with caramelly smooth skin, bright white teeth and glossy black hair that's plastered with sweat to the sides of his face.

"Um, hey," he stammers.

"Hi. Um, you look like you're working really hard. Do you want an iced tea?"

"Uh, sure, yeah. That'd be great. I should be done pretty quick here anyway. My dad just wanted me to do the palm trees, and he said he'd come by later in the day to get the lawn and the rest of the garden."

"Your dad?" I don't follow his train of thought.

"Oh, my dad, Kale. He's the gardener who usually works here. I'm just helping him out a bit while we're still on summer break. Well, he's *making* me help him out. Doesn't want me surfing all morning and napping all afternoon, I guess." He scoffs, throwing his hair back when he says it, and the sun catches on the white of his teeth. I feel a sudden *whoosh* deep in my belly, like an elevator that has plummeted way too quickly.

"Oh, cool. So, you surf?"

"Uh, yeah, of course. Everybody does. Don't you?"

"Well, we actually just moved here from Canada, so there's not a lot of surfing happening there. I've tried snowboarding a couple of times, though. Maybe it's kind of similar?"

"Yeah, maybe. I've never tried snowboarding. Not a lot of snow here." He smiles again and I feel the same *whoosh* pulse through me for the second time.

We stand in an awkward silence for a moment when he suddenly reaches out and plants his thumb square in the middle of my shoulder.

I'm caught off-guard and stumble back a step before he speaks.

"Sorry, um, I was just testing your skin — you know, for a sunburn — cuz you look kind of pink. And sometimes it's hard to tell out here." I get the sense he's just realized how weird it is that he's gone and touched me in a strangely intimate way. I look down at where he pressed my shoulder and see the white thumbprint flood back to a rosy pink.

Immediately, I become keenly aware of my almost naked body, just standing exposed in front of him. My girlie, pink-and-white triangle bikini covered in tiny strawberries seems embarrassingly juvenile. My dirty blonde hair fastened loosely in a ponytail probably looks messy and unkempt. My pasty white — almost translucent — half-naked body does not scream 'tropical beach babe'.

God, I wish I would have thought to grab my cover-up or a towel. I attempt to casually cover myself by crossing my arms in front of my chest, but it's awkward because I had forgotten I was still holding the now sweating cans of iced tea.

"Oh here, I brought this out for you. Sorry, it's probably warm by now." I reach it out to him and his fingertips brush against mine as he takes the can.

Whoosh. Dang, there it is again.

"Thanks. It gets super-hot out here in summer. It's the humidity really, more than anything. Everyone thinks that Maui is the same temperature year-round, but it's the humidity that kills us in the summer. Feels like it's twenty degrees warmer!"

"Why don't you come and sit in the shade for a bit then?" I wave him over to follow me to the pool lounger, where I'm looking forward to finally wrapping my body with a towel. But it sucks to think that he's behind me as I walk, with a clear view of my backside in my teeny tiny, barely-there bikini bottoms. They seemed like a good idea earlier this morning.

"So, you guys just moved in? From Canada?" he asks as we sit.

"Yeah, it's just me and my dad." I hesitate about going on further but stop short instead. I don't even want to go there. The story is too much to unload on an unsuspecting victim.

"This is a pretty big house for only two of you." His eyes are wide as he takes in the expansive yard, the impressive pool, the majestic windows. And for some reason, I'm really self-conscious — embarrassed that I'm now living in this luxurious estate home, while this strange boy works so hard during his last days of summer to keep it looking fabulous.

"Yeah, I know. It's pretty ridiculous. I guess my dad got a raise or something. His company moved him here and put him up in this place. It's pretty unbelievable. It's not like we live like this all the time. I mean, we didn't have a house like this in Canada or anything…" My voice trails off and I can tell by the slight raise of his eyebrows that he doesn't really believe what I'm saying. He probably thinks I'm a stupid, stuck-up, rich tourist who is clueless as to how the majority of people live. I almost defend myself, cataloguing reasons for him to believe me, when he stands up, wiping his hands on his dirty work pants.

"Well, thanks for the iced tea. I've got to get going, as I have a couple of other houses to get to. My dad'll probably be back later in the day, and he'll be the one coming next week, seeing as school starts then. So…nice meeting you."

I have so many questions to ask him — about school, about other kids, about things to do here. But my mouth suddenly fills with cotton and no words manage to tumble out.

He walks over to the ladder leaning against the fence, hoisting it effortlessly under his arm as he strides across the grass, disappearing behind the shade of the house.

No goodbye, no wave, nothing.

Geez, how did I mess this up so badly?

I'm left with an uneasy feeling, like I came across as a preppy bitch, which was not my intention at all. It makes me think back to Marcus' comment to me about pretending not to be noticed, about seeming all pretentious and stuck up when he first met me, even when I didn't mean to be. I'm pissed at myself for not being a little cooler, for not being able to flirt effortlessly, like Maggie always does. I look down at my now-flaming-red skin.

I'm also pissed at myself for not putting sunscreen on, because it means I need to spend the rest of the day stuck inside. Then it hits me.

Damn. I didn't even get his name. I'm really pissed that I didn't get his name.

Chapter Six

I've been awake for what seems like hours. I still haven't gotten past the four-hour time change from home, and it's been causing my brain to snap awake at an ungodly hour each morning and I'm unable to settle back down, no matter how tired I am. It also doesn't help that the sun starts filtering through my bedroom window at about six-thirty a.m., preempted by a large flock of birds racing to be the first ones awake. This morning it sounds like a catfight outside with the squawking that's going on. I thought the magpies and robins back home were bad, but their caws and cries are nothing compared to the *maui alauahio*, which happen to inhabit a large monkeypod tree outside my window. I should be grateful to bear witness to these tiny tropical birds, their vibrant yellow plumage a beautiful contrast to the dark green foliage on the canopy of the monkeypod. They're considered an endangered species and are usually found more upcountry in Maui, where the climate is cooler. But the shade of the large monkeypod, along with the abundance of seed pods it provides, must be appealing enough for these tiny birds to decide that the space right outside my bedroom window is the perfect spot for them to be singing their *whichy-wheesee-whurdy-whew* song endlessly, before the sun has even appeared.

I suppose that's not the only reason I'm lying here, watching the ceiling fan whirl tropical air around my bedroom. Today is registration day at school, the *new* school I'm going to be starting. I'm super-anxious about heading there today. I've never had to 'begin' anything, to start fresh. I've gone to the same neighborhood school, with the same set of friends and the same annoying teachers, my whole life. It might not have been perfect, and oftentimes I dealt with the self-made drama only kids who have grown up with each other can create, but it was what I knew.

Sure, starting a new school can be fun, and exciting and full of possibilities—but it can also be dangerous. One false move and I could end up floating alone through the peripheries of high school's social hierarchy. No one wants that, especially in their senior year.

And really, I don't even know if school is the same here as it was back home. There may be all these unwritten rules I'm not even aware of. I mean, at home I took French because, well, French is the second language in Canada and everyone takes French. I guarantee no one takes French in Hawaii. I start wondering—do I need to take Hawaiian? Will some of my classes be taught in Hawaiian?

I panic for a moment and look down at the registration sheet mailed to us yesterday with Maui Gardens Charter School letterhead. On it, lists my courses — Chemistry, Geometry, English, American History — *Oh Jesus* — and Computer Technology. No mention of Hawaiian anywhere, which I'm relieved to see. The flip side of the introduction letter also includes a list of extracurricular opportunities the school offers. In addition to band, drama, football and all the typical high school activities, I'm excited to see that there's a swim team and a track club. I was one of the top female swimmers at my club at home. My dresser was adorned with trophies and medals in everything from breaststroke to back crawl. A surge of sadness suddenly rushes through me as I think back to all my wins and the trophies I had to leave behind. There were too many for us to pack, even for us to ship with the rest of our belongings. Mom agreed to take them over to Robert's in a large cardboard box that she said she'd store in his garage — all my most precious belongings and shiny memories of childhood, hidden away in a dusty box to collect mold and mildew, left to be forgotten, like Mom has forgotten about me.

I check my watch and realize that I don't want to risk being late, even though it's just registration day. Dad was right. The house is equipped with two matching road bikes, I suppose as an attempt to get us out exploring Maui's glorious scenery. Judging by Google maps, the school should be only a fifteen-minute ride away, so if I leave right now, I should make it in time for orientation.

A little while later, I pull into the front walkway of my new high school, easing to a stop in front of the long row of bike racks adjacent to the parking lot. Groups of kids congregate along the walkway and sit on the front lawn. Out in the parking lot, more kids climb out of fancy sports cars and convertibles, high-fiving and jostling each other with all the excitement a new school year brings. I'm in awe at how the area overflows with pristine, high-end cars, all driven by students, not teachers. At home, less than a quarter of the school's parking lot was filled with students' cars, and even those were usually filthy, dented-up hatchbacks and pick-ups, the result of countless hours working for minimum wage at a fast-food joint. Of course, there were a couple of exceptions. A few of the families from our school had recently torn down old, rambling homes built on double lots, only to rebuild sprawling, new monstrosities, which always looked funny and out of place to me — grotesque mammoths among the quaint and tidy middle-class Victorian homes our neighborhood was known for.

But that definitely wasn't our family. We fell into the category of being completely and utterly plain and middle-class. We fit perfectly into the jigsaw puzzle of our neighborhood, our home not standing out in any particular way at all. We appreciated the quiet contentment that came from living in a home where the floorboards creaked, and the hot water flip-flopped from being scorching to be nonexistent. We were happy just being 'normal'. Well, I was, at least.

Of course, there were kids at my school who craved anything but normal. They flaunted their money with the latest electronics and trips to faraway places. They were the rare ones who could afford fancy cars and designer clothes — the ones who had money to spend every weekend, despite never having had even a part-time job. But everyone knew those kids as the rich ones. As much as they were revered, they were always held at arm's length, too, no one entirely trusting them enough to let them into their social circle. As much as the rich kids at home thought they ruled the school, they sat in the periphery more than they ever knew — because they couldn't be trusted, because they weren't one of *us*.

But here, in this oasis of wealth and money and sparkly things, in this world where extravagant cars matched gleaming new sneakers and designer purses, money is the common thread. Money is the normal. And despite my new home claiming otherwise, I'm not sure whether I'll fit in.

I'm suddenly self-conscious with the realization that my bike is the only one resting against the metal stands, even though I know it's an expensive bike that many of my friends at home would be envious of.

I try to push the feelings of insecurity out of my mind by concentrating on the buzz all around me. There are multiple booths set up all along the front of the school, convincing kids to come and join various teams and clubs. I linger on the large blue sign advertising the school's swim club and decide to wander over. The two girls running the booth could be twins with their long, shimmering blonde locks falling in loose waves around their smooth, tanned shoulders. One of the girls appears a bit taller than the other, although it's tough to tell since they're sitting. But her limbs reach long and lean, the muscles in her legs flexing provocatively as she crosses them under her flimsy sundress. The other girl suddenly laughs at something they're discussing, exposing brilliant white teeth set in a perfectly lip-glossed mouth. I glance down at my sweaty tank top and yoga pants. *It's only registration day*, I think to myself. I didn't realize everyone would be so dressed up. I resent the fact that I'm going to have to wait another full week for the rest of our belongings to arrive, because it means that the entire first week of school I'm going to be stuck wearing a collection of casual T-shirts and cut-offs. I did bring one summer dress, a breezy, flowery one that's fitted and plunging along the top. Maggie always begged me to wear that one because she said it made my boobs look huge.

Maggie... I'd gotten away with shoving her to the back of my mind the last few days, as I focused on moving in my things and settling into the new place. But standing here alone as all these other kids excitedly begin the next year of high school — my last year of high school — well, it makes me homesick for Maggie in a serious way. If I was at home right now, we'd be going back-to-school shopping, convincing our parents that three pairs of new shoes are *not* overdoing it. We'd be soaking in the last few warm, summer days before the chill of autumn falls upon us and causes the city to hibernate until the following spring. We'd giggle in front of our lockers at the end of our first day of school, unfairly separating the new kids into two groups — the ones with cuteness potential and the ones destined for the dork squad.

And now, here I am, walking up to two blonde beauties in charge of the swim team, who are probably casting harsh judgments on *me* this time. *Do I make the cut, or am I destined for the dork squad?*

"Hey there. Um, I was hoping to sign up for the swim team?"

They don't even hide the fact that they're looking me up and down, scouring me with a bristle brush before they respond.

"So, are you, like, an actual swimmer? Because we have a really great team. You need to be good, really good, to make the team. Have you raced on a team before?"

"Uh, yeah. At home, in Canada. I was the captain, actually. I do a one-hundred-meter freestyle in twenty-four seconds. But the breaststroke was always my favorite race. I was being scouted by some of the universities back home—um, before I moved here. I just moved here." I fidget with the bottom hem of my tank top and feel super-dorky holding my bike helmet on my hip. *God, why didn't I just leave it on my bike? Now I have to walk everywhere looking like a loser.*

They glance sideways at each other, an unspoken communication between them. *Do I pass their test?*

"Okay, well, we'll just have to see how you do at try-outs. They start next week. Just write your name here." I bend over the form, awkwardly passing my helmet over to my left hand so I can grab the pen with my right. There's a space for my name, grade and address. *Damn. I didn't think about my address. I forgot to look up my address!*

"Like I said, I just moved here, so I don't know my address yet." *What am I? In third grade?* I try again. "I live up on the hill in Wailea. Um, Kalani Street, I think it's called?"

There's a slight pause, as if my words need a moment to register, then suddenly the tension in the air dissipates, like a heavy fog has been lifted.

"Oh, wow, cool! Well, welcome to Maui Gardens Charter School!" The girl with the long, tan legs smiles wide and tosses her hair over one shoulder. It's as if someone flipped a switch and she has suddenly turned *on*, become alive. The only other person I've ever known to do that is Maggie. She could shine her smile so bright that one would think she was her own energy source. God, if I were Maggie, I'd have the confidence to reflect that smile right back at this beauty queen. *Oh, if only I could channel a bit of Maggie!*

"I'm Callie, and this is Emma. And it's totally awesome here. You'll love it! We're seniors and we head up the swim team, as well as acting as social convenors on the school council. So, anything that's going on with the school, we'll know about it! And we're happy to have you join us. If you live on Kalani Street, you must practically be our neighbors. Which house did you say you moved into?"

"Uh, the big one at the top of the hill, I guess? It has these huge front windows and a rooftop patio thing?"

"OMG, that house is just gorgeous! My parents have been eying it up for weeks. Do you know that a famous record producer lived there before you? Jean Paul something, I think... I don't know, he kept to himself mostly. But we were dying to find out who was going to be next. We totally thought it might be a Hollywood actor. There's been a few who've lived there while filming. So exciting. You are *so* lucky! I'd love to sneak a peek at the inside sometime." The other blonde nods eagerly in agreement, then they wait for me to say something in return.

"Oh, great! Yeah, I haven't really met anyone here yet, so I'd totally love to have you over sometime. I didn't know anyone famous had lived in my house. That's pretty cool. I'm still getting used to it, getting used to everything here, I guess. I'm really excited to be joining some clubs and stuff. I was involved in a lot back home. What types of things are going on at the school? Anything I'd want to be a part of?"

"Well, tomorrow there's going to be a big party at Little Beach. Kind of like a back-to-school bash, I guess?

Most of the seniors will be going. You could totally come to that. Starts at sunset. BYOB, and if you're into music, bring an instrument so you can jam with a bunch of the kids. We're not really into the music scene. We're mainly there for the booze and the boys. Right, Em?"

"Yeah, y'all should definitely come! It's a perfect way to start the year!" She checks my signature on the page then looks up at me again. "Where'd y'all say you were from again?"

I'm caught off-guard by her question, as it's obvious that *she's* the one with the accent. "Um, Canada. Edmonton, Alberta, actually. You probably don't know where that is. I just moved here. My dad and I..." I trail off, not knowing what to add next. Why does this always happen? Why do I feel the need for strangers to know my entire background? My messed-up family? I need to figure out a way of introducing myself without leaving it open to further examination.

It's not lost on me that Callie and Emma's demeanor changed drastically with the mention of my new address in the upscale community of Wailea, of the money it implies. But I can't say I'm entirely comfortable talking about my newfound wealth, because I'm not sure how to explain it to myself, never mind to other people. I'm self-conscious that I'll be judged for where I live and what my dad does. And there's no guarantee that it'll be in a good way.

The boy from my back yard comes back into my mind—how living in that house seemed to make him automatically assume I was a snotty, self-entitled bitch. His sudden, dismissive reaction flashes in my memory like a bolt of lightning—how he got really stand-offish, leaving abruptly without me being able to catch his name. I don't want to have to face that kind of criticism every time I meet someone new, which is why I figure that it's best to keep most of the details to myself.

But with these two girls, hearing about where I live seems to stoke their curiosity and respect, not push them away. It's tempting for me to take the bait.

"So yeah, you guys'll have to come by sometime to see the place. We have the best panoramic view of the ocean! And the pool is amazing — perfect for practicing laps!" I think I've said enough, and now I'm itching to get the conversation circling back to them. I've been in the spotlight for longer than I feel comfortable. "And where are you guys from?" I look deliberately at Emma. "It sounds to me like you're from the south somewhere?"

"Oh hon, what gave it away?" Emma tosses her hair back as she laughs. "Yes, ma'am, been here for almost two years and I can't seem to shake the twang. You can take the girl out of Texas, but you can't take Texas out of the girl!" She giggles at herself.

"Oh, come on. The boys love your accent! You always sound sweet and sassy, no matter what obscenities come out of your mouth!" Callie nudges Emma playfully.

"And how about you?" I ask Callie. "Are you originally from Maui?"

"Um, nobody's *originally* from Maui," Callie responds. "Well, no one who goes to Maui Charter anyway. Most of us are from all over the country and have moved here because, well, who wouldn't want to grow up in this paradise?"

"But what about the locals? The kids born and raised here?" I ask.

"Oh, I don't know where they go, probably some crappy state-run school in Kahului. We don't really have many 'locals' at Maui Charter, so we don't really follow what they do."

She says *locals* with such distaste that it immediately makes me feel uncomfortable. I mean, aren't *we* the invaders of *their* homeland? Shouldn't *we* be the ones paying the original Hawaiians a bit of respect?

"No, ma'am, Maui Gardens'll be the only school you'll want to go to. It wouldn't be worth your time to try any of the ones in Kahului or upcountry. Maui Gardens has, by far, the best reputation."

"Okay, well, that's good to know, I guess." And I do feel relieved that the school my dad has chosen for me is the best on the island, especially seeing as I'll have to start applying for colleges right away. But I also wonder why there's such a discrepancy. I grab the try-out schedule they give me and tell them I hope to make it out to the party.

As I head into the school to get my assigned textbooks and locker, I can't help but linger on the boy from the back yard. *I wonder if he goes to this school?* But then I remember how adamant Callie was that most locals don't choose Maui Gardens. Still, part of me hopes that maybe there are exceptions, that perhaps he *is* the exception.

I spend the next hour or so wandering down hallways and classrooms, trying to orient myself to my new surroundings, but at the same time, I'm intent on finding the curious young gardener. I haven't heard anyone talking about another school anywhere near here, so I'm hopeful he's a student. He must be. Maybe he's just finishing up some of his dad's jobs today, and he'll be back to start school for real on Monday?

The flash of skin under his T-shirt, the flick of his glossy black hair, the intimate press of his thumb against my shoulder...

Whoosh... There's that elevator ride one more time.

Chapter Seven

After wandering around aimlessly on my own, there's finally an announcement for us to gather in the school auditorium so Mr. Rudolf, the balding and robust principal, can perform his welcome speech to new students. I begrudgingly find a seat near the back, anticipating that I'll be itching to bolt out of there before he's even done. He drones on about the school's superior academic achievements, its elite sports and theater programs, and spends another fifteen minutes answering stupid questions about whether quinoa is offered in the school's cafeteria and whether they're installing some sort of security team to keep watch over the student parking lot during the day, to make sure the fancy cars aren't vandalized.

I lose count of how many times I roll my eyes, and I ache to whisper conspiratorially with Maggie. God, she would hate it here. She made fun of kids who wore Apple watches to school because she thought they were too flashy. I glance down at the hand resting on the armrest next to me. Tanned and sprinkled with dark hair at the knuckles, this middle-aged man wears a large-faced, diamond Rolex with a thick gold band. When I peer up at the rest of him, he's exactly as I suspect—lean and trim, wearing an expensive golf shirt, Ray-Ban aviators resting on the top of his salt-and-pepper hair. I also notice that the lady to his left, presumably his wife, is the one who, just a moment ago, cared so passionately about quinoa, but now is scrolling feverishly through her Pinterest page.

I remember my dad's comment about being willing to come with me today if I wanted him here. And I don't know—would it have been better? Would he look the part, play the game? I think of him, with his soft middle and pale skin, his tired eyes and receding hairline. A piece of me cringes inside, because as much as he's the one who got me here, I don't think my dad fits in any better than I do.

I scramble out of my seat as Principal Rudolf starts introducing the teaching staff. I have to excuse myself past Rolex man and quinoa lady, while my bike helmet bumps along their knees. They scowl up at me, and she rubs her leg where the helmet touches her, as if it leaves a trace of dirt on her perfectly tailored pantsuit.

I race to my bike, still the *only* bike sitting at the front of the school, and I can't ride away fast enough. I want the salty air to rush through my hair. I want the burn to form in my legs. I just want to feel a surge of different things than I feel right now—embarrassment, awkwardness, confusion in trying to belong. I want it to blow away in the tropical breeze.

I decide it's time for me to explore—maybe a hike through the hills upcountry or across the lush rainforests to the north. I don't really care where I go. I just need a moment to simply *be*.

Once I arrive back home, I scroll through websites on my laptop, appraising the variety of hikes available on the island. Before coming here, I had no idea that Maui was so full of outdoor activities. I mean, sure, I knew there was surfing, snorkeling, deep sea fishing — but I didn't realize there were so many land activities to do that didn't even involve getting wet.

I discover the island is abundant with a diverse selection of hikes — ones for beginners, as well as ones that look too tough, even for me. I quickly mark down an easy walking trail to do with Dad, a leisurely stroll perfect for his, well...lack of physical exertion. It's down in the Iao Valley, not far from the town of Wailuku, and boasts a twelve-hundred-foot natural lookout point, marking the battle King Kamehameha fought and won, changing the history of Hawaii forever. *Pretty cool*, plus the website mentioned that a few movies have been filmed there, so that's something too.

Then, of course there's the famous Twin Falls hike on the way to Hana. It's relatively easy to get to and promises a picture-perfect waterfall oasis spilling into a deep-set cavern, dripping in vines and greenery. There's supposed to be a stand that sells the best banana bread on the island there. It sounds like the perfect place to spend an afternoon, and my hot, sticky skin is itching for a dip in one of the refreshing pools right now.

But I'm not wanting to drive all the way across the island, so I look for something a little closer to South Maui, where we live. My eye catches on a hike down in the Makena State Park Wildlife reserve, only a ten-minute drive from our home. It's an area sanctioned by the state to preserve the untapped beauty of ancient, hardened lava flows and coastal wildlife. Apparently, visitors park their vehicles or bikes at the entrance lot, then are able to wander through a dry, desert-like abyss, before the terrain gives way to rocky cliffs with magnificent views of the Pacific. The website warns that there's no cell service in the park, so the hikes are not recommended to do alone. But anyone who makes their way through the rocky terrain and down the steep bluffs without toppling into the rough surf below earns the right to explore the untapped beaches that await. The website boasts white-sand beaches that stretch around protected coves, home to coral reefs teaming with sea life not found anywhere else — turtles, manta rays, reef sharks and a myriad of colorful fish, all set in isolated bays, all protected from the world. It sounds like heaven to me, and I can't wait to start exploring.

I snap my laptop shut. *This is exactly what I've been waiting for.*

* * * *

Twenty minutes into the hike, I'm swearing at myself for not bringing enough water. How could I have thought one water bottle was enough? The website said to bring at least a gallon per person! I'm grateful for the hiking boots I'd decided to strap on, though. The rugged lava rocks are far more treacherous and slippery than I'd originally thought, and there's no way I want to risk spraining an ankle out here in the middle of nowhere.

Literally, that is where I am — in the middle of nowhere. It looks as if I've arrived on another planet, like I'm an alien castaway. The endless fields of jet-black lava rock spread out from me in all directions, like a cosmic wasteland. It reminds me of those black and white videos of the first man on the moon, except that I feel the sun blazing on my skin as I take my first steps. The lightly marked trail travels south through piles of large boulders and jagged shards, making it difficult to navigate without stumbling. The dark rocks attract the sun's intense afternoon rays, absorbing its heat and causing the area to feel at least ten degrees warmer than it was back at home.

I read on the website I'd found that the island of Maui was actually created more than a million years ago by the eruption of two large volcanoes—Haeleakela in the east, and Mauna Kahalawai in the west. The hot, molten lava poured out from the volcano peaks, only to stop in an abrupt face-off when it met the cool expanse of the Pacific Ocean. The result was sprawling fields of igneous rock, otherworldly and uninhabitable in their form and vastness. But eventually, much of the volcanoes' lava rock eroded over time, turning into nutrient-rich soil from which Maui's tropical oasis now thrives. That is, except for the untouched areas in this part of Southern Maui, where the lava fields are still only home to roaming goats and tropical birds.

Farther east, the fields give way to the slope of the Haleakala Mountain, with its rich expanse of lush greenery and wildlife. Wispy clouds shield the mountain in mist much of the time, with the peak just poking out above to greet the sun. I imagine the cool crispness of the shade provided by bamboo forests and scented eucalyptus trees, and berate myself for choosing this desert hike, today of all days. The sun hammers down on my neck and shoulders and it seems I can't lather the sunscreen on thick enough for it to actually protect me.

I glance out west and catch the welcome sight of shimmering turquoise water spread out before me. I know that if I can hike to the edge of the lava fields, the rocks will drop off to untouched white-sand beaches below, and I'll be able to get my fill of swimming and snorkeling. The thought of napping in the shade of a giant rock wall while listening to the angry surf lap up against the beach is enough to make me veer off the path and traverse my way through waist-high boulders to find the land's edge. I know I'm getting close when I hear the crashing of a wave through a huge blow hole, and feel it spit out a refreshing ocean spray all over me, its opening hidden among the rock's ledges. The repetitive thump of water slamming into the rocks hypnotizes me, making me feel the weight of the world that is bigger than me. It makes me recognize that my problems, my loneliness, my drama, are nothing compared to the vastness of the ocean before me, the power of the waves.

Despite the beads of sweat now streaming down the sides of my face, drenching the front of my sports bra and sticking my yoga shorts uncomfortably between my thighs, I keep trekking up the loosely made trail. When I glance up at one point to assess how much farther the coastal drop-off is, I notice a dark green pick-up truck parked about a half-mile up ahead off the main path. As there are no vehicles allowed in the state park, so my first thought is that it must be a park ranger out to ticket people not abiding by the rules.

I scour my brain to try to remember the blog posted on the park's website, outlining do's and don'ts, to see if I've broken any rules. Part of me is afraid I'm going to get in trouble, maybe from veering off the main path or for overstaying my welcome. But part of me welcomes the park ranger's presence, because it has been over an hour since I've seen another human being and I'm starting to worry about making my way back. At the very least, the ranger is likely to have a couple bottles of water to share, and if I'm really lucky, he or she will offer a ride back to Wailea.

But as I get closer to the truck, I notice no one is sitting in the driver's seat or leaning up against the truck bed. It looks to be abandoned. I start to worry about why someone would abandon their truck in the middle of this vast desert, when a movement beyond the bluff to the right catches my eye. Three long sticks poke out from beyond the cliff, and they're swaying slightly with the breeze. I can't make out what exactly they are, but considering there's no vegetation in sight, I don't imagine them to be from trees or shrubs poking out from the side of the rocks.

I clamber closer to the ledge, using my hands to help navigate the steep incline as I climb higher. The sharp rocks dig into my palms. At one point, I lose my footing and my right foot slides down the gravelly bank, causing me to tumble forward. I reach out and catch myself before my head knocks into a boulder to the right, but not before my knee slams to the ground, smashing into a shard of jutting rock. A sharp pain slashes through my leg, and it's only a moment until I feel the warm trickle of blood down the front of my shin. Wearing nothing but a sports bra and yoga shorts, I've got nothing to mop the mess up with. Seeing as I'm out of water, I can't even rinse the gash off. I think about turning around and descending the embankment in order to head home, but then I figure I may as well look to see if someone's there to help. I'm just about at the top anyway. It's going to be a long hike back to the parking lot, and another twenty-minute bike ride home. I'm not sure I'll make it without some more water and some sort of bandage to cover the sticky gash.

I balance on the side of the slope for a minute to pick out the pebbles of gravel that are embedded in my palms. I squint my eyes toward the sun, take a huge, deep breath and begin the upward climb once again. By the time I'm at the top of the rock shelf, beads of sweat run like rivulets down my bare stomach and my chest burns with exertion. I brace myself against a large boulder and peer down over the precipice.

I'm surprised to find that the three sticks I'd seen wobbling in the ocean breeze are actually long, thin fishing poles wedged in between sections of a rock crag. They stick straight up so the tips point straight into the sky. Beyond them, down at the far end of the embankment, rests a small, open cooler filled with two cans of beer, two small mangoes and what looks to be a cheese sandwich. The soulful chords of a Jack Johnson ballad dance on the breeze, floating from a small speaker set up against the rocks. And down where the black rocks start to spread out into patches of soft white sand that then extends to a sparkling blue, pristine cove, lies a boy, shirtless and tanned, in a pair of old khaki shorts. He's stretched out on the private beach with seemingly no cares in the world, his hands clasped behind his head, his right foot tapping along with the music. His face, smooth and sun-kissed, is turned upward, toward the sun. His eyes are closed, while his long black hair mingles with the sand to form a shaggy mane around his head. He looks to be one with this strange and glorious world.

I gasp out loud. It causes me to lose my footing and slide a few feet down the embankment. Managing to just barely catch myself, I stand upright again as the boy leans up on his elbows and turns to see who the uninvited intruder is.

"Uh, hi. I, er, saw the fishing poles and heard the music. I couldn't help but check it out. I didn't know someone was down here."

He struggles to a standing position and walks over to me.

His wide grin, lean build and dark eyes are unmistakable.

"Bikini-girl from the house on the hill." He smiles, resting his hands on his hips. "Well, what the hell are you doing out here in the middle of nowhere?"

"Oh...hi. I didn't know it was you." I flush and pray that it passes for a sunburn. "I'm just, I don't know...exploring, I guess? I was just taking a hike. You know, looking for one of the secluded beaches. I saw it on a website." *God, I'm rambling.* Why do I always ramble when I'm nervous?

"Man, there are a million beaches in Maui. You don't need to hike across a lava field to find one." He takes a few steps closer.

"Well, there must be something special about this spot if *you* came all the way out here too." I catch the indignation in my voice, and I'm annoyed by how snotty I sound. But, before I have a chance to soften my words, the boy clambers over, reaching out to me.

"Jesus, what'd you do to your leg?" In an instant, he kneels in front of me as he gently holds on to the sides of my calf. Miraculously, the throbbing pain disappears and is replaced by an electric hum throughout my body. This boy is definitely *not* aware of personal boundaries. This is the second time he's touched me, and I don't even know his name. The mystery excites me more than I care to admit.

"Oh, it's just from hiking. I didn't realize these rocks are so freaking sharp! I'm sure it's fine, though. It doesn't really hurt all that much."

"Yeah, I can't tell you how many times I've messed up my legs on these rocks too. But you really have to watch it. They're super-sharp. We better clean this up to make sure there are no gravelly bits stuck in there."

He reaches his hand up for me to grab, so that I can just hop down the last three feet of the rockslide. I land gratefully on the soft white sand and follow him through a maze of smooth, dark boulders that are worn from years of being washed by the waves.

We stop at a wide expanse of smooth sand where he's already laid out a beach blanket, and he orders me to sit. He walks over to the frothy sea, dips in a fluffy beach towel, and wrings it out as he strides back to me.

"It might sting a bit from the salt, but I think it's supposed to be good with cleaning cuts. Here… Let me just…" His voice trails off as he concentrates on my gash. He holds my leg gingerly, stretching it out along the length of the blanket. He first taps the cool, wet cloth to the area around the cut, then looks up to my face, assessing my pain level. When he assumes it's okay, he presses the towel to the cut itself, gently squeezing the salt water down my leg to rinse away the pebbles and grime. It stings and my eyes well up with tears, but then he transfers his weight to his other leg in an attempt to get more comfortable, inadvertently pressing his free hand into my upper thigh to steady himself — *my bare upper thigh.* The touch is so personal, so unexpected, that it causes a rush of goosebumps to appear all up and down my body. My bare skin has not been touched by another human being since Marcus, and faint memories of him and me sneaking out to the park flood my brain. My body reacts to the touch like a long-lost love, pumping blood furiously throughout my veins and quickening my breath. The touch of his warm hand spread gently across my bare thigh erases any sting occurring in my knee and instead creates a welcome warmth through the rest of my body.

He mistakes this for pain, I think, looking up with raised eyebrows to make sure I'm all right.

"I'm good. It just stings a bit," I lie, relieved he isn't yet aware of the effect of his hand on my leg.

As he bows his head back down to continue working on cleaning my wound, it gives me a chance to examine every part of him up close. His legs look like runner's legs, long and sinewy, and I wonder to myself whether he's on the school's track team. He's got a faint patch of dark, downy hair on his lower back, right where his khaki shorts hang loosely around his hips. His back and shoulders stretch broad and strong, the muscles rippling as they maneuver around my body. He's got an intricate black tattoo wrapped around his left shoulder and bulging bicep, a pattern of interlocking lines, shapes and geometric designs that converge to form the outline of a shark.

"Cool tattoo," I blurt out, surprised I've said it aloud.

"Oh, thanks. Yeah, I just got it a few months ago. But it's true what people say. You get addicted after your first tattoo and no one stops at one. I'm thinking about getting another one on my other arm. You? I mean, do you have any tattoos?"

I open my mouth to tell him that there's no way my parents would approve of a tattoo, but I'm worried it would sound really lame, so I just shake my head instead.

We sit in a contented silence for another moment as he puts the towel to the side and secures a large rectangular bandage to my knee, wrapping it in a clingy gauze.

"There, that should keep it clean and dry for the rest of the day. It doesn't look like you'll need any stitches, but hey, I'm no doctor." He gives me another boyish grin, then runs his hand through his damp hair. I can't help but blush once more.

"Well, thanks. I'm really glad you happened to be here. I mean, that I happened to find you. Not that I was looking for you...but it was a nice surprise. You know, that you were here..." *God, I'm terrible at this.* "Sorry... Let me try again. So, I'm Jess. And it's really nice to meet you, again I mean. It's really nice to see you again."

"I'm Kai. I guess we never got each other's names last time, did we? Yeah, it's nice that you stumbled over here, and I got a chance to see you again too." He offers me a wide and honest smile. I find myself meeting his gaze and smiling back.

"So, school starts on Monday. Argh...where did the summer go?" I look away from him and dig my hands deep into the cool sand on either side of me. "Do you go to Maui Gardens Charter too?" *I hope, I hope, I hope...*

"Me? Ha, right." He tosses his head back and squints at the sun. "Nope. No way. I'm not quite Maui Charter quality. I'm pretty sure the yearly tuition there is more than my parents make put together."

"What do you mean? We have to pay extra to go there?" Maybe I sound like an idiot, but back in Edmonton, we don't really *do* private schools. Pretty much everyone goes to public school, and all the schools are pretty decent. No one has to pay extra for anything. It shocks me to think anyone has to save up money just to go to school. *How can one school end up being that much better than another?*

"Yeah, you've got to pay to go there—a lot. Basically, only the rich kids from out of state go to that school, no offense or anything. That's just the way it is. No, I go to Kahului High. It's where most of the locals go. It's all right there, though. The teachers may be crap, but the kids are cool."

My heart sinks at the thought that I won't be seeing him at school on my first day. It would have been nice to see a familiar face, especially *this* familiar face.

"So, what are you doing way down at this end of the island then? I'm guessing this isn't anywhere near your home?" I ask him. If there's one thing I've learned from the last couple of days riding my bike around Wailea, it's that a person needs to have money to live there. Dad was right. As lavish as our home is, it doesn't even stick out here. I'm guessing there isn't a single home under a million dollars in this whole area of the island. I glance at Kai's dirty sneakers and think back to the beat-up pick-up truck I first saw parked off the trail.

"Well, I helped Dad finish up with a couple of his jobs for the day, so he said I could go fishing. And it's not a well-known fact, but this here is pretty much the best fishing spot on the island."

"But I thought this was a natural wildlife reserve? Are you, like, actually allowed to fish here?"

"Nope, not at all. And I'll probably get fined if the park warden comes by. Although they're a little more lenient with the locals than they are with the tourists. But I've been coming out here long enough to know their schedule pretty well, and they don't like to be out patrolling the lava fields in the middle of the day—too hot for them. I don't think many of their trucks have A/C. Plus, they end up spending more time saving dumb tourists who don't bring proper supplies than they do catching bad guys like me." He smirks, and although he's trying to make a joke, the 'dumb tourist' comment stings a bit. I fumble for something to say.

"I'm not a tourist, you know. Well, not anymore. We live here now. So, I guess I'm kind of a local now, like you."

"No offense, Jess, but no matter how long you live here, you'll never be a local. You can't bring your stacks of cash and your whitey skin from the mainland, buy up a sweet property like the one you live in and think that you're going to just fit right in. Nope. As much as you try, you'll only ever be a guest on this island."

And for the second time today, I've found myself peering in from the outside.

Chapter Eight

"Jess, what the hell are you doing?" Kai lies stretched out on the beach blanket but snaps his eyes open when he feels me rush past him into the surf. We've finished the beers and the cheese sandwich, and have lounged out on this private beach, away from the rest of the world, for the last couple of hours.

"I want to go for a swim. That's why I came all the way out here in the first place. There's supposed to be amazing snorkeling and swimming out in these private coves. I want to see some sea life. Don't worry. I'm an awesome swimmer. I was even captain of the girls' swim team back home!" My brain swirls from the beer and I feel inexplicably charged, like the air right before a big thunderstorm. I want the waves to wash all over me, to clean the sticky sweat from my skin. I want to keep on feeling alive.

I take a few more steps farther into the waves when Kai snatches my waist and pulls me back.

"What are you doing? You don't want me to go swimming?" I try to respond sharply, but the beer has made me slur my *m*'s, and it comes out as a garbled mess.

"For one thing, do you not remember the giant gash on your leg? The one I just cleaned up an hour ago? Secondly, Jess, take a look around you right now. A really good look…" I follow his gaze down into the azure water lapping around me.

At first, I just see patches of dark rocks, like the ones up on the beach. Then my vision becomes clearer as I stare into the waves and I realize that all of the rocks have spiky little mounds around them, poking out into all directions.

"What are they?" I stammer as I freeze my legs into place, too scared to take a step.

"Those are sea urchins…thousands of them. They don't really do much other than glue themselves onto the rocks, but if you step on them, or worse, fall right on top of them, their barbs will puncture your skin in a hundred places, and you won't be able to pull them out. Forget stitches for your knee. We'll be rushing you to the hospital to have these little suckers surgically removed.

"Do you have porcupines where you live? I mean, in Canada?" he asks, as if to make his point clearer. "Imagine a whole neighborhood of porcupines waiting to shoot their quills into you. Not fun, trust me. I've been struck more than a few times while surfing."

"Oh, I…didn't know. The website said…" I trail off, not wanting to risk sounding even more ignorant. His comment about me never becoming a local rings through my ears.

"Come on. Follow me back out. Just watch where you're stepping." I turn gingerly in the waves so I don't topple over, then I trace his footsteps carefully back to shore.

"I just wanted to go swimming and find a special spot. I didn't know…"

"Yeah, I get it. All the tourists want the same thing. I guess we all do. I'll show you a different spot for snorkeling and swimming, I promise. But not today. We should get going. It's getting late anyway, and I've got to make it all the way back to Kula. Come on. Help me pack up, and I'll give you a ride back to your *palace*." He smirks when he says this, and it gives me the courage to slap him back playfully on the arm.

"What the princess wants, the princess gets." I retort. I can play at this game too.

The hike down the embankment to Kai's truck is a lot easier than the hike to get there. Kai seems to know his way around each rock and boulder and bypasses the steepest slopes, so I don't bail and hurt myself again. I'm in awe at how effortlessly he navigates his way, especially seeing as he's carrying the cooler, a beach towel, three fishing rods and another cooler filled with his catch of the day. I offer several times to help, but I get the sense that he doesn't think I'm the most coordinated person in the world, because he keeps insisting that he's got it. Or maybe he's just a gentleman. I like to think of it that way instead.

When we get to his truck, he throws over a large bottle of water he had lying in the front seat. I open it eagerly and guzzle the whole thing at once, letting the water drip all down my chest. We each had a beer down by the ocean, but instead of quenching my thirst, it just left me feeling lightheaded and dizzy.

"Thirsty maybe?" Kai laughs as he opens the car door for me. *He opens the car door?* Okay, maybe he is part gentleman.

"Yeah, sorry. I guess I'm just not used to the heat and humidity. You know, coming from Canada." I sit gingerly on the cracked vinyl seat of the truck, cringing as it burns the back of my thighs. "Have you ever been there? To Canada, I mean?" I ask.

"No, I've never actually left the island. Why would I? When you live in paradise, there's no reason to leave."

I suppose he's right. But still...I wonder whether it's true that he's never had the desire to see what else is out there, to explore the world. As much as I was initially freaked out with the idea of moving here, it's exciting to start something new. And next year, we'll both be off to college. The promise of endless possibilities and newfound independence makes me giddy with excitement.

"What about for college next year? Where do you want to go?"

"Well, I'm not even sure about college, to tell you the truth. My grades aren't super-great. But I don't know, the University of Hawaii has a college campus here. It's pretty small, but I think I'd get in, especially since I'm a local. They hold a ton of spots for people born here. I'm just not sure what to study. They've got a decent automotive program and I'm pretty good with my hands. What about you? Have you thought about next year?"

"Not at all, really. God, I haven't even started this year yet! I'm still worried about my first day on Monday. I met a couple of girls from the swim team at registration. They mentioned something about a party tomorrow. It sounds kinda cool. I've never been to a beach party before. It would be great to meet up with people before starting class. You know, so I can see a familiar face on day one. But it's not like I want to go alone. Who would ever want to go to a party alone?"

"Yeah? So, where's the party at?" he asks casually.

"They mentioned it's going to be at Little Beach? And to BYOB. Oh, and they said to bring an instrument if you have one…but I don't. Well, not unless you count the recorder I learned to play in sixth grade. But no one wants to hear that."

"Seriously? *Little Beach*? How tacky! Let me guess… The girls who invited you are self-obsessed, celebrity wannabe's, who are here for a year or two while their rich *daddies* are working on some big business venture, probably taking away jobs from the people who *actually* live here? Am I right?" His words are bitter and harsh.

Suddenly, it's like he's insulting *me*.

I am one of the self-entitled snobs he's referring to.

My dad is the rich businessman taking away all the jobs.

And I'm pissed. Because even though he hasn't directed the comment at me—God, I don't even *know* these girls—it's true. All of it. I know it, and I'm ashamed of it, even though I've done nothing and there's absolutely *nothing* I can do about it.

"You know, it's just a party that I was invited to. Sorry I don't know the ins and outs of the island. You don't have to be so freaking rude about it." I turn so Kai can't see the wetness in my eyes or the scowl of my eyebrows, but also so I can take in the expanse of the ocean shimmering under the setting sun and feel the breeze from the open window caressing my loose hair.

"Sorry… I didn't mean to piss you off. I've just seen it before, is all. People come. People go. People take while they're here. And the rest of us are still left, picking up the pieces."

From the wobble in his voice, it sounds like there's more to what he's saying, but he's holding it back. He's locking it away for now. I can tell he does feel bad, because through the reflection in the side window, I notice him giving me a sideways glance every few seconds, as if he's willing me to come around.

I also see his hand on the gear shift of the old truck. His fingers tap up and down, and twist on it — restless, waiting to be calmed, waiting to be held. But I'm not giving in.

"You know that Little Beach is a nude beach, right?"

My head immediately snaps to attention.

"What? What are you even talking about?" I stammer.

"Check it out. Google it." Now that we've finally arrived somewhere with cell reception, I'm able to grab my phone and connect with the world for the first time all afternoon. Sure enough, when I google 'Little Beach, Maui', up pop blurry pictures of naked blobs walking up and down a pristine beach with crashing waves.

I burst out laughing, covering my mouth as I do, because I don't trust myself not to snort all over Kai's truck. He erupts into a fit of laughter too, the sound spilling out of the open window like wind chimes tickled by the breeze. I scroll through the pictures on my phone, turning them to him as I go, each picture more horrendous and obnoxious than the last.

After a few minutes, I'm laughing so hard that the phone slips from my grasp and lands on the bench seat between us. As I pick it up, my hand brushes against his on the gear shift, and instead of moving it away, I let it rest there. I let the weight of my hand quell his fidgety fingers.

"So, you want to go to the party with me?" I beg.

He looks at me sideways and gives me a devilish smile. "Hell ya. I thought you'd never ask."

Chapter Nine

Dad and I sit out on the rooftop patio eating a quickly tossed-together pesto pasta dish and well-intentioned barbecued steak. Mom did most of the cooking at home and now Dad and I flounder together like two fish out of water in the kitchen. He has claimed the BBQ grill, and I'm in charge of the stovetop. Together, we attempted to pull off a somewhat balanced meal. He's been working late every evening since we've arrived, so tonight's meal of pasta and steak is a welcome change from the sandwiches and store-bought potato salad I've been eating all week.

"Well, I think we did pretty good for ourselves tonight, kiddo," he comments with a mouth full of noodles. "It's not your mom's roast beef, but I think we're going to make it all right, you and I."

The way he says "*you and I*" feels so lonely, so pathetic, that it makes me cringe inside — because I'm doing everything in my power to dampen this feeling of isolation, to find someone else to be with other than him, that I forget he's got no one here either. His wife of eighteen years just walked out on him, with another man—carrying another man's baby, for God's sake!

"Dad, how are you doing with everything? I mean, I know work has been busy, but how are *you* doing? Sometimes I'm all focused on me and I forget to ask."

A shadow crosses over his face and he takes another sip of his drink.

"Honey, you don't have to worry about me. I'm good. Well, I will be good, just need time to move on is all. We're on to a new adventure, you and me. And I kind of like that it's just us. You know, I wouldn't want anyone else in my passenger seat." He reaches across the table and squeezes my hand.

When I was little, Dad would sometimes let me ride in the passenger seat of his sedan when Mom wasn't around. He knew she forbade it for safety reasons. But he used to tell me that I was his favorite co-captain. I would sit up there, barely able to see past the dashboard, and he would let me press all the buttons on the radio and heat controls, pretending we were in a cockpit and I was in charge of the instrument panel. He always pretended there was enemy fire when we started down our street and would jolt the steering wheel back and forth, as long as there weren't any cars around. I would jostle in my seat, trying to hold on, and I would inevitably erupt in a fit of giggles. Then he would pretend we'd been hit by an enemy plane, and he would pull over to the side of the road. He'd tell me to put on my parachute and jump to the back seat before he drove up to our driveway. He always wanted me back in my regular seat when we got home, in case Mom was out and could see. He knew she'd be mad, and that it was better to just keep it from her—our secret. It made me feel special, as if I were a little higher on my dad's affection meter than my mom. I loved it. I held it over my mom as if it were a contest where she was always getting second place. Maybe that was what finally blew up their marriage. She wanted to be the co-pilot all along, and he never gave her the chance. But Robert did.

"Have you talked to her yet? Since we've been here?" I ask him quietly. He clearly knows who I'm referring to without even asking.

"Yeah, I have, a few times. Jess, I was with your mother for almost twenty years. A relationship that long doesn't just disappear, even if we're all the way across the Pacific. We've had a bunch of loose ends to tie up with the house and some of our banking details. I wanted to make sure she was settled okay with Robert—that it was a done deal. And of course, she's been asking about you like crazy."

There's a long pause. I know he's expecting me to jump in and say how much I've missed her and how much I love her and all that bull. But I don't—even though one miniscule part of me *might* feel a pang of longing for my mom.

"You really should call her, Jess. She's never gone this long without talking to you—ever. She didn't do any of this to hurt you. You know that, right? It was all about her and me. And we're working that out. There's no reason for you not to be connecting with her."

My brain keeps going around in circles, because I do miss her. I miss our little family. But then I think about how she's the one to blame for the dismantling of my life and I get pissed off again, so pissed off that it makes me want to punish her and never talk to her again. I know how much that hurts her, but it hurts me too.

"Yeah, well, I'll think about it. I'm just not ready yet, okay, Dad? Maybe you can forgive and forget that easily, but I'm a Taurus, remember? I hold grudges...for a long time." I give him a teasing smirk and start piling up our dishes.

"You know, the other thing we have to start talking about is colleges. Now's the time to start applying, you know."

"Oh, I just sort of assumed I'd go back home for college. I guess I always figured the University of Alberta, to tell you the truth. That's where most of my friends would be going."

"Well, your mom and I had always assumed that too. It's a great school and we figured you could save a bundle of money by living at home with us. But now, well, now you have all sorts of new opportunities!"

"What do you mean? Why now?"

"Well, Jess, now that I have a green card, you have the opportunity to apply to all of these US colleges you wouldn't have qualified for in the past. They only reserve so many spots for foreign exchange students. And, to tell you the truth, we just wouldn't have been able to afford them before. But now? Well, now we have access, plus we have more money to spend. If you keep your grades up, you have so many options to choose from!" He pulls a stack of pamphlets from a drawer in the dining hutch that sits against the far wall.

I browse through them, various school names I've only vaguely heard of on TV shows and movies dancing through my brain—USC, Chapel Hill, University of Florida—all these places seem so far away, so foreign. Panic rises inside me.

"Dad, I'm going back home for school. I don't want to have to move again in less than a year. I'm not even settled here yet!" An unjustified angers seeps through my skin. Is he forcing me away? Does he not want me here with him?

"Relax, honey. You don't have to go anywhere you don't want to. It's just nice to keep your options open. Apply to the University of Alberta, then, for me, apply to a few others too, okay? Your opinion of where you want to go might well change in a few months, and by then, it'll be too late for you to apply."

I respond with a hesitant 'okay', as I sort through the stack a little more thoroughly this time. I pull a few pamphlets aside that look somewhat appealing. Then I stop when I see one with the University of Hawaii splashed across the cover.

"What about here? What do you think about me staying here for school?"

"Well, it's not my number one choice for you. I don't think it's rated as a top school or anything. But I suppose it can't hurt for you to apply. And the good thing would be that you'd still be close to me. I would absolutely love that." He reaches out to squeeze my shoulder and I soften toward him once more.

"Okay, I'll take a look at these this week and start the application process. I'm leaning toward the University of Alberta, though, just so you know. It would be nice to be back home with my friends, where I know my way around. And I'm starting to miss Maggie."

"You haven't spoken to her yet?" He's shocked. "Honey, you guys have been best friends for so long!"

"Yeah, she and I had a disagreement before we left, and we didn't have a chance to clear things up." I don't dare tell him that she was fooling around with my boyfriend. I'm close with my dad, but not *that* close.

"Well, whatever it was about, I can only imagine it's been resolved by now. I really think you should give her a call. Maybe around the same time you call your mom, okay?" His look is pleading, but kind.

"Okay, okay. I'll call her. And I'll *think* about calling Mom soon, too. Is that good enough for you?"

"I suppose, for now." He winks. "So, where's this party you're off to tonight? I have to admit that I'm pretty impressed you've been invited to a party before the first day of school has even begun."

"Well, it's not a big deal. It sounds like all the seniors go, so it's not like I got some sort of special invite. Some girls just mentioned it at registration. But it'll probably be lame. Did I tell you I signed up for the swim team, though?"

"No, you didn't, honey. That's fantastic! What a way to get yourself involved on day one. I hope they realize they've got a new breaststroke champ joining their team. Did you tell them how many races you've won?"

"Well, I mentioned I was on the team back home. But I still need to try out. It's not like I'm a shoo-in." As I turn to walk the plates back into the house, I see a dark green pick-up truck weaving its way up the hill to our place. I don't want to risk Dad asking questions about Kai, so I hastily leave the plates on the edge of the grill and grab my bag.

"Hey, Dad, are you okay cleaning up tonight? I think I see my friends pulling up to the house and I don't want to make them wait." I pray that Kai pulls right up onto the curved driveway, instead of parking at the edge of the gate. That way, the view of his truck will be obscured from where we're sitting on the rooftop patio. It's not that my dad would be judgy about me going to a party with a boy in an old pick-up. It's the fact that

I'm going with a *boy* I barely know that'll be the problem. Moving to Maui has not changed my dad's stance on dating, unfortunately.

"Okay, so you've got your phone, Jess? And your friends will drop you off by midnight? I don't know my way around the island all that well yet, so I don't want to be sending a search party out for you, all right?"

"Yes, I promise I won't be late. Love you, Dad." I bend down to kiss his stubbly cheek, then race down the staircase that leads to the back lawn. I want to hurry back toward the front and catch Kai before he has a chance to ring the doorbell.

I'm panting as I approach the truck and Kai steps out to greet me. I'm thinking he's coming out to hug me, and my palms get all clammy as I stand frozen, like a dummy. But all he does is walk around to open my door, sweeping his arm dramatically.

"Your chariot, my lady." I blush for the billionth time in front of him and wonder if he thinks my face is naturally the color of ripe strawberries.

I'm grateful the vinyl seat isn't scorching like it was yesterday, but I notice that the discarded water bottle I guzzled after our hike is rolling around on the floor. It makes me laugh a bit to think that Kai's room is probably as messy as mine. He slams his door after walking back over to his side of the truck and turns to me.

"So, we're good to go? Recorder and all?"

"Well, at the last minute I ditched the recorder," I tease, "but I was able to grab these instead. I figure I owe you." I open my shoulder bag to reveal a six-pack of Longboard Ale. When Keanu stocked our house, he stocked it full of beer, without realizing that my dad only drinks wine and hard alcohol. So, I've got at least six cases of beer to claim without anyone even realizing they're gone.

"Sweet, because my older brother Danny wouldn't buy me any tonight, you know, since I'm driving. But maybe just one won't hurt."

Kai turns the truck around and we weave down the zig-zag road of the hill. The houses we pass are still monstrous dream homes, but the shock value of them has dissipated the more I've seen them this week. I wonder if Kai still sees them the same way too, or whether this looks like a regular neighborhood to him after coming here all the time.

He expertly navigates the road, seeming to know exactly where this Little Beach is located. Once at the bottom of the hill, we turn left onto Makena Road and enjoy a drive south along the ocean. As the sun sets, it casts a golden glow that spreads out from the horizon. Swirls of pinks and oranges melt into the clouds, reminding me of the sunrises back home—which reminds me of Marcus—which reminds me that I am alone with a boy. A very cute, very available boy.

As if he knows I'm thinking about him, he looks over and smiles at me.

"Nice dress. Is it new?" I glance down at my overflowing cleavage and think maybe I overdid it with the dress. It's a beach party, after all. Was I supposed to wear my swimsuit? Kai is wearing a plain white T-shirt, a pair of chinos and flip flops, which is pretty much standard attire here.

"Yeah, I didn't really know what to wear. It's not like I've been to a beach party before."

"Seriously? Never?" he scoffs.

"Well, it's not exactly like there are a lot of beaches where I live, unless you count the parties that happen at people's lake cabins. But the water is always murky, and there's always a ton of gross seaweed stuff floating around."

"Yeah, here that's all we do. No one really hangs out at house parties, even when you're older. People just meet at the beach and party there. My family has a huge cook-out on the beach every Sunday. It's like…tradition. You should come sometime." The offer lingers in the air for a moment, but I don't act on it quickly enough, because suddenly the car is in park and Kai is unbuckling his seat belt.

"*This* is Little Beach?" I look around, not seeing a single patch of water anywhere. We're parked in a giant gravel lot, with a couple of porta-potties sitting on one end and a fish taco food truck on the other.

"No, *this* is Big Beach. We've got a way to go before we get to Little Beach. Come on. We have to walk."

I climb out of the truck, still unsure about how exactly it is that we are at the beach. We passed a dozen beautiful, pristine beaches on the way here, and *this* is the one they call Big Beach?

Relief finally washes over me when I see groups of people streaming from a wide pathway on the far end of the lot. They're all sun-kissed and struggling to carry a day's worth of beach gear back to their vehicles.

"We just missed sunset, which is too bad, because you could have heard the conch being blown."

"The *what* being blown? The *gonch*? As in *underwear*?" I start laughing out loud. This evening just started, and it's already bizarre.

"No, *conch*, not *gonch*! I believe the word you're referring to is *ginch* anyway. You Canadians have weird words for things. A 'conch', as in a type of seashell. It's Maui tradition that it's blown at sunset, kind of like a horn. It signals the end of a day and is a symbol of gratitude to the gods. Like, our way of saying '*mahalo*' for giving us this gift of beauty." He spreads his arms around the treed area where we're walking. I'm in awe of his love for this island—his admiration and gratitude for it. I always thought I loved my home in Edmonton, and I was certainly not keen to leave it, but I was never *mesmerized* with it the way Kai is with Maui, as if he truly feels blessed to be here. The way he speaks about his home makes me more and more mesmerized with him.

Then, right as he finishes his wide-armed spin, the pathway through the trees opens up to the most beautiful, wide-open beach that I've ever seen. The silky soft sand stretches over a hundred feet wide and must go on for more than a mile. There's a deep ledge where the sand drops down to the surf, a result of the powerful waves smashing into it all day long. The waves roll in like angry white giants, rising up and gaining momentum, then crashing with a fury as they meet with the beach. Even with my strong swimming skills, there's no way I'm jumping into that water.

A few families still linger about, but the beach is mostly empty by the time the last of the sun dips below the horizon. The moon already hangs up in the sky, dangling like a dim nightlight. The clouds have rolled in over the last hour, leaving hardly any stars in sight. I make a mental note to come back on a clear night. I bet the stars are spectacular out here.

"So, where do you think the actual party is?" I ask out loud. Part of me kind of hopes the party was just a sham, because it would mean Kai and I could hang out alone for the night on this utterly perfect beach. But then that would mean I've been ousted before school has even begun, so that would sting a little too much for me to handle. No, I need to find some friends.

"Just wait. Be patient, young one," he jokes and waves me forward. We take off our shoes in order to walk more easily along the soft, warm sand. I'm happy I chose to wear the sundress, which allows the breeze to float airily between my thighs and around my shoulders, helping me to cool off. Then it hits me.

Little Beach is a *nude* beach, as in *naked*. My mind flashes to those pale blobs on the website we laughed at, then to my ghost-like reflection in the mirror after my shower this afternoon. Shoot, why didn't I think more about that, before agreeing to come? Am *I*...Are *we*...expected to take off our clothes when we get there?

Lost in my thoughts, I stop walking. Kai is already a few steps in front of me and turns around.

"Jess, are you okay? What's wrong?"

"Uh, I just remembered, I mean I just realized... that..." I don't know how to say it without sounding like a loser. Why can't I loosen up for once?

"Jess, the party is *not* going to be naked. At least, I'm pretty sure it won't be. That would be *so* weird—and super-gross. No, kids use Little Beach for parties all the time—*after* the naked people leave. Trust me. It's just a perfect spot to use because it's a little trickier to get to, so the cops don't usually break the parties up as often as they would in other places. And even if they do come, we hear them a mile away, so we have time to scatter. Come on. We're almost there."

Relief rushes over me because, well, as much as I'm starting to *like* Kai, I don't think I'm ready to go there. There's no way I want to be naked in front of him—not yet anyway.

We reach the end of the beach, and it looks like there's nowhere else to go. But Kai expertly starts to climb a rocky embankment that looks to be about forty feet high. I'm impressed that he thinks of me in my bare feet and sundress, turning to reach his arm down to hoist me up. He's even stronger than he looks, and when he pulls me, I stumble into him, causing him to fall back against the large rocks at the top. I brace myself against his chest—his very strong and hard chest—and I catch a whiff of his soap or deodorant, crisp and woodsy.

As I push off, my hand grazes down his forearm, lingering for a second longer than it should. My face is only inches from his.

"Uh, thanks. Didn't know if I could make that ledge without a little help."

"Anything for the princess, remember?" His teasing smile beams at me. It's the kind of smile that could be spewing profanities, but it wouldn't seem offensive coming from that warm and soft mouth, those gleaming white teeth and the dimple that just barely peeks out on the left side. I think about what it would feel like if those lips were to focus their attention on mine, how it would taste and how it would make my insides explode.

But I wipe my palms on my thighs instead of lingering them any further on his arm and turn so I can see out from the vantage point we have at the top of the ridge.

A scattering of trees dots the area just beside us, filtering a faint drum beat and a few guitar riffs floating up from the other side of the hill.

"Party down there?" I ask, pointing to a narrow path leading back down through the trees and rocks again.

"You got it," he agrees. "Ladies first." He waves his hand forward, allowing me to step in front of him.

I stumble down the far side of the slope, sliding a little on the gravelly bit at the bottom, and arrive at an enclosed beach with a roaring surf on the one side, facing a giant rock wall on the other. It's almost like a private little sanctuary, and I immediately realize why people always have parties here. The rocks offer amazing acoustics, and the beach is so cut off from the rest of the world that it feels like a planet of its own.

There are only a few small groups of kids milling about. I check my watch. It's only seven-thirty, so I suppose it's pretty early for the party to be roaring full force. I secretly pray for the girls I met to be here, so I don't feel like an idiot not knowing anyone. God, what were their names again? Em and Callie? Carlie? *Crap, I don't even remember.* But, before I have a chance to stress too much about it, a high-pitched, tinkly voice calls over to me.

"Hey, girlfriend! Yo, Canada! Over here!"

I turn to see one of the blonde beauties walking over with an equally attractive blond guy at her side. I remember the lip-glossed mouth and automatically remember her to be Em — I think.

"Oh, hey. How's it going? Thanks for inviting us. Um, this is Kai…" Then I'm stuck, because I'm not one hundred percent sure this is Em — it could be Callie or Carlie, after all — and I panic not knowing what to say next.

But Kai jumps to the rescue again, chasing after my words.

"Hey, I'm Kai. Nice to meet you. What was your name again?"

"I'm Callie, and this is Connor. And welcome to our senior year kick-off bash!" She throws her arms up high into the air when she says it, exposing a tan and very taut stomach.

I give a half-hearted, dorky *yay* while pumping my fist in the air, then immediately regret it. But Callie giggles a bit, which allows me to relax. She puts her arm around me and pulls me toward the other kids.

"Canada, come meet the rest of the gang."

Connor leaves to throw a Frisbee with another lanky kid ankle-deep in the water and Kai is left to trail behind us.

Chapter Ten

I'm three beers in, and life is a delightful bowl of cherries right now. Some guy in a Grateful Dead T-shirt and dreadlocks strums a ukulele by a blazing fire, and I can't help but sway to the Jason Mraz cover. I close my eyes as I enjoy the warm breeze, the sound of the waves lapping in and the feel of alcohol coursing through my veins.

I notice a half-empty sloshing sound as I swing a beer bottle back and forth and decide to pour the remainder of it into the sand. It's warm as piss. I peek into my shoulder bag. Only two beers left. So, that means I've had how many? Three, four...?

"Ninety-nine bottles of beer on the wall, ninety-nine bottles of beer..."

I'm pretty sure the song just plays in my head, but I start swaying to the melody regardless.

"Take one down, pass it around..."

I need a beer in my hand to sing this song. Yep, just one more beer...

I reach into the depths of my bag to grab another one, but it's a lot more complicated than it seems. My hand keeps getting caught up in the fabric, and suddenly the patch of sand I stand on seems to shift unexpectedly beneath me. I stumble backwards as I finally find my prize.

"There you are, little one. Hiding from me, were you?" The single bottle I'm speaking to blurs suddenly, and doubles in my vision. I have difficulty focusing on it enough to twist off the cap.

"Whoa, whoa, whoa, Jess. I think that's about it for the night." Kai appears out of nowhere and gently removes the sweating bottle from my outstretched hand.

"But I'm just getting going!" I declare. A stream of spit sprays out of my mouth and dribbles down my chin.

"You know, how about I take you home, Jess? I remember you telling me earlier that your dad wanted you home by midnight anyway."

But I don't *want* to go home. The party is really roaring now. There've got to be almost a hundred kids here, and I wonder if they all go to Maui Gardens. When I first showed up, Callie whisked me off to go meet a group of kids — Connor, Andy, Sydney, Benny... *Why do they all have 'y' names?* Oh, and Luke. There was a Luke too.

They all seemed like nice kids...sort of. There was a lot of talk about cars and trips and grades, but they welcomed me with open arms. At first, I was irritated that Callie introduced me over and over with the same spiel... *"Hey guys, this is Jess from Canada. She's the one who lives in the beautiful glass house on the hill."* It irked me that she could sum me up in a simple, one-dimensional comment. And as I stand here now, I wonder whether she actually knows anything else about me.

But I have to admit that everyone immediately knew the house she was talking about, and everyone's attention toward me noticeably amplified with the comment. There were a lot of questions about my dad and what he did, which I effectively brushed off with non-committal responses such as, *"Oh, he's in real estate."* Because in reality, I don't have a clue what he does all day.

Then they all paused and waited for me to talk about my mom. I let the pause extend longer than it should have, while I took long, deep swigs of my beer — hmm, come to think of it, *that* could be the reason behind the six-pack disappearing act. Eventually the other kids got tired of waiting in an awkward silence for so long, and someone changed the subject.

I liked tonight. I felt good tonight. I enjoyed being caught up in the familiar camaraderie of hanging out with friends who know each other so well — the banter, the rough-housing. Even though I was still an outsider looking in, it felt so reassuring to be part of a normal Saturday night with friends. I could almost imagine Maggie here with me.

Oh, Maggie.

Maggie would definitely have a crush on the guy named Luke, with his curly hair and dark, bad-boy eyes. She would drink too much and touch him more than necessary. She'd probably run drunkenly into the waves at some point, then run back with her beautiful red hair dripping down her back like a mermaid, her white tank top clinging to her breasts, leaving nothing to the imagination.

And I would feel a bit like a third wheel hanging beside them, but I wouldn't have the confidence to actually go off on my own. That was, until Maggie would nudge Luke to go grab his friend Benny, or maybe Andy — whichever she deemed had the nice-guy patience to sit through my awkward small-talk before sloppily making out with me for an hour. Then we'd say our drunken and lengthy goodbyes to the boys, and we'd stumble home together, dropping with exhaustion onto her double bed. Her ginger hair would splay across both pillows, and I would be okay with that because it would remind me that she was right beside me, a bright and vivacious ball of energy who always had enough juice to keep me charged as well.

Oh God, I miss Maggie — except that I'm still rip-roaringly, unforgivably pissed at Maggie for stealing *my* boyfriend.

Or am I?

I feel like I still *should* be devastated right now, although admittedly I haven't thought much about Marcus at all lately. But *she* doesn't know that. And at least right now, feeling like I *should* be mad seems about equivalent to actually *being* mad.

"Jess? Are you coming?" For a second in my alcohol-induced fog, I think it's Maggie's voice calling to me. But it's deeper, more gravelly.

"Huh?" I turn my head over to the sound, but I must have moved too quickly because the world tilts at a forty-five-degree angle and I catch myself stumbling again. I finally home in on the source of the voice and am surprised to see Kai standing there. *Was he there all along?* I don't remember, except I do notice that he's holding the beer bottle I *thought* was in my hand only a second ago.

"Uh, no. I can't go with you. You've been drinking." I say sloppily, tripping all over the words as if they can't quite roll off my tongue properly. I turn to go and find someone else to talk with—someone who is *not* insisting I go home.

"Jess, I haven't had a single drink. I'm pretty sure *you're* the one who almost crushed a six-pack. I really think it's probably a good idea for us to go now. You're not doing so hot. I should probably get you into bed."

Now things are starting to turn around! Did he say he wants to take me to bed? Mmm, I could make out with that face for a long time—and that chest. I could run my hands down that chest and feel that fuzzy patch down on his lower back...

In my mind, Kai is right there along with me, imagining a hot and intense make-out session. I reach out to pull him to me, to finally lock my lips down on that gorgeous mouth of his. I close my eyes in order to relish the moment of our first kiss, when suddenly a powerful fury rumbles through my insides and pushes up into my throat.

"Oh God!" is all I manage before a volcano of vomit spews from my mouth. As if he saw it coming, Kai has already sidestepped and is gathering my hair up and off my face.

"Yep, saw that coming. Let it out. You'll feel better after, I promise. What were you thinking, drinking an entire six-pack yourself? God, even *I* couldn't handle that."

The heaving continues, but Kai has considerately sheltered me from the majority of the party, which still bustles full tilt.

When the worst of it has subsided, I wipe my mouth with a light sweater I'd thrown into my bag, and I unsteadily stand up. Kai hands me a bottle of water and gives me a half-smirk.

"So, now do you agree it's time to go?"

I'm absolutely mortified. I mean, I'm not only disgustingly drunk with dried vomit down my neck, but I actually went in for a kiss in that state. What was I thinking? How did I get *that* off-track with things? If I were Kai, I would be so grossed out that there'd be no way I would ever come near this mouth again.

My rancid, putrid breath…it smells as if there are dead animals buried in my mouth. There will be no kissing happening on this mouth tonight, that's for sure.

I look down and glimpse pieces of dad's barbecued steak among the sandy vomit, and my stomach threatens to perform an encore.

Oh God, how disgusting.

Like the gentleman he is, Kai kicks sand to cover the puke.

"Hey, Canada, are you leaving so soon?" Callie walks over with Sydney and Em.

"Uh, yeah. I had one too many, I guess. Time for bed." My hand reflectively shields my mouth as I speak.

"Oh, too bad, the party was just getting going! Well, come find us at school on Monday. We always sit outside together at lunch, so we'll save you a spot." She beams her glossy smile at me, then it dampens slightly as she glances uneasily at Kai.

"And nice to meet you, er…. Kevin?" She fumbles.

"Kai," he corrects. "Yeah, you too."

There's a weird chill in the air, despite the roaring fire and the humid breeze. Even though my brain feels like soggy bread, I can tell something weird is transpiring between them.

We walk back in silence down the beach. The rocky embankment lurks threateningly to me, but somehow, I manage to scramble my way up more easily than I expected. I try not to think of the fact that Kai is below me, getting an exquisite view as my flimsy dress ruffles in the breeze. Wearing a lacy thong doesn't seem like the greatest choice of underwear right now.

I had such high hopes for this evening. I know I haven't known Kai for more than a few days, but the time I've spent with him has been electrifying and comforting all at the same time. He seems to know all the right things to say without ever pushing. He's interested in me without expecting something in return. He is a true gentleman. I've never really met one, but I'm pretty sure he's the real deal. And I've gone and messed it all up. *Why? What was I hoping to prove tonight?*

The rest of the walk back to the truck is silent and awkward. Every time I try to think of something witty to say, my brain swirls again and my thoughts lose their coherence. I can't wait to get home and just forget this night ever existed.

As we ride back past lavish homes and irrigated lawns, the ocean stretches out dark and eerie to our left. I find it weird to think that there's an entire world of living creatures still swimming and eating and existing right now, oblivious to the monumental lapses in judgment I've recently made. At night, the ocean mesmerizes me—so vast and empty, like an abyss. I wish it would just swallow me whole, right this very second.

Kai hasn't said a word since we left the party, and I'm getting a weird vibe from him, like he's pissed at me but doesn't want to show it. I mean, I get it. I just about threw up all over him and embarrassed us both in front of a new group of people. If he's anything like me, he had hopes of this evening going in an entirely different direction than where it went. But I wonder if there's something more.

"Hey, I'm really sorry about tonight. I mean, I'm really glad you came, but it just didn't turn out like I expected. I'm such a mess. I went way overboard. I guess I was just eager to start things fresh here...and, maybe a little nervous that I wouldn't fit in right away, you know?"

"Oh, you fit in just fine, trust me — a little more than I thought you would, to tell you the truth." He runs his hands through his long hair, then says quietly under his breath, "Such a freaking disappointment."

"Huh? What? What do you mean by that?"

"Nothing. Just that I thought you were different."

"Different from what? From who?"

"From every pompous hot shot who shows up on this island and thinks that they own it — from those stuck-up jerks at the beach, all of them."

"What are you talking about? I'm not like that. And *they're* not like that! I thought they all seemed great! Cool, even. How can you say that?"

"Right, they're so nice, and welcoming, and authentic." Sarcasm drips off his words. "With their talk about cars and money and private colleges. They're so caught up in their own bubble that they don't even recognize the rest of the world exists. Didn't you notice that not a single one of them talked to me? Not even once? And you know why? Because I'm a local — a local who has no money and who's here to cater to them, as if I were a part of the surroundings and not a person at the party—like I was there as their pool boy, or their waiter, or their *gardener*."

He says the last word with such venom that the stab of pain cuts beneath my skin. Is that what he thinks? That I just see him as the hired help? There's nothing further from the truth.

But I think back to the evening and how I got caught up in the whole scene. I didn't think to turn around and check to see if he was okay. I guess I kind of forgot about him, what with the music and the drinks.

Crap. Where *did* he go during the party? Callie whisked me away and I sort of lost him in the excitement.

I try to lift the fog from my memories of the evening. Let me see… As soon as we got to the party, Callie took me over to meet Sydney and their boyfriends Connor and Benny. Em was already making out farther along on the beach with her boyfriend, Andy. Then Luke walked over—*shit*. Maybe that's why he's pissed. It didn't seem like a big deal at the time, but looking back, I suppose it looked like we may have been flirting, just a bit. I remember Callie and Sydney getting pulled away to do shots at some point in the evening, and it was just Luke and me, although I can't be sure for how long.

We just chatted… Well, maybe that's not entirely true. It's fuzzy, but I remember his arm being draped over me at one point, the loose curls of his hair tickling the side of my face, him tracing his finger in small circles on my shoulder. Was I crying? Yeah, I think I was crying—about my mom…or maybe Maggie? Oh geez, I wish the evening would come back into focus so I can remember exactly where things got out of line.

I reach back further in my brain to try to picture Kai during the party. He's right. I sort of ditched him, but I had no idea I'd even done that. I'm the one who brought him there in the first place, the purpose being to make *me* feel less alone. A heavy pit of regret and shame weighs in my stomach as I think of him sitting alone on the side of the beach, while this party of strangers thunders around him. And there *I* was in the middle, basking in all of its glorious attention.

I'm a super-crappy friend. Ugh.

"I really am sorry, Kai. That was awful of me — to invite you there then to ditch you. I don't know what I was thinking. I promise, I'm not like that. Truly." I bore my eyes into him, willing him to look at me, to glance away from the road for one second. The car rolls slowly to a stop and I sense the looming presence of my massive home.

He still says nothing.

"Okay, well, thanks. Thanks for coming with me. Thanks for driving. Thanks for holding my hair back, and for the water, and for putting up with me. I'd love to hang out again, someday — if you want. I promise I'll be different."

I notice the flicker of his fingers tapping the steering wheel. Then he shifts in his seat. And *finally*, he turns his body to look at me square on.

"Yeah, I get it. Like I've said, I've seen it a thousand times before. And you know what I think you need?" He pauses for just a second. "You need to see what this island is all about, for real — for the people who actually live here and know and love it. Next weekend, I'm taking you out, my style. No flashy cars or club memberships needed. Think you can handle it?"

A gigantic smile spreads across my face.

"Oh, and don't bring any beers," he adds and laughs a real laugh — that generous and free, warm and open, *real* laugh with his gorgeous mouth and dark, glimmering eyes. My heart almost explodes out of my chest.

"Got it, no beers. I promise. Thanks again. Talk to you soon."

I wobble into the cavernous house, trying to be as quiet as possible. I don't need my dad tearing into me right now about why I'm a half-hour late or why there's a splatter of vomit all down the front of my dress. I tiptoe up the stairs, not quite as in-tune with the groans and creaks of this house as I was with my home in Canada. When I get to the landing, I'm relieved to be home-free until my dad's voice booms from his bedroom. He strains to be heard over the continuous wheezing of his CPAP machine.

"Jess, is that you? Are you home now?"

Don't come out. Don't come out.

"Uh, hey, Dad! Yeah, it's me. Sorry, I'm back a little late. We had to drop a couple of other girls off first."

"Okay, well I'm just glad you're home safe. Did you have fun?"

"Yeah, it was a great party. Fun times."

"I'm so happy, honey. Your mom was all worried about you acclimatizing into a whole new school environment, especially without Maggie and your other friends. She thought it would be so tough on you. But I knew you'd handle it. You're tough like your dad, and you can fit in just about anywhere. I'm proud of you, kiddo. See you in the morning."

"Thanks Dad. Night." I turn off the last of the lights and walk through the silent house alone.

Chapter Eleven

I spend all morning lying in bed, nursing an excruciating hangover, made worse by the fact that I'm agonizing over whether to text Kai or not.

Did he mean it when he said for us to go out? Or was that just small talk?

Exactly how disgusting was I last night? Was he really holding my hair back as I puked up six beers and a grilled striploin? *Please say I'm remembering that wrong.*

My resolve finally weakens around eleven a.m., about the time that the Advil and strong coffee finally kick in. I figure short and sweet are my best bet.

Thanks again for coming last night. And for the ride.

...

And sorry I was such a mess.

I know he's reading my text and starting to respond because I see the three dots, but no response comes. My phone remains a blank screen. I close out of it and go back into my text messages a dozen times, worried that maybe my wi-fi is splotchy and I'm just not receiving messages. But still nothing, which makes me feel neurotic that I've been misreading his signals all along. Maybe he's not into me at all.

But then, an hour later, when I'm helping my dad put up a new piece of artwork, my phone buzzes in my back pocket. I'm eager to pull it out to see if it's him, but the expensive painting balances precariously above my head. I'm trapped. It takes another forty-five minutes for my dad to be happy enough with the placement, and I'm able to sneak off to relish Kai's response in private. But it wasn't Kai. It was Maggie.

Hey, J. Haven't heard from you. Just wanted to make sure you got to Maui safe.

Maggie. Maggie, my ex-best-friend-turned-ex-boyfriend's lover, who I still secretly talk aloud to eight billion times a day when no one is listening because, well, no one listens to me better than Maggie.

But in reality, I haven't talked to Maggie at all since coming here—since finding out she was banging my boyfriend. Well, at least that was what Marcus Crowley claimed. I've been starting to question his authenticity in the whole matter. Maybe he was just exaggerating the whole situation? *A girl can hope.*

I suddenly feel so guilty about how I left things with Maggie. I didn't confront her about the whole ordeal. I didn't even say goodbye to her when we left. I just took Marcus' word for it. And now I feel really crummy about that. Best friends for thirteen years and *pouf!* She just evaporated from my life in an instant—except that

I didn't count on the permanent mark she'd made on me to still be there, like the water stain accidentally made on a fancy coffee table after forgetting to use a coaster. No matter how much it's scrubbed, the mark will always remain as a reminder of what had once been there.

I read the next text bubble.

And FYI, Marcus is a douche. Found out he was banging two girls from La Tapas while he was stringing us both along. So yeah. I guess he wasn't that into either of us. Sorry. It still sucks that I was a bitch. And a terrible friend. And I get that you hate me forever.

In that instant, I realize I'm not mad at Maggie anymore. Maybe I never really was, because instead of bringing up feelings of betrayal, the thought of Marcus and her—the thought of Marcus *period*—makes me kind of gag. What was I thinking being with him? Why did I think he was so cool? It was the mysterious-guy-from-a-different school thing that got me hooked—that, and as much as I hate to admit it, the fact that he was into me instead of Maggie. Or at least it seemed like that. That makes me feel even more guilty. I was so jealous of my best friend that I would be with a so-so kind of guy just because he picked me over her?

Now I actually do feel bad for Maggie, because at least I didn't sleep with the guy. I mean, don't get me wrong. We did stuff, *lots* of stuff—stuff that involves clothes strewn around the room and sharp intakes of breath and tickly pringles of electricity down to my toes…but not sex. There was no actual sex happening between the two of us, and I'm happy to say that I'm still a virgin, *so* happy to say that Marcus Crowley was not my first. Because that would be a very tarnished memory to have.

I'm relieved not to have to worry about the STDs he could have passed to me, or *God*, that I could be *pregnant* with his baby, especially if he was sleeping around with two other girls at the same time. *Gross.* I really hope Maggie didn't go all the way with him. Maybe Marcus just wanted me to believe that—I hope.

I take a deep breath and respond.

Hey. Yeah, got in ok.

I pause, wondering how to ease into things, how to gauge whether we're okay.

Super crazy here. Like living in Real Housewives. *Seriously. We have an ocean-view, rooftop patio. A pool. A cappuccino maker!*

She replies.

WTF?

I knew the cappuccino maker would get her. I exhale the breath I've been holding, because I feel like I've gotten my best friend back, even if we're two thousand miles apart.

So, he was seriously sleeping with two other girls from Tapas? Pathetic. What a prick. Bet it was that one with the fake boobs and the other one with the cheesy lower-back tattoo. How could he think he's such hot shit? Please tell me you didn't screw him. Plz!!!!

Nope. Did other stuff but not the real deal. You?

No way.

See? We're better than that… Miss you.

Miss you too. It's weird here. So beautiful, but not real. You know? Worried about school tomorrow. I have to learn American History!

WTF???

I know. Better than French though, maybe? Met a cute guy.

Already? He a surfer?

LOL, yeah. You know me too well.

Cuz you're my BFF.

And that one text makes me feel better than I've felt the entire week I've been here. I sign off with a heart emoji and a kissy face, feeling good she's there. Even if she's not *here*, she's there when I need her.

Chapter Twelve

"Dad! When does the rest of our stuff get here?" I am so beyond irritated right now. How the hell am I supposed to start fresh at a new school without anything to wear? I glance down at the outfits I've laid out on my bed, neither one looking appropriate for my first day at Maui Gardens.

Jean cut-offs with a plain yellow T-shirt, or black biking shorts with a tight yoga tank. God, I'm probably going to get kicked out of this posh new school for an inappropriate wardrobe on day one. I eye the flowery sundress from Saturday night hanging half out of my hamper. Everyone already saw me in it, but it has to be a better option than cut-offs or exercise wear, right? I've almost convinced myself to put it on when I catch the rancid stink of old vomit and remember how it dribbled all down the front of me Saturday night.

Why didn't I do the laundry yesterday? Ugh!

"You're sure there's no uniform at this school, Dad? I thought all private schools in the States needed uniforms. How come we don't get one here?"

I would have been destroyed at home if anyone suggested we wear a uniform. It's just not a thing in my hometown. I don't think school uniforms even exist in Edmonton. Well, unless you are one of the badasses who get sent to a *boarding* school. But seriously, I don't even know anyone who's been to boarding school before. Maybe they're just urban legends, come to think of it?

Anything I've heard about American schools has come from years of watching *Riverdale* and *Gossip Girl* on Netflix. Fun drama, but both seem a bit too pretentious for most of us in Canada. I'm a little more used to kids rolling out of bed into jeans and sneakers to go to school—no high heels, no miniskirts and definitely no uniforms.

Then, the day before registration last week, Dad mentions that I'll be going to a *private* school in Maui? Okay, technically, Maui Gardens is a charter school, not a private one, but I'm hazy about the difference. As if I weren't already nervous about fitting in! My only consolation was that if it *was* a private school, then for sure I'd be wearing a uniform, which would at least mean I wouldn't have to stress anymore about my lack of clothing choices.

Wrong.

As it turns out, at Maui Gardens they like to be a little more 'liberal', a little more 'progressive'. They like students to express themselves— 'to be free to be who they want to be', which makes me want to gag. It also means I'll be stuck with my sparse wardrobe until the rest of my stuff gets shipped.

Crap.

I let out a final groan and hesitantly grab the cut-offs and T-shirt. I decide to go shopping immediately after school as a consolation.

The bike ride to school is quite glorious. School starts super-early here because it gets sweltering later in the day, so the sun is just peeking up over the horizon by the time I leave my driveway. The morning sea fog hasn't even lifted entirely, so the sky looks almost overcast. But I can tell it's going to be a scorcher, considering it's already hovering around eighty degrees.

I fly down the steep hill, enjoying the predictable switchbacks and the smooth ride on newly laid asphalt. A few of the neighbors are out on a walk or a jog and I wave as I pass them, although I'm thankful to have my Air Pods in so I don't have to stop and chat. The morning smell in Maui is heavenly — the last remnants of night-blooming jasmine mixed with the sweet scent of gardenia blossoms and salty air. It's fresh and clean and invigorating as I ride. At this time in the morning, most people head to work, so the road is congested. Well, busy for Maui, that is. During rush hour, the main Kihei road and Piilani highway teem with vehicles — tourists on their way to the beach and people off to work. The employee parking lots at the luxury hotels I pass start to fill as people begin their day catering to the three million visitors that come to the island each year.

I think about what Kai said, about me never being a local. And I wonder whether that's true, whether I'm going to be destined to remain in this limbo between tourist and native, not having been born here but needing to feel like this is my home. *If I'm not allowed to claim this island, where do I call home?*

Dozens of trucks crammed with gardening supplies pass me as I ride, workers sometimes riding in the bed of the truck too, squished between rakes, ladders and hoses. Eager to get going while the weather is relatively cool, they all stay covered from head to toe, like Kai was the first day I saw him. The scorching sun and overgrown brush are unforgiving when you're outside all day, especially when you're spending day in and day out laboring away in expansive gardens and hedges. I've spent the last few days eyeing the workers as they tend to the immaculately manicured lots around our neighborhood. They work tirelessly and are so meticulous in their endeavors, taking such pride in making their precious island come to life for those who visit. The people who do come here as tourists seem oblivious that there are sweat and tears behind the colorful walkways and perfectly pruned trees. Kai's right. People pass by the gardeners and groundskeepers as if they're a part of the surroundings, instead of the people who create the beauty, the true masters of this incredible island. This is *their* home. *They* were the ones to claim the land years before anyone else thought it would be a lovely place for a family holiday.

I make a vow as I ride that I will *see* them, *appreciate* them and *value* them for enhancing the beauty of the island for me.

Fifteen minutes into my ride, I pull up to the school — *my* school — and lock up my bike. Today there are at least a few more bikes sharing the rack, so mine isn't looking quite so pathetic and lonely. And today, I'm set on shoving my helmet into my locker the second I get to it. I definitely don't need to advertise my embarrassing method of transportation. My first class of the day is Geometry, and I find the classroom without much problem at all. I'm one of the first kids in the class, which gives me the advantage of scoring a seat near the back, as well as scoping out the other kids as they come in. I pretend to scroll through my phone, but the whole time I'm actually glancing up to see if anyone I know walks through the classroom door.

I'm immediately relieved to see that everyone is dressed pretty much the same as me—well, close anyway. There aren't any high heels or miniskirts, and most of the kids are just in shorts or sundresses. Except that, if I look really closely at their outfits, I see small emblems of *D&G* or the Gucci 'G' somewhere on their clothing, small but identifiable markings of how rich they are—like gang symbols for the wealthy. A *G* is better than a *D&G*, but an *LV* is pretty much top tier. And my *H&M*? Well, let's just hope it stays hidden.

It's like the affluence here is understated. Everyone *has* money, but no one wants to outwardly admit to others that they want it to be known that they *have* money. I find it to be a very confusing world.

Seconds before class begins, I hear the unmistakable high-pitched tinkle of Callie's laugh and look up to see her walking in from the hall. She hesitantly says goodbye to Connor with a kiss, and as they step apart, they continue holding hands for as long as possible before letting go. It would be cute if it weren't seven-thirty a.m. It just looks a bit pathetic at this hour of the day.

I look back down and stare intently into my phone, because the next two minutes are everything. The next two minutes are *make it* or *break it* for me in the high school world. If Callie comes in and walks right past me as if I don't exist, it'll mean I start my senior year off in lonely desperation. But if she rushes up to me with a big hug, happy to see we're in class together, it'll mean things are going to be okay. I'm nervous about the outcome. There shouldn't be this much drama this early on a Monday morning, as if my bike ride didn't make me sweat enough already today.

I'm suddenly pulled back to the party on Saturday night, the way I left by puking my brains out all-over Little Beach. Yep, pretty sure I'm stuck in the realm of lonely desperation, which really sucks.

"Hey, Canada!" she suddenly trills and rushes to the seat next to me. "How are you feeling? Saturday was a bit rough for you, I heard. Glad to see you today, though."

I'm thrilled she's chatting with me, but also a bit horrified that the first thing she wants to bring up is Saturday night.

"Hey! Yeah, I guess I went a little overboard. Must have been enjoying the vibe a little too much." I smile weakly. "But it's all good. Kai made sure I drank a ton of water and got me home safely."

"Kai…?" She furrows her brows.

"Yeah, Kai. Um…the guy who came with me on Saturday?"

"Oh, yeah. Right. What was he again? Your housekeeper's son or something?" She starts scrolling through her phone, her attention pulled elsewhere.

"Um, my gardener actually." As soon as the words come out of my mouth, I regret them. Why did I label him like that? Why didn't I just refer to him as my friend or a guy I like? Even as the thoughts drift through my brain, I know why. I know exactly why and the shame I feel suffocates me.

It's obvious by their raised eyebrows, whispered exchanges and their cool greeting toward him at the party that Kai is not welcome. He's not one of them. Like he said himself, he's not Maui Gardens *quality*.

I'm happy the teacher begins talking and passing out textbooks, because it means we have a reason not to continue the conversation. Callie simply leans over to me, whispering conspiratorially, "Remember to meet up outside at the picnic tables at lunch, okay?" Then she turns back to her scribbler and starts writing out today's notes on quadrilaterals.

For the rest of math class, I'm content and relieved that I'm not going to be facing this year alone. But there's also a nagging feeling inside me too, because every time I let my mind wander just a little bit, it's Kai's face that flashes before me — his silky black hair and smooth skin, the way he held the door open for me, not once but twice, getting into his truck, the weight of my hand gently resting on his, the feel of his rough and calloused hand stretched out against my thigh and his offer to take me out next weekend and show me the island.

Mrs. Carlisle shoots me threatening looks about a half-hour into class. At first, I'm not clear why, until I notice my phone is still out, sitting on top of my desk. I didn't realize one of the rules here is to tuck it away during class time. I grab it to stuff it back into the pocket of my knapsack when my hand vibrates.

Dad wouldn't be texting me during the middle of the day.

Maggie and I already caught up last night.

There's only one person left it could be…Kai.

I risk getting into further trouble by flipping the phone over, peering at the screen while pretending to put it away.

Hey. Sorry I didn't respond yesterday. Got caught up in a family cook-out. Hope your first day is awesome. Mine sucks already.

OMG, it is him. He actually texted. I try to play it cool so as not to attract any more attention from Mrs. Carlisle. Her back is turned as she writes out equations on the whiteboard.

Hey. No prob. So far so good. First class is geo. Blah....

Better than me. Found out I have Foods instead of Shop cuz I sent in my reg choices late. Ughhh. Today is quiche Lorraine. I hate eggs. At least I get credit to eat.

I tap-dance my thumbs across my phone. I wouldn't be surprised if somehow little balloons begin popping up all over my screen.

You'll have to try your new recipes out on me sometime.

Oh God, that was so cringy. Did I actually just text that? Why don't I think before hitting send?

You still want to head out this wknd? I can come get you Sat. a.m.

Yeah, sure. That'd be great.

K. Bring your swimsuit.

Doesn't everyone just live in their swimsuits here?

Pretty much. Lol. Can't wait to see you then.

Suddenly, I'm flying. I'm no longer in Mrs. Carlisle's boring math class. I'm not sitting in a new school where I quite possibly might be known as 'the drunk, puking girl'. I'm not worried about my jean cut-offs, my lack of name-brand accessories or my lame transportation to school. Kai Kamealoha is picking me up on Saturday and "*can't wait to see me then*". Life is a freaking bowl of cherries again.

Chapter Thirteen

The morning passes quickly in a blur of new textbooks, syllabus sheets and getting-to-know-you activities. The only class Callie and I are in together is Geometry, but I'm in English with a couple of other kids from Saturday night. We didn't chat much, but they smiled and waved, so at least that's something.

I packed my own lunch this morning, as I wasn't sure what the school cafeteria offered. So, when the bell rings, I head back to my locker to grab it. Kai's text has kept me in la-la-land all morning, and I've avoided having to think about what to do during unstructured time. Callie did mention sitting with her and her friends at lunch again this morning, but it still feels a bit weird for me to just show up. What happens if they all stop talking, then just look up at me as if to say, "What the hell is she doing here?"

I decide to grab my entire knapsack, that way if I walk out and no one pays me any attention, I'll just pretend it's been my plan all along to sit out on the grass by myself and do some homework—not like there's any homework on the first day of school, but still... It's better than sitting alone in the cafeteria.

The dazzling glare of the midday sun practically blinds me when I first step outside. I had almost forgotten all about the heat this morning, since Maui Gardens uses its A/C so liberally. *Must be to keep us alert*, I think.

I pull on my sunglasses, which allows me a bit more freedom to look around. Several different groups of kids loiter around the green space. A few play hacky-sac near the parking lot, and a couple of kids lounge in someone's pale blue convertible, listening to heavy-thumping house music. A group of younger-looking girls lie on their stomachs in the middle of a small patch of shade just west of the gym door entrance. Off to the far-right side, beyond the empty basketball courts, sit a handful of wooden picnic tables, filled with a mixture of guys and girls giggling and joking around. I spot Callie and Connor right off the bat, mostly because they look like some sort of bizarre alien creature. She's straddling his lap with her face literally sucking on his, as if she's attempting CPR. Their matching blonde hair is so tangled up together that it looks like one monstrous head. Their arms are all gropy on each other's backs, and with their bare legs both in flip flops, it's kind of hard to tell which leg belongs to whom. *Hmm... I guess public displays of affection are allowed in this school?*

Em and Sydney sit on the picnic table one over, where Em absentmindedly braids a strand of Sydney's long, dark locks. Luke and Ben sit opposite them and are the only ones who look to be actually eating.

The walk over there feels a hundred miles long, as if every piece of me is being analyzed while strutting down a New York fashion show catwalk. I feel judged, exposed, vulnerable. Other than abruptly stopping to pretend I'm there to play basketball in the empty court, without an actual ball to speak of, it's pretty obvious I'm coming over to sit with them. I just hope my open invitation still stands.

I plaster a confident smile on my face, incredibly relieved that my sunglasses shield the true angst in my eyes.

"Hey guys, what's up?" I swallow hard.

"Hey, Canada, how y'all doin'?" I smile to myself when I hear the southern drawl in Em's voice again. Callie's right that it's the perfect mix of sassy and sweet. *Where was she from again? Louisiana or Alabama? Oh, Texas, that was it! You can't take the Texas out of the girl.*

"Oh, hey, Em." I try to play it cool, but she's got to be able to hear the tremble in my voice. "How's it going? It's super-hot out today, eh?"

Everyone erupts into a fit of hysterics, and I'm not sure why. Even Callie and Connor take a breather from sucking each other's faces and look up at me, incredulous.

I knew this was a bad idea. I look down at myself, checking to see whether I've got a stain on my T-shirt or something gross stuck in my hair.

"What? What's so funny? What are you guys laughing about?" I chuckle as I say it, hoping that it makes it look like I'm in on the joke, when, in reality, the inside of my brain is on an SOS alert, scrambling to figure out what I've done to cause the hysterics. They all continue laughing, even harder now, and I'm about to just turn around and walk away. I knew this was stupid. I've totally set myself up for this.

Then something surprising happens. Em jumps up and gives me a super-tight side hug, causing my arms to dangle helplessly at my sides.

"OMG, Jess. You are too funny! We can't get enough of that cute li'l accent of yours. 'Eh' and 'about'... I didn't even know people from Canada actually spoke like that!" Callie pipes up with multiple attempts at impersonating my 'about', making Sydney and Em giggle further. *I have an accent?* In my head, I sound the same as everyone I've met on this island, with the exception of Em and her noticeable Southern twang.

"Well, *I* think it sounds super-cute, Jess. Bet you didn't think you'd come to Hawaii and be the one sounding *exotic.*" It's Luke, and he's smiling expectantly at me with a mouthful of potato chips. He shifts his body over on the bench to make room for me to sit down.

Memories of me and Luke at the party flash through my mind. We were talking, then his hand was on my shoulder, on my back. I was at the party with Kai, but why wasn't Kai around? Why did I go off with Luke? I remember being so upset that I was drunk-crying all over his shoulder. He hugged me and kissed away my tears and I never once pushed him away or went to find Kai. Guilt floods my veins to think of how Kai must have felt. I feel Luke's appraising eyes on me now as I take the seat next to him. He's so close that the warmth radiates from his body, but then he scootches even closer until his leg presses firmly against my own.

"So, how's your first day been so far?" Sydney's question pulls my attention away.

"Sorry, what?" I manage.

"Have you had Mr. Collins yet for American History? *So* boring, seriously. I think it's his voice they use in those old World War II documentaries."

"And what about Mrs. Carlisle?" Callie jumps in. "You don't want to get on her bad side, trust me. I spent half of last year volunteering to help out in math club because she caught me cheating on my Calculus exam. Worst...punishment...*ever!*" She punctuates her last words with an epic eye-roll and an exasperated throw of her hands. "I was forced to spend one lunch hour a week hanging out with the world's biggest dorks!"

So, I guess now isn't the best time to tell them I was in the math club at home, although it wasn't even all that dorky. At least, it didn't seem to be at the time. I mean, we got extra credit for it, and on the last Friday of every month, Mr. Soba would bring in pizza. But somehow, I don't think free pizza would give math club any kind of street cred with this bunch. I decide to keep that little tidbit to myself for the time being.

"Speaking of which... You were *very* close to hearing one of Mrs. Carlisle's famous speeches about the atrocities of social media. You were on your phone for like almost the whole period today, Jess! Trust me... If she catches you on Snapchat, you better say your prayers. She will eat you alive! She must have been easy on you today since you're new. Who were you so eager to talk to? It's like you couldn't pull your face away from the screen!" When she finishes talking, she eyes my phone, as if the answer will jump out at her.

I instinctively flip it back over, hiding any alerts from popping up.

"Uh, Kai was just texting me. You know, to check how my first day was going."

"The guy from the party?" They exchange mystified glances.

"Yeah, he's cool. Or at least he seems super-cool. I don't really know him all that well yet."

"So, does he go to Kahului High or what?" There's that edge to her voice again, like she's prying the lid off a can of paint, and in just a moment the whole can is going to spill all over the place.

"Uh, yeah, I think that's what he said. I'm still trying to figure out all the places here. The words all sound so foreign to me."

"Yeah, well, that school may as well stay foreign to you. No offense, but the kids there are pretty sketchy. I'm sure Kai is *nice* and all…" She says it like lemon juice is being squeezed into her mouth. "But honestly, it'll be a waste of your time. Once you start hanging out with him and his friends, you'll know exactly what we mean. Trust us." The other kids all nod in agreement.

Then there's a thick moment of silence, where I'm pretty sure I'm supposed to say something resembling gratitude for letting me into this holy clique of theirs. But the words just seem to sit at the back of my throat. Luke senses the tension and lifts both his arms up, pulling Sydney and me against him at once into a giant three-person hug.

"What she means is, you've already found the coolest group of friends the island has to offer."

All I can do is nod, because I don't know… Maybe he's right?

Chapter Fourteen

It's Wednesday morning, the day of swim team try-outs. I've been super-pumped for this all week. This whole move to Maui has felt like one big try-out, and so far, it seems I've just barely made the cut. But swimming is something I'm made for. I know I'm good at this. If there's any place I feel at home, it's in the water.

When I was a toddler, my parents took me to Cancun for a family vacation. It was the first time I'd ever seen the ocean. My parents said that from the moment I saw the roaring waves and felt the sand between my toes, my whole body erupted in a fit of giggles that only toddlers are capable of — as if it takes every muscle in their body working in unison to create a full-body laugh. Before my parents could even wrangle me out of my cute, pink-polka-dotted sundress, I darted toward the raging surf and just plowed right in. Of course, the waves toppled me backward immediately, tossing me around like a ragdoll, while my mother ran in desperation to the water's edge to pluck me out. My dad has the whole thing caught on video, and I sometimes wonder how he just stood there filming, while I was *literally* almost drowning.

My mom cried hysterically, swept me up from the waves and held me to her chest. Thinking I'd be permanently scarred for life, she turned back to where my dad was situated on the beach blanket and screamed at him to start packing up our things. She figured our day at the beach was done. But, not a second later, I squirmed my slippery, wet body from her arms and once again bolted for the water. So, in ran my mom to save me for the second time. On and on this went for most of the morning. They couldn't even wrangle me out of the water for long enough to change me out of the soaking wet, sagging diaper that hung around my knees. Finally, at some point I'd tuckered out and fell asleep on the beach blanket, cooing happily. My parents went out that afternoon to buy me a set of turtle-shaped water wings. They still say it was the best eight dollars that they'd ever spent. For the rest of the vacation, they'd strapped on my water wings first thing in the morning and plopped me into the hotel pool. The only way I would come out was with the promise of an ice cream cone. My parents said it was the most relaxing vacation they'd ever had, and that all the other parents in the resort, struggling with their temperamental and whining children, simply looked at my parents with awe and envy. The water was where I wanted to be.

My dad knows me well enough to guess I'd be nervous about try-outs this morning, and when I get downstairs, I see that he's gotten up early to make me my favorite breakfast—French toast with strawberries and maple syrup. Sometimes my dad surprises me like that. He can be so distant and detached, but when things count, when things *really* matter to me, he always finds a way to get it right.

"So, try-outs. How's my star swimmer feeling about it?" He flips the French toast.

"Good, I think. I mean, I'm nervous, but I *was* the captain of the swim team back home. And I held the school's record for breaststroke. So, I've got to be decent, right? I'm trying not to get myself all worked up about these rich, preppy kids. I don't think it means they're better swimmers, does it? Just because they have money?" I say it for my own benefit, more than his.

"First of all, stop thinking of it as 'them vs. you'. You live here. You belong here as much as anyone. And I happen to think you're going to be spectacular! I can't wait to watch you race. In fact, maybe we can celebrate you making the team this weekend? You up for a dinner date with your dad?"

I know it might not be cool. It might even be a bit pathetic, maybe. But the thought of Dad and me hitting one of Maui's best restaurants together sounds like the perfect date to me. I wince a bit, thinking that Mom should be celebrating with us. That pang of missing her still simmers in my subconscious. I'm pretty sure the only way I'm going to get over it and onto a fresh start is if I actually allow her back into my life, from a distance at least. I vow that I'll find the courage to call her tonight—at *Robert's* house. *Ugh.* Just a quick call. Not a full-blown, I-forgive-you-and-everything-is-back-to-normal call. But maybe just a brief check-in, a small peace offering to smooth things over.

Dad scrolls through his phone, then looks up at me with a frown.

"Oh, honey. I'm so sorry. I forgot to let you know, and I just saw it in my calendar. I have an important meeting with the CEO in Honolulu this weekend. I'm supposed to fly there Saturday to get a tour of a new hotel they're putting up—kind of a prototype of what we're hoping to accomplish here. I'm so sorry. It's just for the night and I'll be back Sunday afternoon. I hate to leave you alone here, considering we've barely gotten settled. But I don't think I can turn this down." He runs his hands through his receding hairline. "I'm really sorry, honey. How about we do a dinner celebration on Sunday night instead?"

I'm disappointed, but I don't want to show it because I feel like a baby. So, I just smile and mumble for him not to worry about it.

He must sense my angst because he scrambles for more to say.

"How about you make plans with some of the new friends you've made? It sounds like you've really put yourself out there, and I'm so proud of you. I don't mind if you have a couple of people over. Not more than two or three though, okay?"

To my surprise, instead of picturing an evening of painting toenails and gorging on pizza with Em and Callie, my mind automatically flashes to Kai and his warm smile. I remember he's supposed to be taking me out all day Saturday, and for a moment, I allow myself the fantasy of bringing him back here afterward—to an empty house. We could drink some of my dad's expensive wine in the hot tub, then lounge in my room on my king-sized bed. I envision him shirtless, with his hands clasped behind his head like they were on the beach that day I discovered him. I see the ripples down his stomach, the trail of hair that leads down from his belly button. I imagine that I crawl up on the bed beside him, then playfully toss one of the overstuffed goose-down pillows on him. He grabs my arms as we fake wrestle for a bit, just for the excuse to touch each other. He ends up pinning me, his weight pressing down against the length of my body. I feel his breath hot against my cheek. Then he releases the grip on my arms and pulls my lips up to meet his.

Yes, my dad being away this weekend might be the best thing to happen to me yet.

"Sure, Dad. I'll ask a couple of the girls I've met to come over. It's no big deal, I promise. We'll go out Sunday instead."

"Thanks, sweetheart, I owe you one. I promise, once I've got this big deal settled, I'll be around more, and we can start to enjoy this place together. I've just got a bunch of moving pieces to work on right now —"

"Honestly, Dad. It's fine. I'll be fine. I'll maybe grab take-out from that fish taco place we've been eyeing, and I'll let you know how it is."

I finish the last few bites of my French toast and pack up my stuff for school.

"Okay, I'm off. I'll see you after try-outs tonight, okay?" I kiss him on his stubbled cheek. "Wish me luck!"

"You don't need luck," he says, grinning. "You've got this in the bag."

* * * *

Later in the day, as I strap on my swim goggles and desperately squish my hair into my latex swim cap, I feel good, confident even. I look out at the outdoor, Olympic-sized swimming pool, perched high up on the hill behind the school, so that the aqua blue of the ocean spreads out beyond, as if it's an extension of the pool itself. It's almost like this high school swimming pool offers a secret entrance to the warm, tropical waters and the sea life that abounds.

I strut across the pool deck in a plain black swimsuit and look to see where other kids would be gathering for try-outs. A large group already congregates on the far side of the pool, swimmers busy doing arm circles and neck stretches to warm up.

I approach a middle-aged woman with a short crew cut and track pants and tell her my name.

"Hi, I'm Jessica Kennedy. I signed up for the swim team? I'm here for try-outs?"

"Hi there, Jessica, you said? Let me just take a look at my list." She runs her finger down the clipboard. "Ah, yes, there you are. A senior, are you? Great! I'm the coach, Mrs. Wilson. And you said you have experience? Okay, just sit on the bench and wait until you're called. What are your best events?"

"Uh, well, I'm pretty good all-around. But I like breaststroke best. I'd like to compete in everything, if possible." She arches one eyebrow, as if she highly doubts my abilities. But I want her to doubt me. I'm going to rock this and show her that I'm going to take this swim team by storm.

I take my place on the side bench with a dozen other nervous-looking kids. I'm starting to wonder where Callie and Em are, seeing as they made sure to brag about being the swim captains. But a second later, I hear voices coming from the girl's change room and it's obvious by everyone's reaction who it is that's coming out.

Every single person on the bench cranes their necks toward the noise, and even Mrs. Wilson looks up from her clipboard with an expectant smile. Two kids that are in the pool doing warm-up laps pop their heads up and wave their hands in the direction of the voices.

I turn, along with everyone else, to see Em and Callie striding across the pool deck, like two princesses arriving at a ball. They have yet to put their swim caps or goggles on, and their glossy, golden locks shimmer in the late afternoon sun. It reminds me of one of those cheesy slow-mo shots in a raunchy teen comedy. Callie wears a bright pink one-piece that looks just half a size too small. Her perky breasts bounce suggestively with each step, her long, tan legs carrying her as smooth as a gazelle. Em struts right alongside her in a teeny-weeny pair of running shorts over her swimsuit. I suppose she's covered more than Callie, but the crease of her bum peeks out from under her shorts, somehow looking incredibly inappropriate. I never understood why girls wore those types of shorts, the ones where their butt actually hangs out of them and, if they sit down, their underwear shows. I mean, I'm all about trying to look cute and sexy, but anyone wearing those just seems to look way too desperate to me. *Who needs to advertise their ass? Most of the rest of us try to cover it up.*

It's obvious by their entrance that Callie and Em don't feel the least bit worried about try-outs today. I wonder if they automatically make the cut or something. Maybe Mrs. Wilson has some sort of secret agreement with them? Maybe they're *that* good? But, after a minute of chatting together, clearly in an amiable way, Mrs. Wilson points them toward the rest of us on the bench, and they grab their gear out of their swim bags. *I guess they have to try out after all.*

Up until now, neither girl has noticed me on the bench. But as they approach, their faces light up, they reach their arms out to me and they race the last few steps.

"Canada! We're super-glad you came to try-outs! We need a new ringer on our team!" Callie reaches out to squeeze my hand. "Can't wait to see our new little superstar!"

I catch the other swimmers eyeing me suspiciously as we chat. I haven't met most of them, and I'm sure they're wondering who the new girl is who's already found an *in* with the queen bees of Maui Gardens. I feel confident and brazen, like I've been given a coveted invitation to the party everyone wants to be at. I'm still nervous about my swim, but I feel so much more at ease with things, knowing I have the support of these two.

I make room for them beside me on the bench, and we wait as Mrs. Wilson runs through how the try-outs will work. As it turns out, I'm second to last on the list, so I'm going to have a while to wait. I wrap myself in my towel and let a quiet contentment settle over me.

Amanda Jensen is the first to go. She positions her feet on the diving block and leans in toward the pool with her arms taut above her head. The coach announces, "Ready, set, go!" and I hear the click of the stopwatch a split second before Amanda's body shoots through the air. Her dive is long and smooth. I'm baffled by how far she glides beneath the water, before surfacing to start her front crawl. Her strokes are powerful and deliberate, ripping her through the water at a breakneck speed. The predictable rhythm of her head bobbing up for air is almost hypnotizing. I just can't grasp how fast she is. *Who is this girl?* She must be new too, because no one seemed to make a big deal about her before she started. I look around at the faces of the other swimmers, but no one exudes any sense of astonishment. In fact, the other swimmers look to be bored and distracted, some even playing on their phones. I can't rip my eyes from this beast of a girl and almost gasp when I see the stopwatch freeze as she slaps the pool edge.

22:04 sec.

Holy shit.

"Not bad, Amanda. Not as good as your typical times last season, but I'll give you a break since it's been a few months." Coach Wilson pats Amanda on the shoulder as she pulls herself out of the pool.

Not as good as last season?

The next swimmer bullets through the water just as effortlessly, and she's only a junior. I'm speechless with the times I see. 22:13, 23:01, 21:46. Every one of them is better than my own personal best. And the guys…? Well, the guys smash those times even further. A couple of them even break the twenty-second mark. *Who are these people?*

When it's Callie's turn, she glides into the water like her body is a silk scarf. She barely makes a splash as her arms slice through, her legs kicking furiously behind her. I hear sharp intakes of breath each time she gulps air, but her breathing is strong and rhythmic. She pushes effortlessly off the far pool wall to do her return lap, and I only seem to blink once before she slaps the edge with an exuberant squeal.

"Yes! I didn't think I'd beat 20:30 until later in the season! This is awesome! I'm going to have to set some higher goals for myself!" Coach Wilson congratulates her with an exaggerated high five and scribbles a bunch of stuff on her clipboard. Em gives her a quick hug before diving in the water for her own turn.

"Wow, that was super-impressive. You are..." I don't want to sound too envious. "You're really fast."

"Thanks. Yeah, I've been training all summer long. After all, I am the swim captain. It would be super-embarrassing if, like, I sucked, you know?" I nod in agreement, but a heavy pit grows exponentially in my stomach — because I *was* the swim captain at my school. I even bragged about it to these girls. And my all-time best was nowhere near the scores these girls are getting. How in the world am I supposed to go now?

I sit there anxiously for the next half-hour while Callie and Em chirp in my ear. Thankfully, Em's time was not as fast as Callie's, but she still beat twenty-two seconds. My knee bounces frantically, and I catalogue excuses in my mind of why I should pull out of try-outs altogether.

But I want this. This is the one thing I've always loved. And part of that love has come from the knowledge that I'm good at it — or at least I thought I was. I suppose it makes sense that Canadians, who spend eight months of the year trapped in a snow globe with not a single coastline in sight, wouldn't measure up compared with these kids, who spend every day of their lives living in the water. I should have known. I shouldn't have come here all cocky and smug. Now I'm going to have to eat my own shit.

The coach calls my name, causing Em and Callie to hoot and holler for me. A few other kids follow suit, even though they don't know who I am. I guess that's what it's like to be the leaders. It's a giant game of 'Simon Says'.

At home, Maggie and I had fortified ourselves into our own private bubble, so being a part of this game was never a thought. We did what we wanted and hung out with who we chose. It wasn't really something we ever had to think consciously about. I've never had to claw my way through the social hierarchy before. I was just always *there*. But now, here in this new world, I've already unintentionally announced my arrival on the top tier so loudly and boisterously that everyone is paying attention. But in about two seconds they're all going to see me as a fraud, and my little matchstick castle is going to tumble beneath me.

There's not much I can do other than just swim my freaking heart out.

As Coach yells *go*, I gulp in as much air as I can handle and push off the platform with every ounce I have in me. Every muscle in my body stretches and reaches as I slice through the water. I pull, pull, *pull* the water down around me with every stroke, like my life depends on it. My legs kick with a fury, at some point becoming so numb with exertion that I have to believe they are in fact still kicking. Each breath that I gasp feels like it's just not quite enough. Oxygen is my fuel, and I can't seem to keep my tank full. After the turn, I put things into overdrive, doing the last ten meters or so without taking a single breath. As the tip of my middle finger finally grazes the pool's edge, I let my face explode from the water so I can drink the warm, humid air.

I look over at the time clock. 22:20.

My best time ever.

Sadly, dejectedly, one of the worst times of the whole group.

Instead of cheers when I pull out of the pool, the other swimmers remain silent, even looking away as if embarrassed. *They're* embarrassed? God, I'm the one who just rocked my best time ever, and it's not even worth celebrating about. I decide to save face by pulling the oldest excuse from the book.

I limp from the pool and plop down on the bench, massaging my left calf.

"Oh God. I pulled my calf running a few weeks ago. I thought it had healed up enough, but I could really feel it on that swim. It kept cramping up and it really slowed me down."

Em's face lightens a small bit. "Oh no, you're hurt? That sucks! You should've told the coach and she would've let up a bit on you. But it's okay. Your score was still pretty good." She says it with kind eyes but a tense smile.

"You said you were the captain at home, right? And you guys had an actual swim team? Like, you competed and everything?" Callie is more cynical.

I catch Em nudging her with an elbow.

"It's just that, maybe they do things different in Canada. I mean, it is *Canada*." The word drips off her tongue like she's tasted spoiled milk. "No offense, but it's kinda backwoods up there, isn't it? I heard some people even live in igloos and everything. So, being the captain of the swim team up there is probably way different than *here*. I mean, this is Maui Gardens. We have a reputation."

"Yeah, you're right. I guess our team wasn't quite the same quality as the one here." I swallow hard, my face flushing. "I guess I'm hoping I'll just make the team."

I feel so hurt, so dejected, not just that she's criticizing my swimming abilities but because she's painting this broad picture of who I am, even though she doesn't know me. I am not backwoods, or a redneck or small-town ignorant. Or at least, I never thought of myself like that before. But no one's ever compared me to something else before. Her words make me feel miniscule and laughable, like I'm a little kid trying to eat at the grown-up table, even though my feet don't touch the ground.

"See, Jess? I warned you that Maui Gardens is the best. And not everyone makes the cut. We pretty much kill at everything. You've really got to be special to earn your place at this school." She flashes me one of her beauty pageant smiles, as if she's being positive, but her words sting me. She's clearly testing me, assessing whether I belong in her world. Her gaze lingers on me for a moment more, then she shifts her attention to Em. Em is a little more gracious toward me, shrugging and giving me a hopeful grin, but I can tell their attitude about me is already changing. I've been knocked down a few notches, and now I'm sitting on the sidelines.

The remainder of the try-out progresses in much the same way. Although, I'm pleased to find that my breaststroke doesn't let me down, and I'm at least near the top of the pack in that event. As we head to the showers, I question whether my races, put together, have qualified me for the team. I am completely deflated.

We stand by our lockers in the girls' change room, and I do my best to scrunch the moisture from my hair with my damp towel. Em and Callie chatter about their plans this weekend, and it's pretty obvious that they've purposely turned their backs on me.

"So, what are we going to do this weekend? I can't believe nothing is going on! Usually, the first few weekends of the year are full of parties! God, what I wouldn't give for a great house party!"

"We could head to the beach again?" Em replies. "Mind ya', I heard they're patrollin' a lot more this weekend."

"And there aren't any new movies out. I guess we could just go for a bite to eat, but it's just so boring. It's our senior year. There's got to be *something* fun out there!"

It happens before I even realize it's happening. It happens because I'm so set on trying to prove myself with these girls, for them to see me in the same light as everyone saw me back home. I know I'm a bit pathetic. I know I just want to feel included. But I say it anyway.

"I was thinking of having a party this weekend. I mean, my dad's going out of town. So...maybe everyone wants to come to my place on Saturday night?"

As soon as I say it, I wish I could gather the spilled words with my hands and stuff them back into my mouth. I think of my date with Kai and how I'll have to pull the plug now because of the party — or invite him. But I think back to last weekend's beach party and how I was being pulled in two directions like a piece of saltwater taffy. The quiet, guilt-ridden ride home... No, better that Kai's not there.

But maybe I can just curtail our day date and make it back to host the party — the best of both worlds, I decide.

The girls look at me expectantly, greedy for the details.

"Yeah, party at my house…seven p.m. And I've got lots of booze too." I throw that last bit in as an extra incentive. Pathetic, I know. But something about these girls makes me want them to like me. I need to feel I belong with them. I thought swimming would be my *in*, but it turned to shit. I need another in, and this may be it.

"Really, Jess? Well, that's perfect! You're sure your dad is gone? And he's leaving you in that big ol' house all by yourself? A senior kick-off house party like nothin' else. It's gonna be epic!"

"Okay, cool." Callie joins in, seemingly not wanting to appear too eager. She's still all bristly about my underachieving swim times, I think.

"Yeah, it'll be great. And you know, invite whoever." I say it casually, but in reality, it's kind of the crux of this whole thing, because I literally have no one to invite. So, if Jess and Em don't spread the word, the party will be a pathetic threesome with just us. And I'm pretty sure that'll be the last time I'm included in any invite.

"Don't worry about that. The text is already goin' out!" Em intently works away on her phone.

Oh God, I'm going to regret this, aren't I?

Chapter Fifteen

"I'm just going to make this short and sweet, rather than keep you all waiting. I'll read through who made it and who, unfortunately, doesn't have what it takes this year. Practice, swim your hearts out and try again next year." Coach has gathered us outside the front entrance of the pool a half-hour after try-outs have ended.

My invitation to the party has softened Callie and Em somewhat, and they stand beside me as we hear the news. But there's hesitation with them as well. It's like an invisible bubble separating us. They hold hands together and bounce around anxiously from one foot to the other. I stand beside them, but just far enough away that I'm not exactly *with* them. And I get it. I know all about living in limbo when waiting to see who's *in* and who's *out*.

At home, our swim coach wasn't quite as gracious as Coach Wilson. She held try-outs then made us wait an entire week for the results. It was torture — not just because we didn't know whether we made the team, but because we didn't know what circle to stand in during the week-long wait. As disappointing as it'd be to find out immediately that I didn't make the team here, it'd be nothing compared to the humiliation I'd feel after hanging with the swim team for an entire week *assuming* I had a spot, only to find out I didn't make the cut.

Because, then what? Where would I go? Other groups and teams would have formed, and the mechanics of the school year would have begun. And there wouldn't be a place saved for me anywhere.

Coach Wilson finishes her rambling speech about trying hard and putting yourself out there, then gets to the good stuff. She starts with front crawl, and quickly moves through backcrawl, butterfly and freestyle. With every name that she calls, a little part of me wilts. And it could just be in my head, but it seems like the space between me and the girls widens with every announcement too. They don't think I've made it either. I brace myself for the inevitable, and brainstorm other clubs I could join that still haven't gotten up and running. Track, maybe? Student council? *Math* club? Oh God help me. This is going to be a long year. Right when I've pretty much lost hope, Coach makes her final round of cuts.

"And for breaststroke girls, we've got Meagan Chambers and Jessica Kennedy. For guys, it's Bryce Cooper and Adrian Curley."

I made the team. I really made the team! I don't know how the hell I did it, to tell the truth. Maybe Coach Wilson felt bad for me? Or maybe she saw something she could work with? Or maybe it was Callie and Em's influence the whole time. I don't want to think it was that — but it could've been.

Either way, I am officially part of the Maui Gardens Elite Swim Team — only for breaststroke, but still…55 I might not be elated about my dramatic dip in swim team title, but I'm relieved I even got a spot. And that's something.

"So, I guess you are Maui Gardens quality after all. Congrats." Callie's smile is smug and cool, but I drink it up anyway.

"Yeah, thanks. I'm super-pumped. It'll be a great year."

"So…your place, Saturday night?" Em jumps in.

"Uh, yeah, for sure. Any time after seven. Do you guys need my address?"

"Oh, darlin', everybody knows where *you* live. We're lookin' forward to the grand tour! See you Saturday!"

They strut off arm and arm with invisible tiaras balancing precariously on their heads, which I find infuriating. *Aren't I the one living in the castle?*

* * * *

Dad gives me exactly the kind of reaction I hope for when I get home. He hoots and hollers across the expansive space, his voice echoing in the halls.

"I knew you'd do it. I knew they'd see you for the superstar you are. See, Jess? You fit just as well into this school as anybody else. You deserve this."

"Well, it's not like I'm swim captain anymore. I'm only recruited for one event. which sucks."

"Jess, that doesn't matter one bit. You take what life gives you and you mold it so it works for you. How do you think I got here? *We* got here? An opportunity came a knocking and I jumped at the chance — made it work for me. It might not be exactly what I expected, but I'm doing my best to stay afloat. And you take after your old dad. You've got my drive and determination. Who says you can't take this position and kick everybody's ass with it?"

I just about spit out the iced tea I've cracked open. My dad never swears — well, at least not around me. He and my mom always had that rule, which I've found hilarious over the last few years, because I've slipped out a few f-bombs around them myself accidentally. They absolutely despise that. Typically, it's a stunt I only pull when they've really aggravated me and I'm wanting to piss them off in return. It always works like a charm.

But, since we've come here, Dad has let up quite a bit. It must be the tropical vibe or something. He doesn't baby me as much as he used to. Like, for example, leaving me alone in this monstrous house this weekend. My mom never would have signed off on that. But here, he doesn't need her permission.

"You know, Jess, what you need to do is work really hard and make them wish they put you in every race. Be the best breaststroke swimmer in all of Hawaii. Show them that you, in fact, were a missed opportunity to them."

"Well, let's not go that far, Dad. These swimmers are good, like, crazy good. Truly, I'm just happy I made the team."

I linger for a moment as a nagging thought comes back into my mind, even though I've tried to push it out all day.

"Um, I'm going to head upstairs now. I have to make a call."

He raises his eyebrows but doesn't say a word. My dad really does know me that well.

"Yes, I'm calling her, *okay*? I know she'd want to hear how I'm doing, and I can't handle any more of your guilt trips about being an awful daughter."

"I didn't say anything!" he protests.

"You didn't need to." I reach out to squeeze his arm, but he curls me in toward his chest for a giant bear hug. His doughy arms wrap around me, and for a moment I'm at home in the smell of his woodsy aftershave and his prickly neck hairs that tickle my cheeks. My dad's hugs have always been able to lift me out of any funk I've been in, as if they melt the grimy stuff from my spirit, making me clean and light again. At this moment, I'm just super-grateful for him. And I finally feel at ease with the turn of events our lives have taken. It's not what I would have expected, even just a month ago, but it's beginning to feel right, normal even.

"Okay, okay. I better go upstairs and get this over with before I chicken out...again. See you in the morning."

"Goodnight sweetheart."

"Dad...I love you."

"Love you too."

I sit on my bed for a full fifteen minutes staring at the contact in my phone—*Douchebag Robert* is the contact I have his home number listed as—before finally getting up the nerve to press *call*.

It rings four times before a deep, rumbling voice answers.

"Yep, hello?" The voice is slow and gruff, like what I would expect from a lumberjack or a truck driver, not what I expect from *Robert from Payroll*. My brain scrambles to recreate my mental image of him from the weaselly nerd of a man I had expected.

"Um...hi. This is...er...Jess? I was wondering if I could talk to my mom?"

"Jess? Oh, my goodness. Well, isn't this the best news of the day! It's so great to hear your voice. Your mom talks about you non-stop. God, she's been missing you. When I heard you were moving away...? Well, let me just tell you that I never, *I never*, wanted to come between you and your mom. You are everything to her. She's been a mess without you here. But you know, she understands that you need some space. And she's been trying to respect that. But boy, is she ever going to be happy to hear your voice. Hang on. She's just in the bath, but I'll pass you on to her."

I hear his laborious breath as he gets up off the couch or wherever he was sitting, and lumbers down the hall. Then he starts calling out to my mom.

"Nicole! Nikki! It's Jess. She wants to talk to you!" I cringe a bit when he calls my mom Nikki. That was what my dad always called her when he was trying to either butter her up for something good or apologize for something bad.

I catch a faint, "What? It's Jess?" in the background, then the splashing of water. It absolutely grosses me out to think that my mom is lying naked in a bath somewhere, with her and Robert at the point in their relationship where he can just pop in like it's no big deal, like he's seen it all a thousand times before and it's all just *normal*. I'm about to hang up, thinking maybe this was a bad idea, maybe this is still too soon for me. But then —

"Jess? Is that you?" She sounds exactly the way I remember her. It's been a little over three weeks since I've heard my mom's voice, and I hate to admit it, but it's the best sound in the world. The way she says my name with such care and gentleness brings me back to a thousand memories—her checking on me after I've fallen off my bike, her checking in on me after my first day of school, her checking to see how it went on my first date. She's always checking on me. I can't believe how much I've missed that.

"Hey, Mom. I just wanted to call and, I don't know, see how things are going?"

As soon as I start talking, I hear her starting to weep on the other end. I can tell she doesn't want me to know, because every so often it sounds all muffled, like she's covering the phone with her hand. And of course, that makes my eyes well up too, a large pit forming in the back of my throat.

"Oh, honey, I can't tell you how much I've missed you, how good it is to hear your voice. How are you doing in Maui? Is it as beautiful as everyone claims?"

"Yeah, it's pretty spectacular. I haven't seen a ton of the island yet, but I plan to do some exploring this weekend." I leave out the part about the boy I'm going to be exploring with.

"I made the swim team! We just had try-outs today. It was tough, really tough. But at least I made it. It's way different than at home. Everything is way different than at home. Mom, I'm in a *private* school." I say it with such distaste that I surprise myself.

"Yeah, I know, sweetheart. Dad's been filling me in on as much as he can. We weren't sure of the school system in Hawaii and didn't want you suffering in your senior year, so we thought a private school would be best. I guess we're lucky Dad is making so much money in his new position there too, so he can afford it." I catch a slight edge to her voice.

"Anyway, are you liking it, at least? The new school?" She says it with so much hope, that I feel like any complaint I have is just going to hurt her.

"Yeah, it's great. It's really great."

"And what about your dad? How's he holding up, for real?" For some reason, that question slaps me in the face. I was really enjoying this conversation until she had to remind me why we're having it two thousand miles apart. It's because *she* made the choice to lie in the bath next to Robert, rather than watch *Law and Order* on the couch with my dad.

I toy with the idea of saying he's been dating a lot, playing the field with some bikini-clad beauty on the island, but my mom knows me too well and can field one of my lies in a second. She's always been way better at that than my dad. So, I settle on providing as little information as possible. I know that will hurt her almost as much.

"He's fine, doing well."

There's a moment of silence where I think we both wonder in which direction to take this conversation next. If we choose the wrong path, it could jeopardize everything.

"So, how are you feeling? With the pregnancy, I mean?"

"I'm good...now at least. The last month was excruciating with morning sickness. I don't remember having that with you. Maybe it means I'm having a boy? I thought morning sickness ended in the first trimester, but that wasn't the case with this pregnancy, let me tell you! Constantly eating carbs has been the only way I've been able to cope. But that means I've gained way too much weight, I think. You know that mauve silk dress we bought last year on sale from Ann Taylor? The one I was going to wear to your cousin Lisa's wedding in November? Well, I couldn't even get the zipper up when I tried it on the other day. So, I guess it's maternity clothes for me from now on."

I can't even imagine my mother wearing maternity clothes. Every image I conjure up of a pregnant lady involves a smiley twenty-five-year-old with perfect teeth and long, swishy hair holding her baby bump with eager anticipation.

Not my middle-aged mother and her weaselly, extra-marital boyfriend.

"So, Robert and I were talking, and we thought it would be really great for you to fly back home to Edmonton for Christmas? It'll give you a chance to see all your old friends? See me?" There's an extended pause where neither of us speak. "I miss you, Jess. And I'm sorry. I know I've said it a thousand times before, but I am. I'm sorry. I love you."

With those three words, my insides turn into an ooey, gooey cheese fondue. Because at the end of it all, she's my mom, and I really miss my mom. I'm not ready to give her what she wants, but I can at least throw her a bone.

"We'll see how things go, Mom. I love you too."

I hang up before she has the chance to whittle me away even further. After all, I'm still pissed, and I'm stubborn as shit. If my mother has taught me anything, it's to stand up for myself and hold my ground. She's still got some making up to do.

Chapter Sixteen

I'm just getting ready for bed when I get a text from Kai.

Thinking about u today. How were try-outs? Make the team? If not, I heard the Math Club at Maui Gardens is A+ :)

The text floats into my phone like a salve covering a burn, and right at the perfect time. I've just gotten off with my mother, and the ache in my heart is almost drowning me. How does this boy, who I barely even know, already have me figured out better than anyone?

I text him back, my fingers skittering across the screen in excitement.

Yeah, just got home. Made *it! Not captain, but that's ok.*

Kai responds.

Who wants to be captain anyway? Too much work. You'd just be showing off lol

I can't help but smile as I text back.

True. And Math Club isn't completely off the table, you know...

This ping pong match of wits is a pretty even game until his next text comes in.

Oh? Sexy, sporty and *smart. You're a triple threat!*

Sexy? Did I read that right? He thinks I'm *sexy?* I try not to let the beach vomit scene slide into my mind. I want to savor this moment. He must be wondering if his comment has weirded me out, because he doesn't wait any longer for me to respond.

So, are we still on for Sat?

Yep, for sure. Time?

Be at your house at 7.

As in a.m.???

Early bird gets the worm. Bring your swimsuit, preferably that sweet one with the strawberries all over it. I got everything else covered.

My face flushes an even darker shade of crimson, and I'm grateful Kai doesn't have some sort of x-ray powers to see through my phone. He remembers the bikini I wore on that first day we met? *Hmph.* And here I thought it was so, so, so...*juvenile.*

I pull the bikini out of my drawer and lay it out strategically across my white duvet. I even put my funky Panama hat—the one I wore at last year's folk music festival—on the top and add a dangly gold knot necklace in the middle, with a set of bangles on the side. Once I've arranged it just right, so it looks like a department store photo op, I snap a picture and text it to Kai.

Do you approve of the ensemble for the day?

Already envisioning you in it.

The comment sends a wild rush through my body, and I catch a glimpse of myself smiling in the full-length mirror standing next to my bed.

Okay, Saturday it is.

As I'm lost in my own snowballing reveries, my phone buzzes. I pick it up, thinking it's Kai again, and I giggle at what flirty nonsense he's responding with this time. Maybe he wants me to actually send him a photo of myself *in* the bikini? Okay, that might be too weird.

But when I peer at my phone, it's not a text from Kai. It's a group text from Callie—a group text involving me and approximately *eighty-seven* other seniors. *Oh shit.*

Hey everyone! Just letting you know about an epic beginning of the year bash *for all seniors this Saturday! It's at Jess Kennedy's—you know, the freshest new breaststroke champ on our swim team! Go Riders! Msg me if you need the address. It's going to be amazing, so make sure to be there! Xoxo Callie*

All my excitement and anticipation about Kai has vanished. I'm aware that I'm the one who put the invite out there in the universe. I recognize that there's no one to blame but me. But somehow, I feel completely taken aback by this text and incredibly pissed off. I didn't think the party would actually be a go! Or at least to this degree. Callie, Em, Luke, Connor...? Okay, fine. But not the entire senior class! *How am I going to get myself out of this?*

At the same time, this is my shot—my shot at making it into the circle at Maui Gardens. Swim try-outs were the first cut, but this is the real deal. If I flake out on this party, who knows where I'm going to end up? It's bad enough that I'm having to restart my entire life halfway across the world. It would be hell if I had to do it while totally on the outs.

Then there's Kai to think about. I've been looking forward to spending the entire day with him all week...and the evening too. I still toy with the idea of bringing him over for the party, but I'm afraid that'll just be intersecting too many lines. And I would have to do so much explaining. I still see the scowl on Callie's face when I mentioned his name earlier this week.

No, that settles it. I'm just going to have to hang with Kai during the day, say a quick goodbye and get revved up for the party in the evening. It does mean my dreamy make-out scene likely won't be happening this weekend, but I promise myself that if our date goes well, Kai and I will have a ton of alone time in the near future.

I feel ready to brave the world. Or at least take on Maui Gardens Charter School.

Hey, everyone! Yeah, like Callie said, party at my place Sat. Come any time after 7!

As much as I want this party to be a success, I'm also kind of hoping it's a flop.

Chapter Seventeen

The blare of my alarm swallows the monotonous squawking of the birds outside. I roll over, squinting my eyes open to see the time on my phone. Maybe I set the alarm wrong, and gloriously, I have another three hours to sleep?

No such luck. It's six-thirty on the dot. Thirty minutes to get myself looking half decent before my date with Kai.

I haven't heard much from him since Wednesday, other than a quick text last night to make sure I set the alarm for this morning. He wanted to know if he should call to wake me up. God, he's sweet. His voice would have been a whole lot better than the irritating beeping of my phone. But I'm all about business now. I've got legs to shave, makeup to put on, hair to do *something* with.

I probably don't need to try so hard. I suddenly realize that almost every time Kai has seen me, I've been a sweaty, half-naked, makeup-free mess — except for the beach party. And well, I was throwing up all over him that night, so I like to think it doesn't count at all. It should make me feel better knowing that even seeing me at my absolute worst, he still wants to go out.

But it doesn't. It just adds to my nerves for today, because I want so badly for it to go smoothly. I want him to know what I really look like if I put in some effort, if I try a little. I want him to see me and think, *"Yep, what do I need to do to win this girl's attention?"* I need to channel my inner Maggie today.

I slip into the oh-so-sweet strawberry bikini, then shrug on a loose-fitting beach cover-up made from a light, gauzy material. I don't want to go overboard on the makeup front, so I apply just a little mascara and some strawberry-flavored lip gloss. It never hurts to coordinate. Since moving to Maui, my pale skin has taken on a rosier glow, a smattering of freckles appearing on the apples of my cheeks and across the bridge of my nose. My typical dirty-blonde hair has caught a few golden highlights from the sun, and it brightens my whole complexion. I loosely curl just a few locks of hair, so it has that 'I've just crawled out of bed and my hair always looks tousled like this' look. At least, that's what I'm going for. I throw my head upside-down, shake it from the roots with my fingertips, then quickly toss it back. I look in the mirror as the pieces drape around my face and I give my lips one final pout. I hope that my beach-sexy hair looks so soft and touchable that Kai isn't going to be able to resist running his fingers through it.

When I'm done getting ready, I grab my shoulder bag and stuff it with my phone, wallet, some sunscreen and a towel. Kai assured me he would cover everything else, but I'm not a dummy when it comes to seventeen-year-old boys. They can be pretty dumb and forgetful. I throw two water bottles and a couple of protein bars into my bag at the last minute on the off chance he didn't think of something so benign as us starving to death.

When I get downstairs, I'm surprised to see my dad already sitting at the kitchen table with a cappuccino placed in front of him, and another one in front of my empty seat. *Shit, I thought he'd still be sleeping.*

Last night, I told him in passing that I was going to be going out with a friend to explore the island, but I refrained from offering up too many details. I purposely caught him while he was busy working on a marketing plan to show the CEO of his company today in Honolulu. I knew what I said wouldn't really sink in. I figured I had bypassed the entire conversation, until right now.

"Hey, honey. Come sit. Have breakfast and a coffee with me. I know you're leaving soon, but you must have a minute to spare."

"Uh, sure, Dad." I grab a banana and sit on the edge of my seat.

"So, which friend is picking you up today? I forget if you told me. That girl Callie you were talking about? Or Em? I get them mixed up."

At first, I start talking with a bite of banana in my mouth, hoping he'll just let it slide. But when I swallow, he says, "Sorry, hon. I didn't catch that. Who's going?"

"Er…actually, it's a boy. His name is Kai."

"Oh, a boy. You never mentioned that." My heart skips a beat, because my dad has always had a thing about boys. He doesn't want me dating them. I'm afraid this will be the start of some awkward conversation about 'what all boys want' or something. But he surprises me.

"Oh, well, that's exciting. What's he like? Do you go to school with him?"

I don't really feel like getting into the whole thing about Kai being the gardener's son. Just saying it to myself sounds really pretentious. But it's true that there seems to be some sort of built-in social structure here that wasn't so clearly defined back at home. And I'm worried my dad has bought into it. He'll think that Kai's a waste of my time just because he doesn't go to Maui Gardens, which couldn't be further from the truth. My dad isn't a terrible person, but he does have that snobby streak. What if he says I'm not allowed to hang with him?

The thing is, I don't want to lie to him either. Since moving here, my dad and I have felt more on the same team than ever, and I don't want to break that bond. It would be like backstabbing a teammate. I'm afraid that once the lies start rolling out of my mouth, I won't be able to stop them. I'm afraid of turning into my mother.

I think of how I can spin my response in a creative way. Half-truths are okay, aren't they?

"He's a senior like me." *Simple. Non-committal. That'll work.*

"Well, that's great, then. He's not coming over tonight, though, is he? You know I don't feel all that comfortable with you having boys over in the evenings when I'm not around."

At least I don't have to lie with this one.

"No, he's definitely not coming over tonight," I say with confidence.

"Okay, well, have a great time then. I should go shower myself, as I need to get to the airport a bit early.

Wish me luck with my meeting, and I'll see you tomorrow afternoon. I've got a special reservation booked for us! I'm not telling you where, but let's just say it's not going to be Olive Garden."

"Okay, Dad, that sounds awesome. And good luck. Have a safe trip." I kiss him quickly on the cheek and he squeezes my hand. Guiltily, I slink away, feeling that I'm not quite worthy of the trust my dad has in me.

Kai pulls up to my place at seven on the dot. I'm impressed with his punctuality. I live my life like I'm in the picture book *Ish*, whereas Kai seems so self-assured, so absolute. I'm all smart-*ish*, pretty-*ish*, athletic-*ish*, on-time-*ish*. He is exactly who he is, with no apologies or excuses. He's an open book that I am wanting to bury myself in.

"I wasn't sure what you drank, but I figured caffeine was a must this early on a Saturday morning. I got you the chocolate macadamia nut dark roast from Maui Beans and Brew. It's my favorite spot. I don't know if you Canadians realize this, but Maui's got the best coffee in the country—the world, probably."

I raise my eyebrows, giving him a skeptical look. Up until a couple of weeks ago, my only experience with coffee was the Folgers can my parents scooped from every morning or the donut-house brand Maggie and I slurped during cold winter days. I have to admit that I've enjoyed the cappuccinos my dad has been making since moving here, but still—coffee is coffee. There's not much difference.

"Go on. Drink it. I dare you. I'll bet you five bucks that you can't take a sip without sighing after."

I almost laugh out loud at his suggestion. The thought of any beverage making me audibly sigh is absurd. Kai could make me audibly sigh, but not this coffee.

I pick the warm cup up as steam dances from the lip. The aroma wafting toward me is rich and full-bodied, wrapping me in a velvety blanket. It reminds me of decadent desserts and long walks through rain-soaked forests, all at the same time—earthy and sweet with nutty undertones. I blow the surface carefully, not wanting to burn my tongue with a premature sip. There's nothing worse than that, I think. It robs a person of the pleasure of tasting anything for at least three days, long after the hot cocoa or steeped tea has been forgotten. Having that happen is like a scolding for impatience.

When a few minutes have passed, and I think it's safe to take a drink, I brave my first sip. Without realizing it, I close my eyes as I drink, enjoying the way the luscious, milky warmth coats the back of my throat. Its texture is silky as it swirls around in my mouth, and the taste is strong and robust. The sweetness from the chocolate mixes with the decadence of the macadamia nut to create a taste so rich and delicious that it's comparable to the most indulgent dessert. I swallow.

I sigh.

"All right! The five bucks is mine. Told you not to doubt the elixir of the gods!"

"Yeah, yeah, you set me up with that one. God, that is a good coffee. Why is it so good? How come the coffee back home doesn't taste like that? You sure you didn't infuse it with crack or something?"

"Trust me, no drugs involved. That's just the island. Everything grown from this island has a bit of magic in it, I think." Kai smiles contentedly as he looks out of the open window.

"You really love this place, don't you?" Just for a minute, I want to be in his head, see things through his eyes. I know this island is beautiful and tropical and magical, but there's more to what Kai sees. He sees Maui with pride and devotion, like only a parent can see their own child.

"Yeah, I love this place. It's my home, and I just never want to leave." He looks over at me. "Did I tell you that my family has land up near Kula? That's where I live. It's upcountry. Not many tourists head up there. We've got about ten acres of rich farming land that's been in my family for more than five generations. My *tutu* still runs the farm, but we all help out. It's like it's in my genes."

Kai hadn't mentioned this before. I'm not sure what I thought his family did. I guess I knew his dad did some gardening and I figured that was about it—that they made enough money trimming rich people's hedges to afford to live on this majestic island. Maybe I am completely ignorant.

I look over at Kai and suddenly imagine him in a pair of dirty overalls and a straw hat. I almost spit out my coffee as I laugh aloud.

"What? You don't like farmers?"

"No, it's not that at all. I was just imagining you...you know, in a pair of...wearing some..." I finally get a hold of myself and my guffawing simmers to a giggle. "Oh, never mind. No, I think it's totally cool that you're a farmer. I just didn't think of Hawaii as the 'farming' state. I figured that was Iowa or Oklahoma or something." Maybe I need that American History class more than I thought. "Is it a regular farm? Like, with cows and horses and stuff?"

"Some people on the island have animals, but most of the time they just take up too much space. The farms here are all pretty small because, well, the island is pretty small. We grow vegetables and fruit, some herbs and a bit of lavender — all organic, of course. We sell it to the local restaurants and stores mostly, as well as eating it ourselves. If you think that coffee you're drinking is good, you've tasted nothing yet. My *tutu* makes the absolute tastiest Kalua pork with pineapple and coconut. She serves it with rice and this salad she makes with fresh mango. So good. But really, anything my *tutu* makes is delicious." He stops for a moment and laughs to himself. "You'd even like her Spam sandwiches."

"Oh, disgusting! I could never eat a Spam sandwich. Isn't that *canned* ham? Who eats that crap?"

"I know, and I get it. Sounds terrible, but the way *Tutu* does it, you can't get enough." I love the way the word *Tutu* rolls off his tongue so delicately, like he holds her with such reverence.

"I'm not sure how long we're going to be in the farming business, though. A lot has been changing in Maui over the last several years. Tourism has gone through the roof, which I guess is good for the island in the grand scheme of things... But it makes things really difficult for the people who live here. The cost of living is crazy. That's why my dad has to tend to stupid, rich people's gardens on the side, just to pay the bills."

He catches himself and glances sideways at me. "Sorry, no offense."

A giant chasm emerges between the two of us, right between the two front seats of the truck. It's the same cliched issue, over and over again. I am the spoiled white tourist who doesn't belong, and he is the poor, hard-working local just trying to stake a claim on his land. It leaves me at a loss for words, because really, what input could I give at this point? I don't know anything about this island other than what I've come across over the last couple of weeks. And I'm embarrassed to say that I haven't even left the professionally manicured estates of Wailea.

Kai breaks the silence.

"I don't mean to be critical. And I'm sorry for making you feel awkward. We've just been going through a lot lately at home. Many of the generations-old farms on Maui have been disappearing because they're getting bought out by big businesses, most of which aren't even from here. Plus, big box stores have recently moved in, offering prices on produce that local farmers could never match, even though we grow it fresh here on the island and they ship it all the way from the mainland. We just can't compete.

"Real estate moguls and hotel chains from the mainland, Asia and Europe know that we're struggling, and they rush in as if they're saving the day. But what they're actually doing is pretty much stealing the land from the locals. They come here offering up what seems like a good deal at first. A lot of the young kids my age don't want to stay in farming. They don't want to continue with the family business. So, the elders end up selling for what they assume is a good price, because they've never really had a lot of money before and don't know the difference. Then some monstrosity is built on the land, raking in millions for the big corporation, and all of a sudden, the five hundred thousand dollars that had been offered for the farm is only a drop in the bucket."

"Wow, I had no idea. Sorry." I wish I could offer more to him, but I'm feeling awfully like a part of the problem right now. "So, what can we do to help out? To help these farms stay afloat?"

"Buy local, I guess. Support small businesses. Respect the island and what it has to offer."

I ponder this for a moment and make a silent pledge that I'll be more conscious of where my groceries come from and how my actions affect the people around me.

Chapter Eighteen

We drive up the highway toward the town of Lahaina, farther north than I've ever been on the island. I watch a golden sun rise over the Pacific, turning the ocean into a sweeping blanket of diamonds. We listen to the lazy strumming of a Ben Harper guitar solo coming through the truck's speakers, and I'm feeling chill...content.

That is, until Kai abruptly veers across the two-lane highway and into a gravel lot on the side of the road. The surf is so close to the highway there that I feel like at any moment it could flood the entire area.

"What's going on? How come we stopped?"

"*This* is our destination. Come on!"

He climbs out of the truck, and I have no choice but to follow suit. I stand with him at the back of the truck bed while he fights to unbolt the tailgate.

I'm not sure where we are. All I know is that we passed a dozen pristine beaches on the way here that looked far nicer than this one. If we were going to spend a day at the beach, we could have gone to one a lot closer to home. Any one of the extravagant hotels just down from my place overlooks an immaculate, powder-soft beach. It would have made way more sense to spend the day there.

"Okay… So, where is *here*?"

"Olowalu Beach! Come on. You're going to love it. But leave your shoes on for now cuz the *kiawe* thorns hurt when you step on them." I look out over the sand splattered with shady patches made from exotic-looking trees, their canopies hanging out toward the water. He's right. The sand is covered in small, thorn-covered twigs, making the beach appear littered and unkempt. I look up to see some sort of welcome sign or lifeguard post, anything to indicate this is a beach actually open to visitors. But all I see is a road sign reading *Mile Marker 14*.

Kai plops a huge beach bag and umbrella into my arms and effortlessly slides two brightly colored surfboards from the back of the truck.

"What? You never said anything about surfing!"

"Can't come to Maui without surfing. And you have the best private tutor on the island. Come on. We're not going to have the beach to ourselves for very long. Let's make the best of it!"

He strides toward the sand with me trailing behind. We find a shady spot that's mostly clear of the prickly thorns, and I spread out a large beach blanket. I go to stretch out and relax before the sun gets high enough to do serious damage to me, when Kai grabs my hand and pulls me back up.

"No way. No sitting yet. Surfing takes priority. The surf today is perfect for teaching you how to ride, and

I don't want to waste a second. Take your dress off and grab a board."

His eyes dart away for a moment, like he realizes what he's just insinuated. I pretend not to notice as I scramble out of my beach cover-up. The air is warm, but it's still so early in the day that I'm not eager to get in the water just yet.

Hesitant, I stand at the edge of the water, just letting the waves tickle my toes, when I suddenly jump back.

"Wait! What about those spiky urchin things we saw last time? Don't we have to watch for those?"

"Sea urchins? Yeah, you always have to watch for those. But I'll keep you close to the sand bar. I'd be more worried about the eels or reef sharks...or smacking your head on the sharp bits of coral. But it's all good."

Oh God, what am I doing? I could be snuggled in my soft duvet at home. I look over at Kai with his expectant eyes and mischievous grin. *That's* what got me out of bed this morning. He gives my hand a tug and turns back around to lead me into waist-deep water.

Kai is definitely in his element. It's hard not to get caught up in his passion for the beach, the surf. He expertly navigates around the shallow coral reef that almost juts out of the water in some places. We eventually walk to where the bottom is almost all sand, and there seem to be fewer hazards for us to maneuver around. I look up at the water stretching all the way to the horizon. It's smooth as glass. There's barely a single wave rolling in. *How the hell are we supposed to surf with the water so calm and still?*

"So, where are the waves? This seems pretty tame."

"Of course it's tame. It's not as if I can take you out to Jaws your first time! Trust me. A few good waves will start rolling in, and they'll be plenty thrilling for you."

"What's Jaws?" I ask, the waves starting to lap up a little more greedily, bobbing me from side to side.

"Jaws is the most epic surf spot on Maui. Tough to get to and it's pretty hidden from tourists, which is how we like it. But during high surf times in the winter, the swells can get up to sixty feet. That's like, five stories or something. Even *I* don't hit those waves."

Five stories? Oh God, I can't even imagine waves that high. I look at the rippling water around me. These waves are maybe two feet high? *Baby waves. How humiliating.*

We're out chest deep, a field of crystal-clear glass surrounding us. The water is so clean and clear that my bright pink toenail polish beams up at me like dazzling jewels lying on the ocean floor.

"Okay, lie down on your board like this." Kai lies on his stomach, his feet pointed down one end and his elbows bracing his upper body on the other side. His body glistens with salt water, his shark tattoo grabbing a hold of his bulging bicep.

He waits patiently for me to straddle my board, holding the edge of it so I don't topple off before I've even gotten going. I lean my body forward, bracing the front of the board with my hands as I scoot my butt up a bit so my legs stretch across the other end of the board. It feels scratchy against my bare stomach, and I immediately realize why surfers always wear those long-sleeved shirts when they ride.

We bob gently for a few minutes while Kai teaches me the fundamentals.

"So, when I tell you to, you're gonna press into your hands and scoot your knees up under you, so you're on all fours. You'll want to take a second there to get your balance. Look out ahead of you instead of down. Trust me, you stay more grounded that way. Then, when you feel stable and you feel yourself riding the peak, you're going to pop up with one foot in front, keeping your legs bent and arms straight out to the sides. If you can't pop up in one smooth motion, you can try one foot at a time, but you may lose momentum by then, and your ride'll be over.

"Now, if you do get up," — that wide, all-encompassing smile beams on his gorgeous face once more — "well, you're gonna feel like you own this ocean. You'll be addicted for life."

He's so full of passion for this sport, for everything in his life, that it makes my insides bubble with anticipation too, like a cold soda that has been poured over ice and fizzes up over the outside of glass. How can anyone not be drawn to his charisma?

I rest my chin on top of my forearms and look up at him coyly. "You make it sound so easy, but I'm thinking it's way harder than that. You've got to show me a couple of rides so I can see those moves in action."

"What the lady wants..." He starts to say, but he really doesn't need any convincing at all. He's already let go of my board and is paddling strongly against the current, farther out to sea. When he gets about fifty feet beyond where I'm bobbing, he sits up with his legs straddled on either side of his board and turns himself around, so he faces me again.

I wait for him to do something, to stand up or start paddling again, but nothing. He just sits there with a cocky smirk on his face and his hands on his hips.

"What's the problem? Am I putting you on the spot? Can't perform in front of an audience?" I yell through my cupped hands, but I'm not sure if he's heard. He continues to just sit there quietly for what seems like an eternity.

Then unexpectedly, he glances over his shoulder and flops back on his belly. I look beyond him to see what has made him jump to attention. Out by the horizon, there's a stripe of deep blue that appears to rise out of the ocean. It bulges and expands as it approaches us, looking as if it's sucking more water into its growing belly with each second.

Kai starts paddling fiercely with his strong arms, his back a curved bow on his board. The swell rushes so quickly that it now rolls right underneath him, and he's lifted up to its peak. In one smooth motion, he presses up off his hands, while placing his feet firmly in the middle of the board. He expertly rides the frothy white tip of the wave like a bull rider taming the unruliest bull. The nose of the board carves right and left, Kai navigating the roaring water with muscular legs. As he approaches me, he does a quick one-eighty jump on his board, so that he faces me square on. As he passes, he trails his left hand in the water, then unexpectedly scoops up a handful to splash at me. All I can do is wipe the salt water from my eyes before I see him gliding toward the shore, smooth and streamlined, holding up his right hand with a cheesy *hang-loose* sign.

Yep, the boy can surf.

Once he has turned his board around and is back floating in the chest-deep water with me, I allow a massive smile to explode on my face.

"*That* was amazing. Incredible! You *have* to teach me how to do that!"

"Thought you said these waves were too puny for you! Think you can handle them now?"

"Well, I didn't realize the good ones came out of nowhere like that. How'd you know it was coming?"

"I guess you get sort of a sixth sense about the water when you spend as much time out here as I do." He pushes himself up so he's straddling the board once again. He extends his arms out to either side of him and tilts his face up to the sun. "*This* is my home. Right here. *This* is where I'm supposed to be."

I see it, I believe it—and boy, do I ever want a piece of it.

Chapter Nineteen

After six or seven failed attempts at getting up on my board, the humiliation is starting to wear on me.

Kai is being a good sport about things, but I sense he's starting to feel frustrated too.

"Thought you said you were a snow-boarder, *Canada*? Just pretend you're whizzing down a mountain instead of slicing through the ocean." He smacks me playfully on the back of my leg while he carefully turns me around to point toward the shore once again.

"I said I've *tried* snowboarding before, not that I'm *good* at it! Besides, when you're snowboarding, the mountain is not rolling underneath you."

"Okay, one more time and you got this. I can feel it. I'm gonna give you an extra big nudge this time to help you out. But you've got to pop up fast. Deal?"

"I'll do my best," is all I can promise.

I'm going through the step-by-step sequence in my head one more time. Paddle, scoot, balance, pop up. Sounds so simple.

Suddenly, Kai chirps in my ear.

"Okay, this one is going to be epic. I can see it rolling in. This is going to be the ride of your life."

I reach my arms forward as if I'm in the front crawl race of my life. I pull the water back quickly and forcefully, then feel Kai give my board an extra little shove forward.

"Okay, pop up *now!*" he demands.

I go into automatic, focusing my gaze on the shoreline. Scoot, balance, pop up. *Scoot, balance, pop up...*

And suddenly, inexplicably, I'm standing on top of my board, racing on the crest of the wave toward the shoreline. The sheer force of the wave is menacing, threatening to tear me off at any moment. But that's what makes it exhilarating. It's like *I'm* controlling the wave. *I'm* controlling nature. I'm not like Kai, who can carve this way and that. I'm concentrating on just keeping my feet planted on the board, the nose facing forward and my body staying upright.

But I'm surfing. I'm actually surfing. I love it.

Kai whoops and hollers behind me, clapping his hands and whistling through his fingers. I feel like I need to acknowledge his cheers, and maybe show off just a little. So, I take a page from his playbook, holding my left hand up to give him the same *hang-loose* sign he dangled in front of me.

I should have known that a small movement like that would throw me off my game, disrupt my focus. The board wobbles at first, then the nose of the board gets caught up in the rushing water, toppling end over end, with me still on top.

The force is more powerful than anything I could have expected. I have zero control as I flail into the roaring water. The board falls on top of me, its edge cutting a deep gash in my shoulder and pushing me farther underwater. I'm a rag doll in a washing machine, unable to gain control of any of my extremities. My head whips back and there's a sharp crack at the base of my skull, like a baseball bat has struck a homer all the way to the outfield. I instinctively gasp, but a rush of saltwater fills my mouth and lungs, instead of air. I try to reach for the surface, to grab something that'll propel me out of the swirling water.

A moment before my vision fades completely to black, I feel a strong weight beneath me, lifting me out of the waves. As soon as my head is above water, a terrible bout of uncontrollable coughing begins. Saltwater streams from my nose and mouth. The back of my head throbs, but my lungs are so grateful for air that I barely pay attention to the hammering in my skull. I try to open my eyes, but they quickly squint shut when faced with the bright morning sun.

Kai holds me close to his chest, carrying me like a baby as he wades out of the shallow water. He doesn't say anything until he's got me lying safely on the beach blanket up on the sand.

"Shit, Jess. I'm so sorry. That was so stupid of me. I shouldn't have let you ride that big one. And I should have checked to see if you were pointed toward the coral. Jesus, I'm so sorry. Let me see. Are you okay?"

He races to the first-aid kit he has stashed in his beach bag and grabs a large bandage to tape over my arm. The gash stings and is bleeding, but thankfully it's not as deep as I thought. Next, he grabs a handful of ice from the cooler and wraps it in his thin cotton T-shirt. He tucks it under my neck and lays my head gently on top of it.

I think back to all of the times Kai has needed to play nurse to me — checking my shoulder for a sunburn the day we first met, cleaning out the gash on my knee when I ran into him in the lava fields of Makena, holding back my hair as I barfed all over him at the beach party. I suddenly feel akin to Humpty Dumpty. *How is it that this boy keeps finding a way to put me back together again?*

I take a quick scan of my physical state — my lungs burn, blood oozes from the cut on my shoulder and my head pounds like a herd of bison.

I feel absolutely fantastic. I feel alive!

"What are you talking about? That was epic shit! I was surfing! Did you see me? I was surfing!" All I can do is beam my widest smile at him. It must be contagious, because eventually a grin overtakes his face as well.

"You were a freaking rock star out there — practically pro. Honest! You were carving that mother up! I am so stoked for you." He nudges me. "Must have been your master coach."

"I like to think of it as natural talent." I gingerly lay my head back down on the ice pack and close my eyes to the hazy blue sky. Kai shifts from his squatting position and lies down next to me on the blanket. We stretch out like that in silence, letting the sun evaporate the patches of saltwater from our skin. My shoulder stings and my head aches, but overwhelmingly what I feel is an invisible pull between Kai and me, like there's an imaginary elastic band strung around both of us, the tension pulling us closer together.

The warmth of his shoulder radiates to mine as we lie side by side. He's so close that I hear his breathing, deep and even. I lift my right arm from where it rests on my stomach and stretch it down by my side instead. Then I slide it out slightly, so it points diagonally from my body. I relax my legs and let them turn open naturally, causing my toes to inch that much closer to him.

Magically, as if he's feeling the same pull as me, he shifts his arm almost undetectably as well, his pinky now brushing mine. I take this as an invitation to lift my hand, placing it fully on top of his. We interlace our fingers and let our toes just graze each other at the end of the blanket.

The surf continues to sing its rhythmic background music while the fresh morning air fills our lungs. And in this moment, I am at peace with the world.

Chapter Twenty

"Oh my God, I'm ravenous! Who knew surfing made a person so hungry!"

After my epic battle with the waves, we agreed that my surfing adventures had probably reached their quota for the day. Kai happened to have some painkillers in the truck, so my headache has subsided somewhat. He told me he had the perfect place to take me for a late brunch and prefaced our arrival by warning me that the diner was a little sketchy-looking at first but promised that the food would more than make up for it.

We pull up beside a run-down looking restaurant with a sagging roof and open-air seating area. People were sitting shoulder to shoulder at aluminum tables in an outdoor courtyard, and a long line zigzags all the way out of the door. Servers bustle through the maze of tables carrying overflowing trays piled with breakfast burritos, French toast and bacon and eggs with home fries. As many people as there are streaming through the establishment, I think there are double the number of birds. They swoop down from the eaves and peck under tables, hoping to score a few bits of lingering scraps and crumbs before they're cleaned up. At one point, I think I spy a random chicken pecking around the tables, stopping for a moment underneath the chair of a man eating what looks to be a plate of fried chicken. *How ironic.* Admittedly, this place does not look to be in the same classification as the five-star restaurants I've gotten used to eating at with my dad, but I decide to bite my tongue and trust Kai's judgment.

"I know you're thinking it looks like a dive. And I get it. I would think so too. But it's so good! You see this line? It's like this straight from five a.m. till three p.m. when they close. This place is packed non-stop."

"You mean it doesn't open for dinner?"

"I think it's just so busy all morning that they don't have to do dinner. I've been trying to talk Charlie into keeping it open for dinner service for years, but he says the surfers and the early blue-hairs are his favorite customers. He says it doesn't do him any good to be open to late-night partiers. Personally, I think he just likes his evenings off to sit on his *lanai* with a cold beer, enjoying the sunset. But who could blame him?"

Almost as if he senses that we're talking about him, a barrel-chested, middle-aged Hawaiian man with short, spiky black hair looks up from the register on the other side of the cramped restaurant. He stops punching in the current customer's order and puts his hand up, urging us to just hang on a second.

Before long, he threads his way through the snake-like line, untying his greasy white apron as he approaches.

"Kai Kamealoha. Aloha! So good to see you, buddy!" He reaches his thick arms around Kai's slender frame, almost picking him up off the ground.

"Uncle Charlie, hey!" Kai returns the intimate greeting with an extra squeeze of the older man's shoulder. "How's it going?"

"You know, busy as shit, hot as hell — but loving life. It's crazy today, bro. There's a convention at one of the hotels up the road and Sean Lugka — you know Sean, the guy who works security there — well, he sent everyone this way for brunch. Told them we had the best *Loco Moco* on the island. So, you know, we had to accept the challenge!"

"Well, Uncle, they're not going to be disappointed." Kai looks around at the crammed tables. "Looks like we picked the wrong time to come, though. We'll come back another — " Before he's even got the words out, Charlie begins steering us toward a table that's just been vacated.

"No nephew of mine is gonna leave my restaurant hungry. No way!" He starts clearing the dishes left by the previous customers. "And who's this lovely lady you've brought out for brunch today?"

"Uh, this is Jessica...er, Jess. She's a friend." I might be mistaken, but I think I see his brown cheeks flush with a hint of pink.

"Let me guess? A Hawaiian native?" Charlie laughs when he says it, letting me know he's teasing.

"The oh-so-tanned skin must have been what gave me away?" I think he appreciates my self-deprecating sense of humor, because his smile widens. "I actually just moved here from Canada, so I'm still trying to get a sense of the island. Kai's been nice enough to show me the hot spots." I'm eager for more of his approval. "And he says this is the hottest spot around!" I add.

"Well, if Kai is an expert at anything, it's food, let me tell you! That and surfing. But by the looks of it, with your wet hair and that terrible gash on your upper arm, I'm guessing he's already schooled you in the art?"

I instinctively touch the bandage on my arm, the stinging sensation suddenly coming back to me.

"Yep, it is definitely not the same as snowboarding at home, that's for sure. But I loved it anyway."

Kai jumps in to interrupt. "Stop being modest. You were ruthless out there! You're gonna own those waves in no time." When he says it, he reaches across the table and gives my hand a reassuring squeeze. Then, instead of pulling it away, he just leaves his hand resting on mine. The unexpected touch sends a warm rush all the way up my arm and seems to rest as a rosy blush on my cheeks.

"So, Uncle, can we get two orders of your famous banana-macadamia nut pancakes and two house-blend coffees?"

"You got it! Nice to meet you, Jess." He does one more swipe of the table with his kitchen rag then turns to wind his way back into the kitchen, stopping to smile or chat with almost every table on the way.

"He seems great. Charlie, I mean. He's your uncle then?" I ask.

"Yeah. Well, not my *uncle*, uncle—not by blood anyway. Everybody here in Maui calls everyone else 'Uncle' and 'Auntie'. It's a sign of respect, a sign that we're all in it together. But I've grown up with him as a part of my family for as long as I can remember. He's great. He lives in Kula, a few homes down from us. He even uses our spinach and tomatoes for a few of the dishes here. He's great about supporting locals. So, you know, we like to support him too."

"Yeah, that's great," I say. And I mean it. *How cool is it, as a farmer, to know exactly where your produce is going? And as a business owner, how amazing would it be to have a relationship with the people who provide you with food, or with the security man at the hotel down the street, with the park rangers who turn a blind eye when you fish in restricted areas?* It's like the Hawaiians who live here are all somehow related, and they all look out for each other.

I gaze out beyond the edge of the patio we're sitting on and take in the beauty surrounding me. There's a lush green park across the road from us, kids running amuck in the playground and a dog chasing a Frisbee on the grass. Just steps beyond that, the grass turns to soft beige sand dotted with beach umbrellas and blankets. A trio of small children wearing brimmed hats and sun shirts run back and forth from the lapping surf to their crumbling sandcastle, eager to keep its draining moat filled with water. A young couple, beautiful and vibrant in their tan skin and expensive sunglasses, bob farther out past the white caps, the woman's arms draped around the young man's shoulders in a private embrace. He holds her around the waist, and although I can't see beneath the water, I imagine her legs wrapped around his torso, water swirling between their pressed bodies. I catch him nuzzling her neck and she tosses her head back with laughter, then teasingly steals his sunglasses, placing them on her own head. She dips in to kiss him as the water ebbs and flows around them, and they are oblivious to the other beachgoers.

I feel as if I owe them a small gift of privacy, so I shift my gaze to a family huddled on beach chairs under a large banyan tree with a canopy that sprawls out above the grass. The sun is high in the sky at this point in the day, and I can tell they're greedy for whatever shade they can find. I realize how grateful I am that Charlie chose to sit us at a table on the far side of the patio, shielded from the sun by a large, overhanging plumeria tree.

A slight breeze blows in, carrying with it the delicate floral scent of the plumeria blossoms. It brings me back to my childhood, to the endless Saturday mornings of Dad and me wandering the botanical gardens. At the time, I thought of that warm and humid place as a magical, mystical world where my imagination could run rampant. I never dreamed that a world like that existed for real outside of our glass bubble of early Saturday mornings.

Yet here I am, sitting in the shade of a plumeria tree as I hear the gentle surf in the background and the calls of tropical birds fluttering in the air. I finger the delicate petals of one of the blossoms and it pulls off its branch, falling gently to the table.

Kai is the one to pick it up. He twirls the tropical flower between his fingers, lost in thought.

"Have you ever heard the myth about plumeria flowers?" he asks. Before allowing me to respond, he continues.

"Legend has it that when sailors were leaving Hawaii to go fight during WWII, they would set sail and pass Diamond Head. It's kind of like a military outlook on the island of Oahu. Anyway, as they passed the edge of the island, they would toss a plumeria into the waves. They would watch it for a while to see which direction it floated. If it drifted out to sea, that meant the sailor was never coming back home, that he was going to be killed at war. But if the plumeria floated back to shore, it meant he would return home to his family."

"Wow, that's so incredibly sad—to go off to war thinking your fate has already been decided for you?" I think about what it would have been like to leave this beautiful island for the first time, to fight in a war for a country I feel so detached from. Because here, in this paradise, it *does* feel like a world of its own. So rich in culture, food, and tradition... This place doesn't compare to any other places I've been. I think back to the vacations I've taken with Mom and Dad to different cities in the United States—Orlando, Seattle, Boston, New York. No matter where in the country they are, the hustle and bustle of being productive, 'getting things done', overrides everything else. Only Maui has this casual, island vibe. People here seem to enjoy each moment for what it is without striving for *more* all the time.

As much as I fought coming here, I realize now how much I'm falling in love with this island. I always figured that this was temporary, that once I graduated from high school, I'd race back to Canada—back to my *real* life, my *real* friends. But now, I don't know. I imagine myself as a plumeria drifting among the waves. Will I be washed back to shore or be destined to float aimlessly out to sea?

Charlie bustles toward our table, two plates of towering pancakes balanced on one arm and two mugs of steaming coffee in the other. Then he reaches over to grab a couple of different syrups from another table and puts those down as well.

"Well, folks, banana-macadamia nut pancakes. Made with a little extra love, of course." He winks at

Kai. "I recommend slathering them in the coconut syrup, but as a Canadian, you may be partial to maple?" He again gives me his easy smile.

"I always go with the chef's recommendation." I grin.

He turns to leave, and I look down at my overflowing plate. I don't even know where to begin. There are five massive, golden-crusted pancakes stacked on top of each other, with a mound of melting butter in the middle. Sprinkled all over the top are heaps of pale macadamia nuts that Kai soon reaches over and covers with a generous helping of rich coconut syrup.

"Dig in!" he says eagerly, and we both shovel bite after bite into our mouths.

Twenty minutes later, I've pushed my half-finished plate away and I slump back in my chair.

"Thought you were famished?" Kai jokes. He's polished his plate off completely, every last bite. *What's with teenage boys and food?*

"Honestly, I don't know how you did that. I only ate half of mine and I'm completely stuffed. I feel like I'm going to explode!"

"You have to admit that it's good though?"

"Good? Those were by far the best pancakes I've ever eaten — even better than my dad's Nutella-stuffed ones. And trust me, he doesn't fool around with those!"

"How about we walk it off a bit? There's a great beach walk that goes all along the water right over there." He points past the seaside park. "If we're lucky, we might see some dolphins jumping or some turtles out near the cove."

"Seriously, you can see turtles right from the beach?"

"Oh man, you haven't been here long enough if you haven't seen turtles. They're everywhere. Let's go!"

"Okay, but I'm warning you. You might need to roll me there!"

Chapter Twenty-One

After Kai pays the bill and we wave goodbye to Charlie, we find a break in the ever-flowing traffic on the main Kihei road and quickly scoot across. The beach is still jam-packed with tourists and locals alike, it being a Saturday.

"So, do you go to the beach often? Like, just to hang out, I mean? Or does it lose its appeal when you live here and you get to see *this*" — I wave my arms in a 360-degree spin — "all the time?"

"Are you kidding me? My family practically lives at the beach. Well, on the weekends at least. They're too busy working during the week to make it out all that often. But yeah, on Sundays we basically set up camp on the beach for the entire day. My dad brings out a hibachi and he grills chicken wings and hot dogs all day. Mom makes the best pasta salad. And *Tutu* always makes up a big jug of iced tea. My cousins are a little crazy and end up wrestling each other at some point. We hang until past sunset. It's the best. You'll have to come sometime."

"Yeah, that sounds really great." And it does. I've never had that sense of tradition before or an abundance of family like Kai does. I imagine what it's like to have uncles, aunts, cousins all talking over each other, building sandcastles, playing catch in the waves. I think of the sprawling estate home I share with Dad, how we haven't even stepped into some of the rooms. I think of Mom and Robert and the beginning of their new little family, about how I don't quite belong. I'm suddenly feeling very homesick, but for *which* home I'm not sure.

"Okay, over there! Quick, look!" Kai exclaims, pointing out to a rocky bay not far from where we stand.

"Huh? What am I looking at?" I respond. We've stopped our walk along the path. Kai urges me to follow him across a small patch of grass and down a rocky embankment. As I clamber through the rocks, I need to use my hands for support. The black rocks are slick with water. The tide must have recently gone out, as it's left dozens of small tide pools among the boulders. Tiny fish dart in and around the rocks, and I see a squishy sea cucumber nudged in beside one. I stop to hunch over it to get a better look.

"Hey, Kai, take a look at this!" But he doesn't stop to look at what I've found. Instead, he grabs my hand and pulls me past the small tide pool.

"Trust me. What I see is way better!"

So, I follow him beyond even more small pools of water, watching that we don't accidentally step on one of the many sea urchins poking out from the rocks. Finally, on the edge of one of the largest tide pools, he stops and points into the water. The waves rhythmically thrust into the pool, then greedily sweep a rush of water back out as the tide pulls into the sea.

At first, I'm not sure what I'm supposed to be looking for. The tide pool appears to be full of the same dark, round rocks we've just finished maneuvering around. But then I see it. A small round head poking up to the surface of the water for a moment, the splash of a flipper, the sheen of a smooth shell in the afternoon sun.

"OMG, is that a turtle? A real sea turtle?"

"Not *a* turtle, an entire family of turtles! See?" And like an optical illusion, the half-dozen boulders I'm staring at all turn into turtles, some the size of large coffee tables, nibbling on the seaweed and algae around the rocks.

"Wow, look at them..." I breathe, unable to take my eyes off the magical creatures for even a moment. Every time a wave crashes and tumbles into them, I fear they'll be pulled back into the sea. But then I blink again, and there they are, calmly paddling along the rocks.

"Cool, huh? We're technically supposed to keep our distance because they're an endangered species. But I love just sitting out here watching them. They don't even care that we're here. They're just doing their thing, riding the waves."

We stay for a few moments more before we start making our way back to the truck. I'm lazy and content from my day with Kai. I feel like our day was so full, so perfect. It doesn't seem like our surfing adventure was just this morning. It feels like ages ago. But when I lift my hand up to the back of my head, a large goose egg is there, raised and swollen. *Yep, that epic fall was definitely this morning.*

We sit in an easy silence driving along South Kihei road, then up Kalani Drive. I've had such a great day that I'm hesitant to let it go just yet. I lean my head against the window, noticing that the sun is just starting to leave its post for the day. Wide strokes of yellow stretch across the horizon, fading to orange, red then the most magnificent color of coral. I breathe a satisfied sigh as I realize our perfect day is ending. Then it hits me.

Shit. The party. Tonight is the night of the party.

I glance at the digital clock on the dash of the truck. 5:58 p.m. Almost six o'clock. Okay, one hour until the party. How am I going to do this? *Why* am I going to do this?

Shame and regret fill me as I look over at Kai. He's absentmindedly whistling an island tune as he slowly creeps up the steep incline home. I've spent the entire day with him, laughing, talking, flirting. I've heard about his family, his passions. I've shared with him all my anxieties about swim club, about my mom. And yet, I didn't even bother to mention that I'm having a massive house party tonight? I haven't even invited him!

I tell myself that it's because I don't want him to feel pressured to come, that I know he has schoolwork to do. I know Sundays he gets up early to surf, and I don't want to keep him out late partying. But I know none of these reasons are why I don't invite him. In reality, I've kept the party out of my mind all day because I don't want him there — because to have him there means my two worlds collide and I'm not sure how to navigate that. The kick-off party last week was a disaster, and I still remember the looks on Callie's and Em's faces when I brought Kai. I remember Kai saying that he's not *Maui Gardens quality*. I'm terrified to have a repeat of that. So, I sit there, beside this gorgeous one-of-a-kind boy, who beyond all odds, seems to *actually* like me, and I stay silent. I crimp my lips together, an attempt at preventing an impulsive invite, while my insides swirl worse than a riptide.

"So, that was an awesome day today." Kai shifts the truck into park, then runs his hands through his hair like he always does when he's nervous. As if he doesn't know what to do with them next, he rubs them across his thighs, then rests them on the steering wheel again.

"Yeah, thanks so much for taking me. I had such a great time." I feel awkward. *So awkward* — like the air in the truck is dead still, and every word we say causes the molecules to shift suddenly.

"So, do you feel like you know the island a little better?" He gazes at me inquisitively. As he turns his head, a small piece of his hair falls down over one of his eyes, despite his constant attempts at pushing it back.

Before I realize what I'm doing, I reach to push it back myself. I can't even help it. I just want to be able to see both of his eyes. I'm caught off-guard by my own spontaneity. I think he's taken aback too, which is crazy. I mean, we've been touching each other all day — him helping me on and off my board, me helping him hoist the equipment. Earlier in the day, when the sun was at its peak, we even stood in the shade, slathering sunscreen on each other — and I didn't feel this crazy, stupid, clumsy pull then. None of those acts were deliberate, thoughtful moments. They were just part of the day's activities. But now there are no distractions. Every slight movement is magnified, its significance impossible to ignore.

He shifts sideways in his seat and I catch him swallowing. My heart gallops in my chest, a stallion racing to the finish line. Now I'm the one not knowing what to do with my hand. It lingers by the side of his head, and I'm not sure whether to pull it back or rest it gently on his shoulder. Before I've decided exactly what to do, Kai reaches up and clasps it with his own. As he does it, he tugs gently so that I have no choice but to let my body fall forward as well. I know what's coming and my insides bubble uncontrollably with anticipation. I've stared at those soft lips all day. I've imagined my fingers running through his dark hair. I've wanted to grasp those arms that held me so strongly in the water.

I notice his breath, warm and sweet. I feel it, soft puffs landing on my upper lip. And from this close I see the slight stubble from where he'd shaved this morning. He flickers his focus from my eyes to my mouth, letting me know what he wants, what he's asking for. But he's too much of a gentleman to close the slight gap that remains between us. He wants it to be my choice, my move.

So, I tilt my chin up and shift even closer. When our lips connect, it's soft and sweet and delicious. He's gentler, more delicate, than I ever would have imagined, letting me take my time and asking for permission with each minute movement. I think back to Marcus and the urgency, the passion we had. We clawed at each other like we couldn't get enough, like we were struggling for air, stealing each breath from each other as we constantly wanted more and more. But now, with Kai, it's like we're giving each other new breath, new energy. The touch of his lips surges my body with endless electricity, making every synapse fire all at once.

I reach my hands behind his head and pull him closer. I stroke the soft spot behind his ears with my thumbs, and he releases a gentle sigh from his lips. He cups my face, like he wants to take in all of me. I open my mouth slightly and let my tongue gently graze his. The connection sends goosebumps across my body, despite the late afternoon heat. We stay like this, exploring, tasting each other, until the colors in the sky smudge together and the sun has disappeared.

Finally, I pull away, feeling the weight of my upcoming party ruin the moment.

"So, that was a pretty great end to a pretty great day." I feel silly, clumsy.

Kai sits back into the driver's seat, an exhausted, contented smile creeping across his face. I slump back in my seat too, trying to talk myself into ending the evening with Kai. I suddenly notice the plumeria bloom that he'd grabbed at the restaurant, lying on the truck's console between us. I didn't realize he had brought it with us on our walk back to the truck. Its white petals glow in the silver dusk and I almost smell its intoxicating scent. Kai looks over at the plumeria too. He picks it up and twirls the stem between his thumb and forefinger.

He wants me to invite him in. I know it. I can feel it. And every part of me wants it too. I remember the fantasy I had earlier in the week where he and I were sprawled out on my white duvet. But I can't do it. I can't invite him in. And what's even worse is, I can't tell him why.

He opens his mouth to speak, and I think I've misjudged his demure, gentlemanly persona. He's going to ask to come in, and I know I won't be able to resist the temptation.

"Um, there's another story about the plumeria blossom, you know," he whispers, almost too quiet for me to hear. I'm not sure where he's going with this, so I stay silent, waiting.

He presses the sweet yellow center of the flower up to his nose then reaches toward me and gently tucks the stem of the flower behind my left ear.

"Do you know what it means to wear the plumeria behind your left ear?" he asks softly, gazing intently into my eyes.

"No. I see tourists wearing them like that all the time, and basically every tourism ad of Maui has a Hula girl wearing one. I figured it was just decoration?"

He looks down for a moment, suddenly unsure of himself.

"If a girl wears a plumeria flower over her left ear, she's pronouncing to everyone that she's in a relationship — that's she's taken." He looks up from where he was staring down at his lap.

As the significance of this sinks in, an eager smile explodes on my face, and I touch the soft petals of the plumeria with my left hand.

"I guess I should keep this one on all the time then?" I say it like a question, like I'm probing deep waters with a shaky underwater camera.

"Only if you want," he answers back with a tentative voice. I reach over to give him one long, lasting kiss so he can be assured that his gesture has been understood.

"Consider me taken," I beam. "I'll call you tomorrow, okay?"

"You're sure you'll be all right with your dad away? I can keep you company if you want? I mean, your house is so big. Sprawling mansions like that can be kind of creepy alone."

As much as I want to say, "*Yes, yes, yes, please come in and keep me company!*" I swallow and tell him I'll be just fine.

"Looking forward to a quiet Saturday night on my own," I lie.

And I hate that I do it knowingly.

Chapter Twenty-Two

It's a little after ten and the party is thumping. Ear-splitting house music reverberates down the halls and echoes through the towering, vaulted ceilings. At this point I'm surprised one of my dad's expensive new art pieces hasn't crashed to the floor from all the vibrations. Beer cans, red Solo cups and cheese puffs litter the hardwood floors. My bare feet make a *thwap-thwap* sound as I walk, forcing me to brush sticky crumbs and spilled booze from my soles every few steps.

Eighty or ninety drunk teens have shown up so far for the party, although more seem to keep trickling in without my knowledge. Someone has braced the heavy front door open with a large ceramic pot from the patio, an open invite for anyone passing. Kids spill out of every door of the house, like a cushion overfilled with stuffing.

A few couples laze on the back grass, smoking dope. Others swim recklessly in their underwear, faint shrieks exploding from the pool every time a new kid unwittingly stumbles in. The living room has turned into some type of make-out orgy room. Pairs of kids couple up on the couches and large recliners, their arms and legs tangled as they clumsily grope each other. I grimace when I think of the five bedrooms upstairs and hope to God they aren't occupied. I'm relieved that I thought ahead to lock both mine and my dad's bedroom doors on the off chance someone would go exploring. Of course, at that point in time, I was still hoping only a handful of kids would show up. *How wrong I was.* I guess the kids at Maui Gardens like to party — whether on a beach or in a random stranger's home, they don't really care.

Callie suddenly appears before me, descending the curved, teak stairway with Connor trailing behind. Her hair is a tangled mess on her head, and her lips are swollen and red. Mascara has smudged across her eyes so she resembles a racoon, and I notice her silk camisole has been put on inside out, the tag flapping from the side seam. Faint outlines of her nipples press into the delicate fabric, making me wonder whether she purposely went braless tonight or whether I'm going to find her bra hiding under a bed or strung across a random piece of furniture tomorrow.

She stops when she reaches the bottom of the stairs. Connor gives her a quick slap on the ass and a kiss on the cheek as he slides past her. He winks at me knowingly, and it makes my stomach turn. Something about him is just so…slimy. When he catches sight of a couple of guys from the rowing team playing beer pong in the kitchen, he raises his arms and races over to them.

"Make way for the beer pong champ of Maui Gardens! Get ready to see miracles happen!"

Callie looks over at him and blushes.

"God, he's great. Isn't he great?" She distractedly pats down her unruly locks.

"Yeah, he's great," I mumble, fighting an eye-roll.

"Thanks so much for hosting the party, Jess. Your place is, like, perfect for parties! It's just so gorgeous! Who decorated it? And what year was it built again? God, I bet this cost at least ten mill." She stares blankly into the open foyer. "What did you say your dad does again?"

"Uh, something with land developing, I think. He builds hotels and stuff."

"Well, he must be doing something right, because this place is seriously dope. Come on. Connor told me Luke has been looking for you all night long. You know he's totally hot for you, right? And he's actually available! He and Jenna Perkins broke up right before school started. He's a super-great catch, Jess. Tonight might be the perfect night to hook up and make it official!" She raises one eyebrow, like this is the best offer I could imagine coming my way. I barely have the energy to smile back at her.

I think about the plumeria blossom that was wedged behind my ear just a few hours ago. *What am I doing? God, am I seriously this pathetic? This desperate to fit in?*

I slide away when Callie gets sidetracked watching the beer pong championship. I sneak out of the side door, hoping there isn't a group of kids huddled there smoking more dope. The night air has cooled a bit from what it was this afternoon, and it's heavy with the scent of night lavender from the bushes that run along the side of the property. I walk barefoot along the spongy grass, tiny geckos darting this way and that with each of my steps. The strip of lawn that leads to the quaint *ohana* is steeped in darkness, affording me the anonymity I desire. The music pounds heavily behind me, along with the laughter and chatter of drunk kids doing dumb things. All I want to do is shut out the noise and wait for it to be done.

The door of the *ohana* is jammed at first and I worry my hideout is locked. But after a couple of tugs, I nudge it open and step inside. It's a small guesthouse but looks like it's never even been used. It still smells of lumber and fresh paint. I decide not to flick on the light, as it might just lure other kids out there. And right now, I crave being alone. There's a small living room set off to the right, with a coffee table, sofa and two wing-back chairs. At the back of the house lies a galley kitchen with a little breakfast nook that looks out over the sea. A half-wall acts as a sort of partition to the bedroom on the left, complete with a king-sized bed and an en suite. After my long day at the beach and the stress of the party, I want nothing more than to climb under the fluffy duvet and fall asleep. Part of me worries that the party will get out of hand, but another part of me hopes for it. Maybe the neighbors will finally complain about the noise and the cops will come to break things up?

My head throbs. I haven't taken any painkillers since this morning. It's possible I have a concussion — I never thought about that until now — and that could explain why I'm so tired. I remember hearing something once about not sleeping after a concussion, but I decide a little catnap won't hurt. I set my phone alarm to two a.m., thinking that the party will hopefully wind down by then and I'll be able to climb into my own bed for the night.

Sometime later, something causes my eyes to snap open. I must have fallen asleep immediately after my head hit the pillow, and I'm disorientated. I feel groggy and half-drunk, for a moment forgetting where I am. The moon has hidden behind the clouds, so the guest house is a murky black. The shadows in the room are all different degrees of gray melting into one another. The music still pulses outside, so I convince myself the extra bass is likely what's pulled me from sleep. I tap the screen of my phone to see the time, and sigh when I see it's barely past midnight. I turn over, inching farther into the covers, willing myself to ease back into a deep slumber.

For a few moments, I'm suspended in that limbo between sleep and consciousness, not sure what's real and what's in my mind. Kai smiles at me on the beach, the same beach where we saw the turtles today. But instead of standing among the rocks, we lie on the beach blanket spread on the sand. The waves lap up gently, just short of where our toes stretch. The sun is hot on my skin, and so bright that I need to close my eyes. We're splayed out on our backs, like we were this morning. Our fingers find each other and intertwine. My heartbeat quickens as Kai's body inches closer to mine. He turns his head, his breath soft and moist against my cheek. He braces himself on one elbow then dips his face down so that his lips graze where his breath has just been. I sigh with pleasure. He continues nibbling on my neck, on my ear, until the heat in me sizzles and pops like cooking bacon. I can't take the teasing anymore, so I turn my face toward him, and my lips find his.

The kiss is long and deep, full of more urgency and need than before. There's no hesitation in his movements, only confidence and strength. He shifts so that his body is now on top of mine, the weight of it pinning me down. I wrap my arms around his back, and he takes this as an invitation to press my thighs apart with his legs. I feel him hard against me, but it's all happening too fast. I try to maneuver myself so I can squeeze my legs back together or slide back onto my side, but his body is too strong and forceful. I move my hands from his back to his neck to nudge him away, ask him to slow down, but I don't feel his silky hair, or his smooth and strong shoulders. The hair is coarse and curly, and the top of his back is covered in a smattering of small patches of acne.

I snap my eyes open. I am not dreaming, and this is not Kai in bed with me. I press against the shoulders of my assailant, eager to get him off me this instant. He's perplexed, hesitant, but he automatically stops when he sees me suddenly flailing beneath him. He sits back on his heels as I sit up, cowering against the carved wooden headboard.

"What the fuck, Jess? I thought we were having a good time."

I reach across the bedside table to flick on the lamp. Luke is the one perched in the middle of the bed, an astonished look on his face. The button on his chinos shorts is undone and his T-shirt has ridden up so his pale waist peeks out from underneath. His curly hair is tousled and messy, his cheeks flushed red with anger, embarrassment or desire—which one, I'm not sure.

"Why did you come in here? *How* did you get in here?" I stammer.

"What are you talking about? Callie said she saw you slip out the side door to the guesthouse. She said you were waiting here for me, that you were wanting this…"

Now I'm the one embarrassed—embarrassed, angry, horrified, disgusted. No, I did not want any of this, and I'm angry at Callie for putting me in this position. Luke must see the disgust in my eyes, because he suddenly looks hurt, deflated.

"I'm sorry, Jess. I guess I just got mixed signals. I didn't know you didn't want to... Forget it. I'll just go. It's about time I head home anyway." He gets up to stand, trying to pat down his unruly hair. It takes him a minute to find both of his sandals as he had accidentally kicked one of them under the bed in the dark. We're both silent and awkward, not knowing whether to apologize to each other or let our words stay unsaid. I still feel his lips nibbling on the hollow of my neck and wonder if there'll be a mark in the morning.

Luke fumbles for the door handle. As he pulls it open, I finally speak.

"Luke, I'm sorry if you thought we were...you know, if you thought I wanted to... I'm actually seeing someone else." This seems to catch him by surprise. He raises his eyebrows at my words but doesn't bother asking who. Maybe he thinks I'm making it up so he won't feel so bad. And maybe it works.

"Can I ask you a favor, Luke?"

"Yeah, what?" he answers, hesitation in his voice.

"Can you tell everyone the party is over? That it's time to leave?"

"Yeah, whatever. See ya."

I'm not sure whether I can trust him to follow through with my request. But a few moments later the music is turned off, and I hear cars pull out of the driveway. It didn't sound like there were many kids still left at the party anyway. Through the small window, I see a handful of stragglers slowly traipse the length of the back lawn to the front of the house. I wait for half an hour anyway, just to be sure, before I let myself out of the *ohana*.

The lights inside the pool are still on, casting an eerie, fluorescent glow from beneath the water to the area directly surrounding it. The house lights beam through the windows as well, and even from here I can see the mess of the interior.

I make my way through the yard, sidestepping broken beer bottles and cigarette butts. I peer into the pool and am repulsed to see bits of vomit floating on the top, a scum of filth covering the surface. I reach down and, with my pinky finger, fish out a white string bikini top. I flick it disgustedly onto the pool deck. A random boot sits at the bottom of the pool too, and for a moment I pause, wondering why anyone would have worn a pair of boots to the party. Then I realize it's one of the hiking boots I wore last week and had left outside to air out in the sun. *Oh, to reverse time and go back to that Makena hike, where I first saw Kai.*

Kai... The thought of him makes my heart ache. I could have spent the night snuggled up in his arms instead of throwing this stupid party. He would be so hurt to find out I didn't invite him. I make a promise to myself not to ever let him know, and not to make a mistake like this again.

Cleaning the house seems too monstrous a task for me to take on right now. Exhaustion creeps through me like worms wriggling under my skin. My dad said he'd be back sometime tomorrow afternoon, so I still have twelve hours to worry about this mess. A few hours of sleep will help to motivate me. Yeah, this task is just too daunting for me to take on at this ungodly hour.

I head up the wide staircase, my legs heavy with fatigue. I strip off my sundress before I even make it to my bedroom, tossing it on the hallway floor beside a used beach towel and a random black T-shirt. I fall face down on my pillow, with nothing on but a pair of pink cotton panties, my last thought being the way the whirling ceiling fan sweeps a soft breeze across my goose-pimpled skin.

Chapter Twenty-Three

Scrubbing dried soda off a kitchen ceiling is a lot more difficult than one might think. I find this out the hard way as I perch on the kitchen island and have to reach up on my tippy toes to wipe the sticky mess. I've never understood the appeal of shaking a can of soda before letting it spray all over the room, but I'm pretty sure that's what caused this mess to form. Maybe kids try to emulate the uncorking of champagne bottles they see in movies, and this is the best they can do, given their inaccessibility to actual alcohol.

Although, no one can complain about a lack of alcohol last night. The cardboard boxes from six cases of beer lie flattened and stacked at the far side of the room. Three empty bottles of cheap wine were out on the patio, and various bottles of hard alcohol still litter the kitchen counter.

I heap a second load of laundry into the washing machine when I hear the chimes from the front doorbell ring. Thinking it's probably someone from the party looking for a piece of clothing they accidentally left, I swing the door open without checking.

"Hey, Jess, how's it going?"

My heart skips a beat at the unexpected sight of him. He must have been out on the water this morning, because his hair is damp, and the usually caramel-colored skin on the bridge of his nose has taken a pinkish hue.

"Hey, Kai. How are you? I mean, what's up? Uh, what are you doing here?"

"I noticed that you left your sunglasses in my truck yesterday after the beach, so I thought I'd bring them by. I was just out fishing in Makena, so, you know, it wasn't out of the way or anything."

His gaze travels from my face to the mess in the house behind me. I pull the door closed a few inches, as if I'm trying to conceal the evidence of a crime.

"What happened to your place? It's a disaster in there!" He looks at me again and I see him putting two and two together — me in my sweats and tank top, my hair piled in a loose knot on top of my head, mascara smudged around my eyes, the four garbage bags piled to the one side of the front door and the three, blue recycle bags filled with empty beer bottles and cans on the other, the mound of cigarette butts and roaches that I swept up at the foot of the stairs.

"Did you have a big shaker last night or something?" The hurt in his eyes radiates from him.

"Well, it wasn't a big shaker. I just had a few friends from school over. Then, well, a few more people came, and it sort of got out of hand." I look down, pretending to examine the chipping nail polish on one of my toes. I use one foot to rub the other, busying myself with the task.

"I thought you were just going to hang by yourself last night? You didn't say anything about a party."

"Well, it's not like I planned it. It just happened." My defensiveness gives me away—because we both know it *was* planned, and what was planned with the utmost certainty, was the fact that Kai had *not* been invited.

"What happened to your neck?" As he says it, he reaches over to touch the soft skin above my collarbone, thinking perhaps I've got a bruise or a bug bite there. His fingertips brush a loose tendril of my hair away from my skin, then he pulls away and takes a step back when he realizes what it is he's noticed.

The hickey. I forgot all about the hickey Luke had made last night during my semi-conscious make-out session with him in the *ohana*—the lucid dream where I imagined Kai's fingers trailing the curve of my back, Kai's lips grazing my neck.

"No, it's not what you think. This guy just… I didn't want him to…"

"What? Did someone hurt you? Did someone force themselves on you? Seriously, let me know who it was and I'm going to beat the shit out of them."

"No, no, it wasn't like that." I insist, then I'm stuck on what to say. How do I say that I thought it was him? That I wished it was him? And that, even though I knew the body on top of me was a foreign imposter, for a few moments I let it happen because I *pretended* it was him.

Absentmindedly, my hand goes up to my neck and hovers there.

I meet his steely gaze with pleading eyes. "Honestly, it's not what you think. I promise." My eyes well up and I blink to erase the tears threatening to spill down my cheeks.

How did I mess this up so badly? Our day yesterday was perfect, and now it feels like a daydream I'd simply gotten lost in.

The silence between us stretches long, like a tightrope threatening to snap. Right when I think he's about to turn around and walk away from me — like Marcus, like my mom, like Maggie — he picks up the four garbage bags, struts back down the front walkway, and throws them into the bed of his truck.

"You're going to want to get rid of the garbage before your dad gets home. That's the absolute tell-tale sign of a massive house party."

His tone is flat, and he has turned away from me when he speaks. But he pauses as he reaches his truck, as if he's making a monumental decision. He runs his hand through his hair, the gesture signaling his immense anxiety, and wordlessly strides back up the walk to the house. He gently pushes past me into the front foyer and starts sweeping cheese puffs off the hardwood floor. I release the elastic from my twisted-up hair, allowing the locks to fall gently over my shoulders, covering the dark purple stain on my neck.

Three hours later, the house gleams, the garbage bags are piled high in the back of the truck, the beds are all made with fresh sheets and Kai and I are enjoying a soda on the pool deck.

"Kai, thanks so much for helping me clean up the mess. Honestly, I don't think I would have had the time to do it myself." My dad just texted a few minutes ago, letting me know his plane had just landed.

"Yeah, not a problem. I know how these things can get out of hand sometimes."

"Yeah," is all I manage. I can't tell if Kai is still pissed at me or whether he truly does get it.

"Okay, well, if your dad is on his way home, I guess I should get going. He wouldn't be all that happy about a guy being here when he arrives, I'm guessing?"

"Yeah, I guess not." I walk with Kai over to the side gate and pause awkwardly, but not the delicious kind of awkward pause before our kiss in the truck yesterday, where the anticipation threatened to overtake me, every ounce of me buzzing with excitement.

No, this awkward pause feels more like watching a ball balance precariously on a ridge, and I'm not sure which way it's going to roll. I'm afraid if I breathe too deeply or move too quickly, the ball will roll away from me and I won't be able to get it back.

"So, I know your friends at Maui Gardens are super-cool and you like hanging out with them, but if you're ever wanting to try something different, do something a little more low-key, you can always come out with me and my friends. You know, see the island from the eyes of someone born and raised here."

This is the golden ticket I've been waiting for, like he's holding a door open for me and asking me to walk through. I don't even think about it when I stretch up on my tippy toes to plant a soft kiss on his mouth. He tastes like salt from sweat and from the ocean, and the skin on his neck radiates heat from soaking up the afternoon sun. It only takes a moment, and he's kissing me back, gently and sweetly. And when his hands grip my waist and pull me closer to him, I know we are good, we are great. Everything is okay.

* * * *

Dad arrives back about twenty minutes after Kai leaves, exhaustion filling the creases on his face and pulling at the saggy skin at his jawline.

"How was your trip, Dad? Everything okay?" I help him with his overnight bag and grab him a cool glass of water.

"Yeah, I'm just tired is all. This job is a lot more demanding than I originally thought. They're making me work for my dinner, that's for sure!" He laughs halfheartedly.

"Well, what's so stressful? Weren't you just there to pitch a new deal you're after?"

"It's not just that. It's how they expect me to go about it. When you're dealing with big trades and acquisitions, these large corporations sometimes forget that they're dealing with real people. It's like they're sharks, and they figure every little fish in the sea is put out there for them to devour. I appreciate my job and what it's given me — given *us* — but sometimes I just get tired of being the bearer of bad news. Sometimes I've got to do things I'm not all that comfortable with, for the greater good of the company.

"You know, maybe your dad is just getting soft in old age, hey? Another ten years like this, and I'm looking at retirement. Wouldn't that be nice? To retire in some place like this?"

I smile at Dad, although I'm concerned about him. It's true that since we've been here, he hasn't stopped working. He hasn't had the chance to enjoy walks on the beach or a swim in our pool. Everything has been work, work, work. I look at how the buttons on his dress shirt pull apart at the waist, how his belt is let out to the last hole.

"Dad, maybe you need to slow down a bit, take some time to enjoy the fresh sea air. It wouldn't hurt you to get a little exercise either, right?"

"Yeah, yeah, I know. And I'll try a little harder. But for right now, I'm starving, and I'm excited to show you the best restaurant on the island. Come on. Put on your nicest sundress. Our reservation is in less than an hour!"

We drive with the top of the convertible down, the wind whipping around my face. Palm trees sway in the early evening air, and the sea stretches out to the west like an unraveled bolt of shiny satin. The indigo blue is dotted with brightly colored sailboats and a few paddle boarders gliding smoothly across the surface. Families pack up their belongings as another day at the beach comes to an end. There's a line snaking outside a popular ice cream joint, and I make a mental note to ask Dad to stop on our way home.

We zip down the highway, then slow as the road winds through a funky little surfer town, up on the North Shore. A haven for beach bums and second-generation hippies, the streets are filled with shirtless guys and bikini-clad beauties, all eager to enjoy a cold glass of beer on a restaurant patio as the sun sets and Maui's tempered night life begins. A few miles past town, the road winds around another bend and a rustic wooden sign emerges, letting us know we've arrived at 'Maui's best restaurant, three years in a row'.

At first, it doesn't look like much, and I wonder why Dad's chosen this place, especially when the five-star hotels down the road from our house are brimming with world-class restaurants. We pull into a dirt-packed parking lot, and a sharply dressed boy around my age walks up to our vehicle. He wears a red, flower-covered Hawaiian shirt and tan khaki pants, and he holds the door open for me as I step out of the vehicle.

"*Aloha*, and welcome!" He reaches over to place a strand of beautifully scented pale purple flowers over my head and bows slightly to my dad. He walks us over to a wooden boardwalk, extending his arm down the length of it to show us where to go. My dad hands over the keys to the convertible so it can be valeted, and gestures for me to go first.

The wooden boardwalk curves around the small parking lot, then over a stretch of powder-white sand that surrounds a perfect little cove. The open-air restaurant overlooks this private beach, with quaint tables dotted all along the sand for patrons wanting a special beach dinner.

As we sit at our table overlooking the ocean, the sun dips below a smattering of clouds to make its final descent beyond the horizon. The pinks and oranges swirl together in the sky, causing every surface to sparkle with a glint of rose gold. The waiter brings over two fancy-looking cocktails, complete with sliced fruit and the stereotypical umbrellas. The alcohol from last night still churns in my belly and I'm happy, for once, that my dad has ordered me the non-alcoholic variety.

We spend a couple of quiet moments browsing the menu, trying to decide which tantalizing options to choose. Then I turn to the last page of my menu and smile at what I see.

All the fresh produce on our menu is proudly grown from local Maui farms and served at its absolute peak in freshness. We believe in supporting local farmers and hope you enjoy the bounty that our island offers. Please do your best to shop local, too!

The menu then goes on to list the various family farms where it gets its meat and produce, and the actual names of the fishermen who are responsible for today's catch of the day. I quickly scan the list and sure enough, I see Kai's family's name near the bottom.

I don't know why, but an immense amount of pride surges through me. I'm about to share with Dad that one of the local farmers is a friend of mine, but he starts speaking at the same time.

"You know, it's too bad about these farmers. I'm sure they've spent their entire lives working the land, struggling to succeed in the market. But really, it's useless. They just can't compete with big corporations. And to be honest, they shouldn't have to. Let the big guns do the heavy lifting, is what I think. I mean, why would you need to struggle to keep a small farm running—work day and night, just to make ends meet—when the land you're on is worth a fortune, in and of itself? Most of these farmers don't even realize that they're sitting on a goldmine. If they'd just let go of this crazy ideal they have of island life in the good old days, they'd be better off. Let the Costco in Kahului do its thing and provide food for the entire island. People can buy their groceries much cheaper there anyway!"

With that, he closes his menu and has me do the same. He says he's going to order for the both of us and knows exactly what to get. I don't get a chance to talk about Kai or his family farm.

The food comes out looking as spectacular as was promised. My macadamia-crusted sea bass is bathed in a rich, buttery herb sauce and sits alongside baby potatoes tossed in fresh dill. I almost feel guilty taking my first bite, because images of Kai's family farm flash through my mind. I imagine his grandmother hoeing the garden by hand, plucking the baby potatoes from the rich soil and dusting them off with her apron. When

I smell the tang of the dill, it bubbles up images of woven baskets piled with fresh herbs, on their way to this, or any one of the fancy restaurants on the island.

Kai carries so much pride about his family and their way of life.

How can I make my dad see this?

Chapter Twenty-Four

At swim practice on Wednesday, all everyone is talking about is my party. Apparently, it's been hailed as one of the best parties Maui Gardens has seen in over a year.

"Jess, that night was super-dope. OMG, I felt like crap the next day. What about you? You slipped off with Luke and we didn't see you after that. So…are you guys a thing now? I knew you'd be a perfect match!"

Callie and I are side by side doing our requisite twenty warm-up laps. We take a break on the side, and I lift the corner of my swim cap so I'm able to hear her more clearly.

"Huh? Yeah. I mean no, we're not a thing. It just doesn't feel right, you know?"

"Seriously? Luke is, like, the best catch around. Really, Jess, I wouldn't mess this up if I were you. Did you know that his dad is a movie producer? He could introduce you to movie stars and everything! One year, his dad even took him as his guest to the Oscars." She whispers conspiratorially. "I even heard a rumor that

Chris Hemsworth stayed at their place once when they were prepping to shoot a movie. Chris Hemsworth! Are you kidding me?" Callie laughs and shakes her head. "If I wasn't already with Connor, I would totally be all over that boy!"

We finish our set of laps and climb out of the pool to do some stretching.

"I hate to keep droning on about this, but I really think you should go after Luke. Seriously. Connor didn't want me saying anything, but I guess Luke was like, telling everyone that you guys made out in the *ohana*. And not just made out, but like...*made out*. If you know what I mean? And you know, fooling around is one thing, but going all the way with a guy you're not even into? Well, that's not so cool, Jess. We don't really do that at Maui Gardens. It'll make people think you're a" — her voice drops to a whisper once again — "well, you don't need me to tell you."

She bores her eyes into me and raises her eyebrows, attempting to fish out the truth.

"Oh, gross! I did *not* sleep with Luke! I barely know the guy!" Rage and disbelief steam off me. "I pushed him off me that night! I mean, sure, we kissed a bit. But I didn't let it go further than that. Why would he tell everyone otherwise?"

"It's just that, Jess, you came to school with that massive hickey on Monday. So, obviously you guys did *something*. Then he started telling everyone... And, well...it's not like you've said anything otherwise."

"This is the first I've heard of all this! I didn't know he'd said anything!"

"Well, Luke said you've been giving him the cold shoulder all week, and I think he's a bit pissed about it. He's basically been telling everyone that you must hook up with random guys all the time — that maybe it was your *thing* back at home. And listen, maybe that *is* how you were back in Canada. But Maui Gardens is different. You don't want to be known as one of those girls who will just get with *anyone*. It doesn't look cool, trust me. You should really try to make things work with Luke. Then this whole thing will just go away."

What the hell? He's telling everyone we slept together? How am I just finding out about this now? And what can I do about it? Despite the cool pool water beading on my skin, a hot mass wells up inside me, as if a ball of molten lava is about to erupt.

"I… Did… Not… Sleep… With… Luke!" I spit out at her, one syllable at a time. My eyes blur with tears, and the raging fireball has made it down to my fists, which are balled at my sides.

"Hey, don't get mad at the messenger!" Callie chirps, setting her hands on her hips. "I just thought you'd want to know. And I'm just letting you know how *I* would handle the situation if I were you, that's all." She's so flippant, so blasé about the whole thing, that it sends me over the edge.

"Well, you aren't me, are you?" I scream at her, and with both hands I push her into the pool. She falls in with a splash and a tiny yelp, definitely not with the grace of her usual dives. I catch Coach Wilson look up in alarm, then stride over to us. I don't wait to explain. I don't want to hear how Callie is going to spin this little altercation. Instead, I grab my towel, rip my swim cap off and march over to the girls' change room. My swim practice has come to an end for the day. I'm reluctant to admit it, but this may be the end of swim practice for good.

I mount my bike and ride home with a vigor I've never felt. Cruising smoothly over the fresh concrete, I pedal hard and fast. The rolling hills slide under me, and I almost feel the same power and freedom as when I was riding the waves out on the ocean with Kai. I start my ascent up the hill to my home, and the burning in my thighs deepens. It's like, if I can concentrate on the ache in my legs and my chest, it takes a bit of the pain away from my heart. My lungs cry for more oxygen, but I don't slow one bit until I hit the crest of the hill. I dismount my bike, feeling an utter exhaustion creep into my body.

He told everyone we *slept* together? Why would he do that? He seemed so apologetic that night, hurt even. I guess guys like Luke Crawford don't get *hurt*, they get *even*. I'm trying to see a way out of this mess, a way to fit back into the puzzle of Maui Gardens. I'm suddenly horrified at my outburst in the pool because, really, that's only going to make things harder for me. I can almost hear Callie's squeal when she was thrown into the pool, and I only imagine how she's going to spin that one. *"Did you hear about Canada's crazy meltdown? She's seriously not stable. No wonder Luke decided not to go for her after all!"*

Yep. My senior year may turn out more pathetically lonely than I ever thought possible.

Walking my bike around the final bend to my house, I try to push the dismal thoughts out of my head. Dad promised he'd be home tonight to cook his famous barbecue chicken for dinner, and I realize suddenly how ravenous I am. I take a few deep breaths to try to slow my racing heart, and I wipe the sweat from my forehead with the back of my hand. I look up as I approach the curved driveway and am surprised to see

Kai's green truck parked there. For a minute, I wonder whether he's here to do yard work for his dad, being that it's Wednesday and everything. But there are no tools or ladders visible in the bed of the truck. Worry and anxiety crawl up my spine. *What does this day have in store for me now?*

I open the heavy oak door hesitantly, not quite sure what I'll be walking into. But laughing and faint conversation trickle in from the back patio door. When I round the corner into the spacious kitchen, my mouth waters with the smell of barbecued chicken. My dad and Kai are sitting outside on pool loungers with two sodas, a bowl of potato chips and a large, empty plate on the small table between them. My stomach rumbles in jealousy.

"Uh, hi, Dad…Kai. What are you guys up to?" I dart my focus back and forth between the two of them.

"Kai here just came by to finish trimming the hedge, as his dad didn't quite have time to get it all done when he was here earlier. He was working so hard that I asked him to sit and have a cold soda with me. Sorry, honey. We may have accidentally polished off the chicken. I wasn't sure when you'd be home from practice." He glances guiltily at the empty plate before continuing. "I didn't realize Kai was the one who showed you around the island last weekend, Jess! He was just telling me all about his family farm and his *tutu*'s delicious macaroni salad."

"Um, yeah. This is Kai. Kai, this is my dad." As if that isn't completely obvious to all parties involved.

I stand awkwardly beside them for a few moments. Neither of them jumps back into the conversation and I don't dare start up a new one. Finally, Kai takes a long gulp of his soda and wipes his hands on his shorts as he stands up.

"Well, thanks, Mr. Kennedy — you know, for the soda and the advice and everything. I appreciate it." He shakes my dad's hand, which to me seems entirely too formal, and he starts to walk back around the side of the house.

This day has been utterly exhausting. I'm grouchy and irritated that I've come home to no supper and my sort-of-boyfriend hanging out with my dad. It's like a double whammy. I just want to go inside, stuff my face with an entire bag of Cheetos and call it a day. But I also need to chat with Kai before he leaves.

"I'm just going to walk Kai out, okay, Dad?"

"Yeah sure, honey. I'll just be in my office. I've got a few things to do before going to bed."

I quickly catch up to Kai, resting my hand gently on his shoulder to slow him down.

"So, you were hanging out with my dad? Wasn't that weird?" I think back to Marcus, about how my dad never even knew he existed, let alone hung out with him. In fact, my dad hasn't met a single one of my boyfriends because, well, I've kept every single one a secret from him in order to avoid this exact awkwardness.

"Yeah, I really did come by as a favor to help my dad out with the yard. He's had a crazy busy week. But then your dad and I got to talking, and well, time just got away from us, I guess. Why? Is it weird for you?"

"Not weird, just very surprising. My dad has barely had time to have dinner with me since we've moved here. I'm just impressed he made time to sit and chat with you."

"He's actually super-smart, Jess, and he was helping me out. There's been talk about some big hotel chain wanting to come in and buy up all the small farms in our community in order to build a massive, luxury hotel. My *tutu* hasn't heard anything directly yet, but she's been a bit torn about what to do if she does get an offer. She'd love to keep it in the family, but it's been a lot of work for her, and the rest of us aren't positive we want to take it on. And well, it would be a lot of money for her, so selling it might be the best thing in the long run."

"But I thought she loved the farm! And it's been in your family for generations! How could she just let it go like that?"

"Jess, you don't get it because you live here, in this"—he stretches his arms out toward our estate home—"fairytale. But the rest of the world doesn't live like kings and queens, and the temptation of money is very convincing."

"But I thought the farm was doing so well?" I ask.

"Well, according to *our* standards it is, I guess. But according to the neighbors, the offer this company is making is close to a half a million dollars per farm. Half a mill? Do you know how much that would change *Tutu*'s life? She won't have to worry anymore. She can finally retire. And this would mean my parents won't have to work so hard too, trying to manage two full-time day jobs, then help with the farm in the evenings." A shadow passes over his face. "I'm not saying it's without hesitation. The farm *has* been in our family for generations, basically since my ancestors came to this island. But maybe it's just time to let go. I don't know." He looks out into the deep purple the ocean has turned since the sun set almost an hour ago.

"Oh, I forgot to ask you. We're doing one of our famous cookouts at the beach on Sunday, then we're heading back to *Tutu*'s for cake. She's turning seventy, although I'm probably not supposed to tell you that. But my parents wanted to know if you'd like to come hang out for the day. You in?"

"You mentioned us to them? I mean, me? You mentioned *me* to them?"

"Of course I did." He reaches out to grab my hand and interlaces his fingers with mine. "Why would I keep someone as great as you a secret? I'll come by around ten a.m., then? I know you like to sleep in…" He smirks at me. "Besides, someone from my family will get to the beach early enough to grab a good spot. They always do." We linger at the front of his truck, weaving our fingers in and out of each other's, putting off our goodbye.

This is why I love being with Kai, because when I'm with him, all the other crap that's going on in my life just magically melts away. It's as if the disaster at swim practice didn't occur. The issue of Luke and the *ohana* has disappeared and Callie's splash in the pool has been pushed to the back of my mind.

"Sure, that sounds really fun. See you Sunday." Kai leans over to kiss me sweetly on the lips, letting go of my hand and gently squeezing my shoulders as he does it. He pulls back for a moment, then leans in to plant one more kiss, as if he can't resist the urge.

"All right, see you Sunday!" I call out one more time. His truck pulls away and I start making my way up the front walkway.

Okay, I'm meeting his parents. And he's already mentioned me to them. *Wow.* A heavy pit of guilt settles in my stomach when I think about how I'd never even mentioned him to my dad. I had actually avoided it altogether. Was it because I was worried he wouldn't approve? That he'd be ashamed? Or—a tiny voice in the back of my mind whispers—is it because I was feeling ashamed of him?

I brush that thought away from my consciousness as if it were a pesky housefly. I walk a little faster into the house, deciding tonight might be the perfect time to call my mom again, to reconnect. I might even have some fresh news for her. Maybe, just maybe, I'll tell her all about my amazing new boyfriend.

Chapter Twenty-Five

Honestly, Sunday couldn't have come quickly enough. I'm so glad to be done with this God-awful week.

Thursday and Friday were two of the longest days of school I've ever experienced. I wasn't really sure what to expect when I arrived on Thursday morning, but it was evident by Em's cold shoulder in the hallway that Callie had already started spreading rumors about Wednesday's practice. There was probably some group text about it that I was being purposely left out of.

It wasn't until noon that I was completely convinced I was being iced out. I grabbed my bagged lunch and headed out to the picnic tables on the back lawn. I passed through the empty basketball court, like I had on that first day, but no one looked up at me or called my name as I approached. I literally came within a few feet of the group before concluding that they were going to pretend I wasn't even there. They kept joking around and chatting together, as if I had never existed.

Luke was seated between Sydney and Em, and when he thought no one was looking, he glanced up at me. His eyes were dark and cold, and I may have imagined it, but it looked like a smug grin started to creep across his face before I turned on my heel and walked in the other direction. I found a shady spot beneath a monkeypod tree, a flurry of geckos darting around my outstretched legs. I spent the remainder of the lunch hour trying not to overhear the laughing and jostling of the group of kids I had thought were my newfound friends.

The day didn't get much better after that. In the middle of last period, I got a call from the office to go and see Coach Wilson. I knew what was going to happen before I even arrived.

I entered her office, and she was sitting behind her desk, lines of exhaustion etched in her furrowed brow.

"Jessica Kennedy, what the hell happened yesterday?" She clasped her hands together on her desk. "Where in the world did you run off to, in the middle of practice? No matter what has transpired, you do *not* walk off in the middle of practice." She stared unblinking at me.

"I know, and I'm so sorry. I was just really upset. I needed some space."

"Yes, Callie told me all about it. She mentioned that you had a little crush on that boy Luke Crawford, and that he maybe didn't feel the same way? She said she couldn't help it that he seemed to have a thing for her, and that you were totally jealous about it. She told me that you called her a slut and pushed her into the pool before stomping away."

What? Callie said *what?*

"No, it wasn't like that. Luke was spreading rumors about *me*. I'm not the one who did anything wrong—"

"Jessica, things might be done differently in Canada, but here at Maui Gardens, when you are on a team like our swim team here, well, we've all got each other's backs—no matter what. We need to know that we can count on each other. There's nothing I hate more than petty rifts between my swimmers. From what I can see, Callie took you under her wing when you arrived. She introduced you to her friends, and she made you feel comfortable... To tell you the truth, she's the one who vouched for you when I was on the fence about putting you on the team. You know your swim times aren't stellar, Jessica, and it was Callie who thought you'd be a great addition.

"Well, now I'm rethinking things. I can't have teammates who are squabbling and spreading rumors. It's just not gonna work that way. And well, Callie is one of my star swimmers. So, I'm sorry to do this, but I'm afraid I have to ask you to remove yourself from the team. It's just not going to work out for us. But really, you only have yourself to blame."

For a moment I tried apologizing, tried getting her to see things from my perspective. But no matter what I started to say, she had a rebuttal ready and waiting, like an all-star defensive back. I eventually lost the motivation to say anything at all, and I left her office feeling deflated and alone. I didn't bother heading back to class and instead rode my bike to the beach down the hill from my place. For three hours, I just sat there listening to the rhythmic lapping of the waves.

With each wave that rolled in, I flip-flopped between wanting to get on the next plane back to Canada and wanting to stick it out in my new home. I just kept thinking about how much I had fallen in love with this island since coming here. Why should a bunch of stuck-up kids in a snotty charter school be allowed to chase me away?

* * * *

Now that I've had a chance to let things settle for a couple of days, I'm even more determined to stay. As I sit on my front step waiting for Kai to pick me up for his family cook-out, I let the warm sun caress my shoulders, easing some of my tension away. Sure, part of me aches to go back home. It's been nice talking to Mom a bit more in the last little while, and I've been realizing just how much I miss her. Surprisingly, Robert seems like a decent guy, and Mom really does seem committed to him. And I have to admit that Dad's forgiveness toward Mom has caught me a little by surprise as well. Maybe he was more at fault in their dissolving marriage than I really cared to see? Because if he can be on speaking terms with Mom at this point, I guess I should be able to get there too.

The one thing—the biggest thing—that keeps me wanting to stay, though, is Kai. I think about his soft eyes and his easy smile, and it puts me at ease. He makes me feel like I don't need to pretend to be someone I'm not. And God, do we ever have fun together. I laugh with him more than anyone else. He always has a way of making me feel better, which is why I've been absolutely looking forward to spending the whole day today hanging out with him and his family.

He picks me up at ten on the dot, but this time I let him come and ring the doorbell. Dad answers in his bathrobe and ushers Kai in. Kai has not only brought me one of those dreamy lattes, but he's brought my dad an entire bag of full bean espresso, to use on his machine here at home. That'll add some extra brownie points in Dad's books for sure. Other than whiskey, good coffee is about the only thing that makes him smile that wide. He immediately makes himself a cup and agrees with us that it's the best coffee he has ever tasted.

I let Dad know that we'll be up on a beach in Kihei, and afterward we'll be spending the evening at Kai's parents' home in Kula. It's about a forty-five-minute drive and I'm feeling a little guilty that Kai has to come all this way to get me then drive me back home again. Maybe this'll work toward convincing Dad that I'm in need of my own car while we're here?

Kai explains that the beach we're going to is only about ten minutes away and happens to be just down from the spot where we saw the turtles the other day. We park across the street from the café we'd had breakfast at, and as I smell sizzling bacon and buttermilk biscuits, I wish I'd eaten a bigger breakfast.

We walk around to the back of the truck, and I help Kai unload the beach gear. This is apparently a decent surf spot, so he's brought his board, but luckily decided not to pack an extra for me. He's also got a cooler and two beach chairs for us to set up. For a minute, I'm worried that the golden sun is going to roast me to a crisp, but then I see that Kai has remembered a beach umbrella as well. He definitely thinks of everything. When our arms are heavy with supplies, we make our way across the busy street and over to a space on the lawn where his family has set up for the day.

"*Aloha*, Kai! Come give your *tutu* a big old kiss and hug!" A wisp of a woman with short, feathery gray hair and tough, sunbaked skin shuffles over to us. Her face is etched with wrinkles, making the skin on her cheeks look like crumpled newspaper. She has permanent laugh lines around her mouth, which give the impression that she's always smiling. This, paired with the crow's feet radiating from her sparkling eyes and her stature at five-feet-nothing, all combine to give her an impish impression. She holds her arms out to me once she's given Kai a giant hug and pulls me in for a warm embrace as well.

"Oh, Jessica, how wonderful to meet you! We have just heard so much about you!" She holds me long and tight, and instead of feeling like an awkward exchange with a stranger, it gives me a comforting feeling of welcome. When she steps away from me, she takes my hand and leads me to where a large gathering of family members has congregated.

"Everyone, this is Kai's lovely friend Jessica. Let's make her feel most welcome here with us today!" At first, I feel a bit strange that Kai isn't the one doing the introductions. In fact, he's still several feet behind us, struggling to get the beach chairs set up on the grass. But with the warm smiles and *alohas* from the group surrounding me, it seems I've got nothing to feel nervous about. The one thing that is crystal clear with this family is that *Tutu* Kamealoha is the matriarch of the entire bunch. Her confidence, warmth and take-charge attitude have me feeling at ease in an instant. *I think I'm going to like Kai's family.*

Twenty minutes after we've arrived, Kai and I are in our swimsuits, bodysurfing with his three little cousins in the crystal-clear water. The waves are quite manageable, even for me, and again and again we let the roaring surf pick us up and throw us haphazardly to the shore. I can't seem to body surf quite as gracefully as the rest of the family and end up tumbling in a whirl of somersaults as the waves crash down on me, instead of *me* riding *them*. As I pop my head up from the surf, laughing at my clumsiness, I always have to make sure my bikini bottoms have actually managed to stay covering my bottom.

I finally convince Kai that I need a break from the water, and we plop down on a soft patch of sand, just away from the water's reach. My hair is a tangled mess on my head, saltwater stings my eyes and I feel the beginnings of a glorious burn forming on my shoulder blades, but I don't even care. I'm having the best time.

"You doing okay? You having a good time with my crazy family?"

"Are you kidding me? I'm having a blast!" I grab Kai's hand and interlace his fingers with mine. As if right on cue, his little cousin Alanna grabs my other hand, pulling me to the wet sand a few feet from where we're sitting.

"Come on, Auntie. We're building a castle and we need you to help with the moat!" I remember Kai calling Charlie *Uncle* in the café that day, so I know this is just a formality for showing respect to an elder. And I suppose in this case, *I'm* the elder. But I still can't help feeling pride at the term of endearment—a sense of connection to this family that I never thought would be possible so quickly. I spend a moment just watching this beautiful little girl scoop sand this way and that, with such abandon, until she cries out that I'm not helping and urges me to dig in. For a little while, I'm lost in this haven of sun, waves and sand, and the world feels like such a simple and beautiful place.

A while later, *Tutu* calls us all back to the grass for lunch. Her invitation is unnecessary, as the aroma of grilled meat has been wafting over to me for a half-hour. I don't realize how famished I am until I spy the mouth-watering spread laid across the picnic table. Mounds of macaroni salad, platters of barbecued chicken and pork, and fresh-baked sweet rolls call to me. I ask Kai about a few dishes I'm not familiar with, and he points to the *lomi* salmon, which is basically what I know of as a poke bowl, as well as a thick paste known as *poi*, a traditional Hawaiian dish made from taro root. He reaches down to a plate stacked high with quartered sandwiches and, without any warning, plops one into my mouth.

The meat is salty and tender, and I taste the tartness of a grilled pineapple mixed with a melty, gooey cheese. It is pure heaven in my mouth, and after I gulp it down, I ask Kai what kind of sandwich he'd just given me.

"Well, you've just had your first taste of one of *Tutu's* famous Spam sandwiches!" Kai replies before popping a second sandwich in his own mouth.

Wow, who knew Spam was so delicious? I'm surprised to find myself stealing a second sandwich to add to my overflowing plate before we find a quiet place in the shade, a little farther away from his family.

"So, you're sure you're doing okay today?" he asks again. I love that he's always thinking about how *I'm* doing, how *I'm* feeling. It gives me the confidence to enjoy myself without having to worry about whether I'm fitting in.

"Yeah, your family's great. They're amazing, actually! I just... I don't know... I guess I've never really had a family like this, so I've never done this before. I actually thought family get-togethers like this were only in the movies." And it's true. I have great childhood memories, but they basically involve me, Mom and Dad. In fact, pretty much every vacation photo of us features me with only Mom or me with only Dad. It was almost never all three of us, because someone always had to take the picture. Maybe that should have been a bit of foreshadowing for me — even in pictures, Mom and Dad couldn't enjoy a moment together.

But here — I look out over the chaos ensuing around me — the beauty is *in* the mayhem. Kai's uncle catches an overthrown Frisbee and topples to the ground. Three little boys under the age of ten pile on top of him for an impromptu 'uncle sandwich', with the family dog hopping up on top. *Tutu* chats in a circle of aunties and cousins relaxing in beach chairs, water bottles filled illicitly with wine coolers. Several of the little ones run back and forth between the waves and the grass, their mothers scolding them to finish eating lunch before they're off again. At every turn, someone is yelling, someone is laughing, someone is cursing and someone is hugging. And I'm wanting a piece of it all.

As the sun starts to set for the day, everyone begins to pack up to make the long drive back to Kula, where the majority of the family lives. I'm so eager to see where Kai has grown up that I have no problem spending over a half-hour in the car to get there.

We drive with the windows open, north through Kihei, allowing the salty evening air to erase the day's sun from our skin. At some point, about fifteen minutes into our drive, we pass the sugar factory we'd driven by the very first night we'd arrived. I remember Keanu, our driver, telling us about the history of the sugar cane industry, and I marvel at how that one crop helped to create Maui as it is today. We bypass downtown Kahului and instead take a shortcut down Hansen Road before joining up to the Haleakala Highway, which travels east through upcountry Maui. Immediately, the scenery changes and Maui is a desert on either side of us. Swaying palm trees are replaced by patches of prickly pear cactus poking up over the dry dirt. The highway twists and turns and the barbecue lunch I had on the beach threatens to make another appearance.

It doesn't take long for the scenery to morph once more. We make our way through foothills covered in pineapple fields, thousands of green tops sprouting from the earth like tufts of hair. Vegetable, herb and flower gardens also dot the countryside, alternating as patches of green, purple and yellow. A few cows graze in a pasture out to the left and a strip of towering jacaranda trees line the highway to the right, their fingerlike branches looking barren and sparse without the lavender-colored blooms they house during the spring. I stretch my neck so my face pokes out of the open window, and I notice the breeze is about ten degrees cooler than it was closer to the beach. When I mention it to Kai, he tells me we've entered a different micro-climate, that we're in more of a temperate zone right now, compared to the desert climate we were in just minutes before.

We continue our winding ascent up the wide expanse of Haeleakela, the road switch-backing this way and that, a never-ending climb to our final destination. We pass the town of Makawao, a real-life rodeo town, steeped in history and culture.

"This is where Maui's original cowboys lived," Kai insists, although I can't help feeling ignorant to the fact that Maui has ever had any cowboys. Surfers, Richie Rich types and wanna-be hippies...sure. Cowboys? Not so much.

"The people upcountry are a little more laid-back, a little rougher around the edges and a little more, well, Country—like, with a capital C," he goes on. "We love it up here. It's a totally different vibe than the rest of the island. Although somehow, Makawao has turned a bit into a yuppie town, with newfound attention from tourists—you know, people who fight to see and do anything off the beaten path." Automatically, Callie and Em come to mind, and I can almost envision them sitting at one of the outdoor cafes on the main street of Makawao, indulging in the fact that they discovered *the* new trendy place to be.

Kai continues. "So now, the town is full of high-end boutiques and galleries, instead of the quaint, small-town businesses it used to have. But I have to say, it still does have the absolute best bakery on the island. Right over there" —he points to a small corner store-bakery right on the main avenue— "are the only stick donuts you'll ever want to eat in your life. So gooey and fresh... But you need to get there early because they sell out every morning."

We make our way out of Makawao, the road climbing through steep, lush hills. Suddenly, a rush of rich lavender fills my nostrils, and I realize we're driving past one of Maui's famed lavender farms. Fields of the luscious blooms envelope the side of the mountain, covering it in a delicate purple blanket. The heavenly smell is intoxicating, and I can't help but stick my head out farther into the evening air.

Eventually, we turn off the main highway, making our way down an unmarked dirt road. Every so often an old-fashioned mailbox pokes out from the trees — now a mix of evergreen and deciduous — marking each farm tucked away behind the groves. We slow and turn into a long stretch of gravel driveway that leads up to a charming little farmhouse. A field of sweet onions sits alongside one end of the tidy white home, and strawberry patches abound on the other side. From where we pull up on the driveway, it looks like the rest of Kai's family has beaten us there, their vehicles parked haphazardly along the front lawn. His cousins are already kicking a soccer ball around, and several adults mill around the front porch.

I'm thankful I thought to bring a light sweater, and I wrap it around my shoulders as we head out to the back. The large patio teems with Kai's family, a flurry of bodies walking back and forth, voices toppling over each other. *Tutu* sits in the center of the bunch like a queen in her castle, enjoying the camaraderie around her. I don't blame her. The noise, the joking, the rough-housing... It's enough to make anyone feel right at home.

Kai's Aunt Linda passes around glasses of sweet tea, then Kai's mom walks in from the house with a giant sheet cake covered in vanilla frosting with buttercream roses. One of Kai's cousins comments on why there are only seven candles on the cake when *Tutu* is turning seventy years old. His older brother swats him upside the head murmuring, "Don't be a dummy. We can't have seventy candles on *Tutu*'s cake!"

The entire group begins an off-key rendition of *Happy Birthday*, while Tutu sits in the middle, pride radiating from her wrinkled face. It comes to me that I've never had this many people sing me Happy Birthday in my life. I had the one party in the fifth grade where Mom and Dad let me invite the entire class, so no one felt left out, but even then, half of the boys ran off to play street hockey, so I was left with just Maggie and a handful of girls hanging behind.

I look back at *Tutu*, her wrinkled hand stroking the hair of her youngest granddaughter, who snuggles contentedly in her lap. *I would be proud of my family too*, I think to myself. As the song comes to an end, she picks the little girl up around the waist so they can both lean over the cake. Together, they take a deep breath in and blow every last candle out, not even leaving one for a lucky wish. *I guess not everyone needs to rely on wishes.*

Kai and I gobble our cake, then he takes me on a tour of the farm. I'm surprised at how much produce a small farm like this can actually cultivate. Along with onions and strawberries, rows of all types of vegetables abound—cucumbers, tomatoes, lettuce, carrots and peppers. My favorite area is the flower garden, where Kai picks me a small bouquet of carnations, tuberose, *ilima* and, of course, plumeria blooms. He tucks one of the blooms in behind my left ear like he did on our surfing date.

We wander in silence from the flower garden to a grove of jacaranda trees. A narrow path weaves through and opens up into a small cemetery, set back from the rest of the farm.

"Oh, wow, super-creepy. Are we suddenly in a cemetery?"

Dozens of modest gravestones mark the area, some looking chipped and worn over years of withstanding the elements. Despite the eerie vibe I get, there's also a sense of tranquility that blankets the space. The grass has been cut low, showing care is taken in preserving the area. Small patches of wildflowers sprout beside grave markers, and tropical birds flit between the trees.

"Yeah, this is our family's communal resting place, I guess. I never thought about it as creepy before, as it's always been here, but I guess I could see it that way. For me, there's a sense of belonging here, believe it or not. This is where all my family is buried — generations of us, in fact. And I don't know... There's a sense of comfort knowing where my final resting place will be and that I'll always be surrounded by the people who love me. It's like my ancestors' spirits are all here, cheering me on, supporting me. It might sound silly, or creepy, or warped" — he gives a self-conscious laugh — "but for me, this is one of my favorite places. It's where I feel at peace with the world."

"Yeah, I get it. And I'm so grateful I got to come here with you." I smile up at him.

"Jess, I'm so glad you came with me today, to get a taste of *my* Maui. Are you having an okay time? I know it's not a luxurious resort..."

"This is even better than any luxury hotel," I reply. "I love this farm, this area of the island, your family. Everyone is so real and so welcoming. It feels like what a family is supposed to be like." I choke up a bit when I speak, visions of Robert, Mom and her growing baby bump floating around in the back of my mind. I think about Dad sitting at home on the sofa, drinking a whiskey on the rocks. Neither place has a fraction of the warmth this day has provided for me.

"Well, you're welcome to hang here with me anytime you'd like!" Kai leans over to give me a quick kiss on the tip of my nose, but instead I pull him in to me and reach my lips up to his. We're out of view from the rest of the family, and I want to show him how much he means to me right now, in this moment. Passion and desire run through my veins, and it's like I can't get him close enough. I play in the soft locks at the back of his head and lose myself in the heady feeling he gives me as he tickles the back of my neck with his fingertips. I'm hungry for him, for him to kiss every inch of me, to make me his. I pull my lips from his mouth for a moment so I can explore his chiseled jaw, and I linger on the sweet spot behind his ear. A gentle sigh escapes his lips and I feel his hips press into me. I slide my hand up his T-shirt and feel his smooth and taut waist. I can't help but graze my fingers along the inside of the waistband of his chinos. He takes a sharp inhale of breath, then pulls away from me suddenly.

"It's not that I don't want to… It's just that this isn't the time…" He trails off, breathing heavily and wiping his hand over his brow. "Another time, I promise," he says sweetly, planting another kiss on my nose.

He's right. Now's not the time for any type of heavy make-out session. I've just been caught up in the beauty of the day, the feelings it has stirred within me. I feel closer to this boy beside me than I ever did with Marcus or any other pathetic boyfriend in my past.

I link my arm around his and steer him back toward the house.

"Okay, let's head back to the fam. But don't think I'll forget that this part of the date will be continued on a different day."

Chapter Twenty-Six

"The hell you're not!" is all we hear as we approach the back deck from the flower garden in the yard.

Kai's dad stands in the middle of the porch, towering over *Tutu*, with his hands thrown into the air.

"You can't do this without talking to us first, Mama." His tone has softened a bit, and a few of the other adults start piping in.

"Yeah, Mama, this has got to be a family decision," Kai's aunt interjects.

"I appreciate what you all are saying, but this is *my* farm and I get to be the one who makes the decisions. I just turned seventy years old, for God's sake. Akela is gone, and this farm is just too hard for an old lady like me. Plus, the money they're offering is really good."

"But *Tutu*, we'll help you out. We'll *all* help you out. We can't imagine not having the farm," Kai's older brother Pikka jumps in.

"I know, sweet boy. You always help me out. That's not the issue. I just think it's time, that's all."

Kai lets go of my hand and marches up to his mom, who's standing just in front of the porch, on the back lawn.

"Mom, what's going on? What's *Tutu* talking about?"

"Oh, honey, it looks like *Tutu* has decided to sell the farm. I guess she's received a handsome offer for it from some big land developer, so she thinks now's the best time to sell. And your dad and your uncles? Well, they're not quite on board."

"What the...?" Kai pushes past his family members that have huddled around *Tutu*.

"*Tutu*, is it true? You're selling?"

"Well, I'm thinking that's best right now, honey. I know you love this place, but I'm afraid if I don't sell now, they're going to take the deal away and I'll be left with next to nothing in the future. Eventually, I'll be forced to sell anyway. Most of the neighbors have taken the deal as well, so it's not like I'm just selling out. It's just not working anymore. The big stores, the big corporations... They always win. What do I have to fight back with? No, it's better if I can at least squeeze a bit of money out of them first. I'll get my own little place in Kahului, help your parents with their debts. I can help pay for your college education, sweetheart!"

"*Tutu*, you can't do this. This farm" — he sweeps his arms out to the sides — "this farm is everything to our family. *Everything*!" He just stands there for a moment, waiting for someone to agree, to back him up. But everything has been said, and with *Tutu*'s look of resignation, it seems that she's done saying her piece as well.

As if grasping for straws to keep the conversation going, Kai snatches the piece of paper from *Tutu*'s hands.

"It just came today. Kai, it's a lot of money…" Kai scans through the paperwork, trying to sort out the details. He's quiet for so long, his attention wrapped up in the legal jargon of the offer for purchase. I make my way up the back porch steps and snuggle in close to him as he reads. I slip my hands around his waist and rest my chin on his shoulder so I'm able to read the paper too. I scan a few phrases… *the landowner hereby relinquishes all rights…. the possession date is deemed to be the last day of the month… The seller agrees to these provisions and to the purchase price of $500,000.00.*

"$500,000? They're willing to pay you $500,000 for this place?" Kai asks in disbelief.

"I told you it's a lot of money, sweetheart," *Tutu* responds.

It does seem like a lot of money…at first. But I remember having that conversation with Dad about big companies dangling what seems like large sums of money in front of hard-working farmers. They snap up the deal, thinking they're walking away with a fortune. But, let's be honest, even a million dollars doesn't last that long on Maui. The corporations conglomerate the land, build massive hotels and box stores, then squeeze millions out of it by the time they're done. And the local produce, local craftsmen, local artists — whoever — start disappearing from the island. Maybe this deal *Tutu* sees isn't all it appears.

I'm about to pipe up, offer my perspective on the issue. But my eyes catch something on the paper that takes all the words right out of my mouth. I see it, right there in front of my face, scrawled out in impossibly illegible handwriting, right at the bottom of the last page, with the words neatly typewritten underneath.

Sincerely,
Mr. Robert Kennedy of CanStar Properties

A tiny gasp releases from my mouth, causing Kai to focus his gaze on the bottom of the page as well. His mouth drops open and he spins around sharply, a look of complete puzzlement on his face.

"What the hell, Jess?" His voice punches into me like icy stabs.

"I... I...don't know. I had no idea. There's got to be some sort of explanation."

The rest of his family looks on with confused expressions, not understanding the implications of what we just discovered.

"Honey, what's the matter? What's going on?" *Tutu* asks Kai, instinctively grabbing the papers back as if the answer might be written all over them.

"Jess' dad is the one pushing us out of the farm."

Chapter Twenty-Seven

Honestly, there's no rule book in the world that tells a person how to respond when they find out their father is responsible for the upending of their boyfriend's family's entire existence. I babble on about not knowing anything about it and offer weak explanations that might help to give us all a new perspective. It seems as if Kai's parents are trying to do the same thing, as they keep taking turns grabbing the stack of papers, trying to find a misunderstanding in the written document. *Tutu* stays quiet, as if she figures this argument has to play itself out the way it's supposed to.

But it's my dad's signature, plain as day. There's no denying that he's the one pressuring *Tutu* to give up this beautiful place, like pawning an heirloom that's been in a family for hundreds of years.

Kai basically loses his shit on me all in one swoop, which I don't blame him for one bit. I stand here, a stranger in the middle of his family, and take the harsh words as if they are lashes being doled out for a crime I can't deny.

"Did you know about this the entire time we've been together?"

"How could you let him do this to us?"

"You pretend to love getting to know my family, when all along you had this planned?"

"So what? Is this how you manage to live in that fucking mansion of yours? By stealing family farms from poor people who are just scraping by?"

Eventually, he loses a bit of steam and stomps around to the front of the lawn in a huff. He calls for me to come so he can drive me home, which is a really awkward thing to have to do in the middle of a monstrous fight, but we really have no other option. Tears stream down my face and I'm in disbelief, at both the thought that my father is responsible for this, and that my boyfriend has just gouged me so gruesomely with his words.

The ride home is quiet and uncomfortable. I'm not even able to find solace in David Gray's soothing voice coming from the island's easy listening station on the radio. I roll the window down farther, hoping the cool evening breeze will wash the feelings of guilt from me, but I find that the minty, pine scent of the eucalyptus trees we pass on our way down the mountain just stokes my anger about why anyone—my dad, in particular—would want to develop over this pristine land. The forty-five-minute drive feels like a billion years, but at the same time, I don't want it to end, because I know it might mean the end of Kai and me as well. As much as I want us to stay together, this impossibly large chasm that has formed between us—

my father and his billion-dollar deal—is creating a distance that seems too vast to overcome.

At last, the truck slows in front of my house, which appears even more ridiculously enormous and empty-looking than it normally does, especially after spending the evening with Kai's boisterous family in *Tutu's* tiny farmhouse.

I've apologized a thousand times and still can't seem to find anything to say that might bridge the gap between us. Halfway through the ride, I tried reaching over to take his hand, which had been resting on the gear shift. He moved it away from my touch so quickly that you'd have thought he was afraid of catching some crazy disease from me. So, I spent the rest of the drive with my hands restless on my own lap.

Now that we're stopped, the temptation is for me to reach out and hug him, to try to show him that I'm on his side. But I'm afraid of getting rejected once again, so I simply turn and offer one more weak apology. He doesn't respond, and instead of walking me to my door or even waiting for me to get inside, I hear the tires spin behind me as he races back down the hill, shrouded in the evening's darkness.

Only one light looks to be on inside the house, and it's coming from my dad's study upstairs. As I mount the curved staircase, rage bubbles up stronger inside me with every step.

How could my dad do this to me?

Why does everyone I care about have to betray me in the end?

How am I supposed to go on living on this island without Kai? Without any friends in school? Without being able to trust my own father?

When I reach the second floor, I race down the hall and barge into his office. He jumps in his chair, causing it to roll away from the desk where he's working, papers strewn across the surface.

"Jesus, Jess. You scared me! So, how was your night with Kai? Did you have fun?"

"What the hell did you do, Dad? What the *hell* did you do?" The fury takes over and turns me into a mess of tears. I don't know why, but when I'm mad, really mad, the anger somehow morphs into crying, with hot, raging fireballs transforming into streams of tears as they leak out of my body. My dad looks perplexed, like he has no idea what's going on. For a moment, I don't say anything, just sob uncontrollably and crumple against the office wall.

"Jess, what is going on? Is it Kai? Is he okay? Are you okay?"

"You... You're stealing their farm from them. You're forcing them out," I babble. "They love that place. It's... It's...everything to them!"

"What are you...? What the...?" he starts to say, then it's like something clicks for him. "Oh, honey, I had no idea Kai's family is one of the farms we're trying to buy." He scans through a few papers on his desk until his finger stops at a name.

"Kamealoha? Shit, I didn't even put two and two together." He pauses, looking over the paperwork. "But, honey, we're offering them a great deal, and it looks like all the neighbors are going to sign on as well. They can start fresh with all the money they're receiving. It's an opportunity for them to try something different. That'll be a lot of money for that family, trust me."

"For *that* family?" I spew. "What, like, they're simple, working-class native Hawaiians who should be *grateful* that some big company is throwing them a bone? As if you're doing this—your company is doing this—as a *favor*? For their *best* interest? How can you even pretend that?"

"Honey, we've talked about this before. The money is in the land, and it's all in what you do with it. That land is invaluable, and truthfully, it's not being used most effectively right now. CanStar has the ability to turn their land into one of the most prestigious, luxurious vacation destinations on the island. People will be flocking to Maui to be able to stay there! Did you know that it's one of the only places on the island with a bi-coastal view? And the natural vegetation up there is just breathtaking. We're hoping to leave a lot of it as a natural preserve for tourists to enjoy. So, it's not like we're ruining it all. We're actually going to be putting in a lot of money to beautify the place, make it a little more alluring for visitors. Instead of Kula being a rustic, backwoods, upcountry part of the island, we're going to turn it into the hottest destination for people to travel to. Trust me… With the restaurants, galleries, boutiques and souvenir shops that open up after the hotel is built, people will be flocking to Kula. You won't even recognize it anymore!"

An image of the quaint rodeo town of Makawao flashes through my mind, how Kai was saddened by the change it was undergoing, the transformation from a quiet, locally owned island town for residents to the trendy, hipster-filled tourist trap it was becoming.

"Dad, that's not what the people who live there want."

"Well, we're offering them more money than they probably deserve for it. And you know what, Jess? Money speaks. That's fine if they don't want to sell, but let's see how long they can hold on. The project is going forward whether they like it or not. And if I were them, I'd take the money that is offered now, before they're truly forced out, and for next to nothing. There's going to be no room for a crappy little vegetable farm there by the time we're through. This *deal* that you're so worked up about? Well, this *deal* is what pays for us to be in this home, to afford this standard of living that you quite enjoy. That car you've been bugging me to buy for you? Well honey, this *deal* is the thing that can make it happen. So get off your high horse for a minute and think about whose side you're really on."

I swallow hard, because I always thought my dad and I were on the same side. But it's looking more and more like we play for opposing teams.

Chapter Twenty-Eight

The next couple of weeks are lonely, lonelier than I ever thought possible. I not only have to spend my days drifting from class to class on my own, but Kai hasn't been returning my calls, so my evenings are vast, endless blocks of time that never seem to end.

After my split with Kai, then my consequential explosion with Dad, I feel like a bubble that has been blown and now drifts aimlessly through an airless sky. Dad won't apologize or slow up on the deal, so he's been avoiding me by working late almost every night. The only thing providing me with any sense of sanity has been Maggie. She's detached from the whole thing, so she provides a breath of fresh air for me, although with our typical conversations revolving around boys, school and swim practice, nothing seems to be safe territory.

"So, you haven't been able to reach him at all, Jess?" she asks over our video call.

"No, he's totally iced me out, which isn't like him at all. But I get it. He's pissed. I mean, his *tutu* hasn't decided for sure what she's going to do, but I think they feel pretty trapped."

"There's got to be something they can do, some way to avoid this whole mess."

"Trust me. I've thought this through a thousand times over, and I just can't figure anything out. CanStar is so massive. It's like David vs. Goliath. There's just no way for them to fight the inevitable. Short of finding an ancient fossil discovery on their land or claiming it to be the remnants of the Lost City of Atlantis, I'm not sure how we could—"

"Wait a sec, Jess. Didn't you tell me that there's a little cemetery on Kai's grandma's land? That everyone in his family has been buried there, for like, *forever*?"

"Yeah..." I say, hesitant to acknowledge the small flicker of hope that ignites in my gut.

"Well, aren't ancestral burial grounds protected by law or something? I'm sure I've heard stories on the news about oil companies wanting to install big pipelines, but Indigenous communities protest because the land is sacred to them. Doesn't this sound like a similar situation?"

"I guess maybe it could be..." I sit up from where I've been lying on my bed, suddenly alert with the new realization.

"Look, Jess. My uncle is a land title lawyer. He lives in Toronto, so the laws might differ in the States from what they are in Canada but let me see what I can find out. Start digging on the web to see if anything's on there about burial rights in Hawaii. I'm not sure where you'd go to look, but there's got to be some sort of record of archives database on the island. At the very least, text Kai and tell him our thoughts. See if he has any more info to support our theory. I'm guessing his grandma needs to make her decision in the next couple of weeks, so we'd better get on this fast. I'll call you as soon as I talk with my uncle, okay?"

And in the blink of an eye, I've got one more teammate on my half of the field. It feels so good to have someone side with me, and I couldn't ask for anyone better than Maggie. All the reasons why she has irritated me in the past — her stubborn, take-charge, lippy, self-entitled attitude — are exactly the attributes I adore at this very moment. I'm so thankful to have her back in my life.

I spend two and a half hours on the computer, scrolling through websites and archived newspaper articles, trying to come up with any information that'll cast light on the early settlers of Maui or ancestral rights the locals might be able to claim on the land. My blood is still steeped in anger and anxiety, but at least I go to sleep knowing that there's a plan and that I'm doing my part to put things into action.

The next morning, I pick up my phone to see a text response from Kai. Right before I'd gone to bed the previous night, I'd texted him to let him know what Maggie and I had discussed. I didn't know whether he'd even bother responding to me, so I'm overjoyed he has agreed to meet me for coffee. I try not to acknowledge the tiny fire burning in my belly that aches for him to touch me and kiss me again. I know this meeting may just be his way of gaining closure, or maybe he really is interested in hearing what I've discovered, but either way, it's likely he doesn't want me back in his life.

It only takes me fifteen minutes or so to bike to the beach café where we went for brunch that day he took me surfing. It's as busy as ever, with a line snaking through tables and overflowing onto the sidewalk. I eye the crowd to see if Kai has already arrived, when Charlie spots me and jogs over with his booming voice and gregarious smile.

"Jessica, my maple syrup sweetheart! *Aloha*, and welcome! Nice to see you're back. Got a craving for one of my breakfast burritos, maybe? Or my famous *Loco Moco*? And where's my bro, Kai? Is he here already?" He looks around to see if he's missed spotting him at a table.

"No, he should be here right away, though," I say softly. It's obvious that Charlie isn't privy to our falling-out.

"Okay, well, let's get you a table and a cup of coffee. I'll show him where you're sitting once he has arrived."

He takes my hand and guides me over to a narrow table inside, next to the kitchen.

"Sorry, my dear. This is not one of my favorite tables in the restaurant, but it's so busy today that it's the best I can do. But as you know, the food always makes up for it!"

After he grabs me a coffee, he scurries off again, taking time to mingle with the guests with a friendly smile. Pots and pans clang behind me, and a soft whistling sound floats in from someone in the kitchen. The coffee is strong and sweet and doesn't help my frazzled nerves or my racing mind. I look over the menu to give me something to do as I wait, but in reality, my stomach can't handle eating a single thing right now. I avoid pulling my phone from my bag, as

I'm terrified there'll be a text from Kai on it with some lame excuse for why he's had to bail.

But then he walks in.

He looks as delicious as ever, his dark hair swept smoothly off to the side of his face, a gray T-shirt tucked casually into his shorts. He catches my eye and walks briskly over to me. Everything about him looks perfect…except for the fact that no generous smile greets me from his handsome face.

"Hey, Jess." is all he says. There's no movement in his arms to imply he's offering a hug, so I stay seated in my place. He takes a seat as well.

"How're you doing? How's *Tutu*?" I ask.

"Fine. She's fine. Just still stuck with the same dilemma." He makes a little grunty noise that's filled with exasperation. "CanStar's pushing pretty hard right now, telling her that she's only got until the end of the month before they go to the courts, mandating her to have to sell. I don't know if it's bullshit or not, but they say that they can take legal action and force her to get off the land if it's in the best interest of 'community development'. They claim *Tutu*'s land blocks the area where the road is going to go that will lead to the hotel complex. So, they say that in the best interest of infrastructure, they'll be able to push her out. And if that's the case, *Tutu*'s looking at receiving less than half the money they're currently offering her. She doesn't know what to do. Take the money now, or try to fight it? It's not like she can afford an attorney, so she's pretty screwed either way."

He looks so deflated, like his passion for life has been stripped from him. I desperately want to bring him some hope.

"See? That's what I wanted to meet with you about. We might have another option. The cemetery on the far side of your property... Who's buried there? From how far back?"

"I don't know. Everyone in the family, I guess. It's been there as long as I can remember. A lot of the grave sites aren't marked, but I'm pretty sure we have ancestors buried there from hundreds of years ago. I know the land has been in our family for ages."

"Well, from what I've read, I think we can get the government to dictate that land as a sacred burial place. Have you ever heard of what happened at Honokahua?"

"Of course I have. Everyone who lives here knows about it. The Ritz-Carlton basically came in and started bulldozing over a thousand graves to put in their new, swanky hotel. A bunch of protestors lost their shit over it, so they had to halt construction. They ended up moving to a new location, and people tried to ceremoniously re-inter the graves that had been removed. But really, the damage was already done. People's bodies were *exhumed*. That's pretty dark shit. Seriously, they desecrated entire generations of people who had been put there to rest. You can't just put them back in the ground, say 'sorry' and think no damage has been done.

"In Canada, you may not have the same history or belief systems that we do, but here in Hawaii, caring for loved ones after they die is central to our cultural beliefs. The *n... iwi* or bones of a person, are considered sacred. They carry that person's *mana*, or spiritual essence. In Hawaiian culture, the *kuleana* to care *for iwi kūpuna*, or ancestors' remains, is serious shit.

"The thing is, they got away with it, basically, by giving some meaningless apology and moving elsewhere to take over some other poor person's land — probably someone who couldn't afford to fight the fight. And really, nothing was ever done. Sacred sites are being destroyed on this island all the time — all the time. Because big, rich corporations, like the one your daddy works for, always win. That's just how it is."

The comment about my dad is a low blow and hits me as hard as it was intended to. But I can tell I've gotten him riled up, which is what I've been aiming for. His hands are restless and there's a fire in his eyes that wasn't there a few minutes ago.

"That is exactly what I'm talking about, Kai! The thing is, they can't get away with it, not anymore — not if we're smart about it and are willing to fight. There are laws in place now to prevent this exact thing from happening!"

"What do you mean? What can we do?" There's skepticism in his voice.

"Well, after Honokahua, legislation was put into place to protect ancestral burial sites and prevent further destruction of sacred land. The NAGPRA, or Native American Graves Protection and Repatriation Act, was established, which basically advocates for the repatriation of sacred burial sites. But Act 306 was also enacted, which gives the power back to native Hawaiians. There's a council who makes decisions about burial sites deemed more than fifty years old. If we can convince them that your family's land falls within the classification of 'venerable', they may be able to prohibit the further development of it by external forces — CanStar included."

He simply gives me a look of bewilderment.

"Wow, someone's done their homework." Then, like the magic of a rainbow appearing after a storm, that wide grin of his appears between those dimpled cheeks.

"Yeah, well, I'm nothing if not stubborn." I return his smile. "But honestly, if this is going to work, we're going to need numbers. We need all of *Tutu*'s neighbors to be on board too. Fighting an entire community is going to be a lot more daunting for CanStar than overtaking one small family farm. Are you up for a little door-to-door canvassing?"

"You better believe it!" The smile stretching across Kai's face spreads down into the rest of his body. His whole demeanor has shifted. His eyes come alive, his shoulders square, and as I stand up from the table to follow him out of the restaurant, he reaches back to grasp my hand in his.

We head back upcountry to Kula to talk to his *tutu* before pursuing things further. We need to make sure she's on board. Bathed in morning sun, the drive is even more gorgeous than the evening I came here with him for *Tutu*'s birthday.

I'm keenly aware of every one of the farms that line the highway and pepper the slopes around us — fields of strawberries, lavender and vegetables interspersed with groves of silver eucalyptus and canopied jacaranda trees, small ranches with rolling pastures and lazy cattle. As we reach the dirt road just outside *Tutu*'s home, I realize Dad is right about one thing. The views from Kula truly are spectacular, sweeping views of the Pacific stretching out from either coast of Maui. It's the first time since being on the island that I'm acutely aware that I am on an *island*, that I'm a tiny human, living an ordinary life on this small parcel of land in the middle of nowhere. It makes me feel so small and insignificant, but at the same time gives me renewed passion to do what I can to preserve this island's beauty and culture.

After spending a few minutes discussing things with *Tutu*, Kai and I get to work on writing up a summary of my findings. Maggie's uncle did a little digging on his own and emailed me some of the information he'd found. We do our best to use the legal jargon and reference materials to make our case sound really airtight, and when we're done, I'm proud of what we've accomplished. At the very least, I feel like we'll be able to convince *Tutu* and most of her neighbors to hold off on selling their properties until the burial councils have had a chance to review our application. In the best-case scenario, our research pays off enough to scare CanStar—or any other interested corporation—away, unless they're willing to get caught up in an epic legal battle. We can only hope we've done enough.

It's late into the evening by the time we're done talking to all the neighbors, and we're both filled with the satisfying type of exhaustion that happens when a person puts every ounce of themselves into a project.

We climb into his battered green truck once again, as it transports us from the simple farm life in Kula to the homes of the rich and famous in Wailea. It's surreal that on a single island, a forty-five-minute drive can reveal a change so drastic. Despite the luxury that abounds in Wailea, I'm surprised at how much I long for the simple beauty of Kula.

I open my mouth, ready to ask Kai if he wants to come in, but then remember my dad as the root cause of the entire mess we're in. I decide my home is probably the last place Kai wants to be. So, I sit awkwardly in the passenger seat, just like I've done many times before. I don't know where I stand with him or what he wants now, so I decide brevity is best.

"Well, thanks again for the ride. I know it's a pain to drive me all the way here, especially when you have to make the return trip back. And thanks for listening to me, for helping me today. As I've said a thousand times before, I'm sorry about what has happened. I wish my dad had no part in it, but I guess I don't really have a say as to what he does. And he has his reasons. I just hope… Well, I just really want…things to work out for you."

I figure that's that. As much as I've pushed to save the farm, it's ultimately not my place to make any decisions. At this point, there's really nothing left for me to do.

I climb out of the truck and walk around to lift my bike from the back. I gently close the tailgate and start wheeling my bike up the front walk. I pause for a moment in order to find my keys. I hear them jingle, but I can't grasp them in the black hole of my bag, so I rest my bike against my thigh and rifle through with both hands.

Suddenly, I feel a pull on my waist that causes me to whirl around. The bike crashes to the walkway and the keys I had just retrieved rattle for a moment, then disappear into the plush front lawn. I hear my own sharp intake of breath a split second before I feel a set of soft lips press against mine. Kai grasps at me with strong hands, like he can't quite get enough, like he is thirsty and I provide him with the water he desperately needs. For a moment, I'm lost in the way he devours every inch of me. It's as if he's apologizing—he's accepting my apology — he's accepting me — all at once, and it ignites a burning fire inside me.

"I'm sorry, Jess..." he manages between soft kisses down my jawline. "I know you are not your dad. I know none of this is your fault." More kisses, more caresses. "Whatever happens from here, I want you to be a part of it. Please be a part of it."

I let him know with my long, deep kisses that I am in it with him until the very end.

Over the next couple of weeks, every molecule in me itches to tell Dad what I've done, to boast and brag that we may have succeeded in upending his plans, his momentous *deal* in the making. I want to hurt him as much as he's hurt the people around me. But Dad and I are no longer on speaking terms, haven't been since that first blow-up. Plus, I figure an element of surprise might come in handy, and I don't want, in any way, to reduce the chances of this working.

Kai and I have had to keep things on the downlow as well. Kai's still pretty prickly about Dad, and it's easier for me not to get into the details of anything if Dad assumes Kai and I have broken up. So, I'm back to using Callie and Em as scapegoats, even though they have utterly and completely iced me out from any social event Maui Gardens has going on.

Kai and I have just enjoyed a lovely dinner at a local fish taco truck and he's dropping me off early, seeing as we both have school tomorrow. I give him a quick kiss and get out of the truck a hundred feet or so from my place, so Dad doesn't spot his truck. I walk the last bit home and let myself in through the front door.

Dad's pacing the front foyer with heavy feet, letting out angry puffs of air with each step. He turns to face me as I enter, and rage billows from his body like dark clouds in a storm.

"Jessica, what the fuck?" is all that comes out of his mouth.

It's then that I know. I know that our plan has worked, that the neighbors have signed on, that CanStar has been forced to back off, that the deal is off. I'm elated and relieved, but also a little terrified. And I can't let him know of any of it.

"Uh, what are you talking about Dad? What's going on?"

"Don't play dumb with me, Jess. I get it. You like the guy, and you like his family. You want to be a hero and save the day. But do you realize what you've done to us? To our family? Do you even know the ramifications of your actions?"

He goes back to pacing. I've never seen my dad this angry, not even when he found out about Mom and Robert and the baby.

"Okay, fine. I helped, but it's not like I did much. I just showed them a way out. Dad, if you would have seen the farm — their land, their family — you would have done the same thing. You've always taught me to stand up for what I believe in, and well, this is something I believe in. I took action. I respected the laws in place, and I found a way to make them work for the people they're supposed to protect. I didn't do anything wrong, Dad. *You're* the one working for an immoral business, working for corporate America. Well, I don't want any part of that. And if it means your company loses a bit of money, then so be it. They're a multi-billion-dollar corporation. They'll get over it."

He looks so distraught, so upended that I decide to take a softer tone.

"Dad, Kai's family is happy there. They just want to continue living the life they've lived for generations, without the threat of a money-grabbing company coming in and sweeping it all away. They don't deserve to be forced out of their homes."

"No? Well, I'm glad you think that, sweetheart," he says bitterly. "Because it means that now we're being forced out of ours. CanStar's sending us back to Canada."

Chapter Twenty-Nine

"Mom, I don't get it. I was only doing the right thing—the good and just thing—so why am I getting punished?"

After my dad laid into me for more than an hour—about how I've ruined his career, how he's done everything for me and I've never appreciated any of it, how he may not even have a job to go to, even after CanStar sends us back home—I locked myself in my room and lay on the bed, sobbing uncontrollably, feeling utterly hopeless.

What have I done?

I needed to talk to someone, hash this out. I almost called Kai, but I knew he'd be devastated to hear the news of me moving, and I wasn't ready for that conversation yet. I tried Maggie, but she didn't pick up. Hesitantly, I called my mom. Funny how, not long ago, she was the last person on the planet I wanted to talk to. But now, when things are at their lowest point for me, she's the one I reach for. I guess that's the thing about moms. They're always waiting in the wings for when you need them.

"Honey, you're not getting punished. I can see how you thought you were doing something brave and just. And maybe it was. I don't know. It's just that things are often more complicated than they originally seem, and usually, someone pays the price in the end. In this case, it's your father. I understand why he's angry with you, with the situation. And I understand your disappointment too. But you're both just going to have to deal with the consequences, even if they're difficult. Like the old saying goes, you can't have your cake and eat it too."

For some reason, this sends a lightning bolt of resentment through me.

"What do you mean, Mom? When you left with Robert, you had your cake and ate it too — and a frickin' baby in your stomach, to top it all off." The acid of my words leaves a sour taste in my mouth.

"It might seem like that to you, honey, but I lost something very important. I lost you."

I guess she did, temporarily anyway. But I'm talking to her now, aren't I? Isn't that something? I came back, I just needed time. Maybe my dad will eventually come around too.

I decide it's best if I steer the conversation back to the topic at hand — my utter desperation.

"But, Mom, I don't get it. Why can't Dad just get a new job here? He loves it as much as I do. I can tell he does. God, I just want to finish out my senior year of high school!"

"You'd think it'd be that easy, but unfortunately working overseas always has its stipulations. Dad was working on a temporary visa, Jess. That means when the work is done, he's done. He always knew this was probably only temporary, but just figured paradise would last a little longer than it did. And at this point, he might just have to head back to Canada with his tail between his legs and do the best he can to build back up his reputation. For now, CanStar's giving him back his old job in Edmonton—and with no penalties—but things could be much worse. I mean, imagine if he were to get fired completely. That would be the worst-case scenario."

I imagine Dad's face, drawn and weary, with no work to go to. Work has always been everything to him. I know this demotion has got to hurt him, and I'm sorry for that. But Kai's family's farm is everything to them too, and they deserve to be able to keep it. At least the one good thing about this whole ordeal is that the council agreed the land is to be protected from further development for the foreseeable future, and the farm, as well as the burial grounds, will stay for good.

"You know, honey, the other good thing about this is that you'll be coming home. I've missed you more than you know. The baby is due in just over a month... It'll be really great to have you around for that. Depending what area of the city your dad decides to move to, maybe we can get you back into your old school? You can join the swim team again, and you can see Maggie. Things'll work out, I promise. They always do."

Although her words provide me with some comfort, it's not enough, because I do love this place and I think I love Kai. I'm not ready to leave either one.

Chapter Thirty

Kai picks me up after school so we can do a hike up in the Iao Valley. His school is off today with some sort of professional development—it seems like he has about ten times more PD days than our school—so we had made plans to do this last week. I've been anxious and agitated all day, not sure how I'm going to tell him the news. After my conversation with Mom the night before, I started feeling a bit better about things. Well, to be honest, I feel more optimistic about the actual move back home and that my dad will one day come around and start talking to me again, but I feel terrible about leaving this place, especially leaving Kai. Is it possible to look forward to going somewhere at the same time as being devastated about leaving the place you're in? It seems like an impossibility, but that's exactly how I feel.

It makes things even more difficult when I step out of the school to see Kai grinning at me through the window of his green pick-up truck. The rusty, dented bumper looks completely out of place among the sports cars and luxury SUVs, but it's the best thing I've seen all day. I've gotten used to my days of quiet solitude at school since Callie and Em have shunned me. I mean, I've started to hang out with a different crowd a bit — *the math club, no joke* — so it's not like I've been spending my days *completely* alone, but I've still been hesitant to really sink my teeth in.

Now, with it looking like I'll be leaving back home permanently in a few short weeks, well, it seems like there's really no point in getting too attached. I've been keeping my head down, doing my work, and that has given me the opportunity to spend the rest of my free time in the evenings with Kai.

My dad doesn't know this, of course. I had to phase Kai out of the picture weeks ago for his benefit — too many questions and too many lines crossed. And now, well… Now, Dad sees Kai as the enemy, and as the one responsible for his plummet through the social structure of Maui. So, it's best Dad doesn't realize Kai even exists anymore. I've been out with him so many nights that it's getting impossible to keep up with the lies I create. So, the math club came in handy on that front. It only took one Saturday afternoon of our living room full of a dozen dorky kids designing sculptures using the Fibonacci sequence for it to be enough to scare Dad away. He's never bothered to try to get to know the math club girls again.

But right now, as I walk down the school's front steps, feeling Callie and Em laugh and whisper conspiratorially behind my back, knowing that my time at this school is almost coming to an end, all I think about is how I'm going to leave Kai.

He must sense something's wrong, because as soon as I get in, he grabs my hand and asks if everything is okay.

"Jess, what's going on? Did something happen at school? Is it your dad? Is he still giving you the silent treatment? Honestly, he'll get over it. They'll give him a new contract soon enough and this'll just be a business deal gone wrong for him. I mean, for my family this was *everything*. For your dad, this was literally just one piece of paperwork that didn't work in his favor."

I stay silent, letting him believe that my severed relationship with my dad is the reason for my melancholy, not my soon-to-be severed relationship with *him*.

We drive in a comfortable silence, Kai jumping in to sing along to the chorus of a song every so often. As many day trips of the island Kai and I have done, we've never ventured out to Wailuku or the Iao Valley.

We drive north on the Piilani highway before turning onto North Kihei Road. It takes us past the tourist shops and beachfront condos of the Maalaea Harbor, the island's port for dozens of whale-watching tours and sunset booze cruises. We continue back on the highway, driving through the small town of Waikapu in central Maui, a once-bustling agricultural community during the peak of the sugar cane industry. All that remains now is a sleepy and withdrawn town of Maui residents, wrapped in the green pastures and rolling foothills of the West Maui Mountains.

From here, it's just a few minutes to Maui's commercial hub and former tourist destination of Wailuku, which sits at the mouth of the Iao Valley. Lush, green hills seemingly rise above the town from every angle, giving it a closed in, claustrophobic vibe. There's a slight fog in the air, and my skin begins to feel dewy and damp. It's hard to believe I left sunny skies and scorching temperatures just twenty minutes ago, as the chill in the air here feels almost otherworldly.

We continue past Wailuku to drive right through the heart of the valley. Dense, green rainforests dominate all around us, as if we've entered a *Jurassic Park* remake. Giant ferns and palm fronds, some bigger than my head, crowd the road, so it feels as if we're navigating entirely untamed territory. After we park in the state-run lot, we walk up the paved pathway and across a small footbridge, which traverses over a rushing stream. Amid a magical mist made for fairytales and dreams, I hear the raucous roaring of the falls before I see them. A thundering spray of water shoots down from the wall of rocks, while the Iao needle, a majestic piece of rock pointing twelve hundred feet into the air, stands as a sentinel to the valley it overlooks below.

"Well, we're here," Kai announces as we take a minute to absorb the beauty around us.

"This place is magical, like we're not on the same planet anymore," I say.

"Yeah, it's pretty spectacular. One of the bloodiest battles in Hawaii's history took place in this spot. The Battle of Kepaniwai. King Kamehameha arrived with his troops in an attempt to unite and protect the Hawaiian Islands. Thinking he was a knight in shining armor coming in to save the day, he never considered that maybe the people here didn't want to be saved. A massive battle ensued, and thousands of people died, mostly the native Hawaiians who had been living here peacefully before that. So, the people he sought to protect ended up being the ones he was at war with.

Doesn't make sense, if you ask me… And it seems that the battle for Maui still continues today."

I automatically think of what happened in Honokahua with the Ritz-Carlton, what almost happened with CanStar and Kai's family farm. The misty fog hangs heavy around me.

"Now, this place is protected as a state park and a sacred burial place. So, the good thing is that it doesn't really belong to anyone anymore, and we can all enjoy its divine beauty."

Kai starts walking again, this time up a muddy path alongside the stream. We stop momentarily in front of a sign that clearly states *No Trespassing: Do Not Enter*, but Kai utterly ignores it, instead hopping right over and inviting me to do the same.

"Are you sure we can go there?" I ask hesitantly.

"Thought you said you were pretty much a local now?" he asks with a smirk.

Now would be the time to tell him that I'm leaving. Now would be the time to let him know we aren't going to be able to do this anymore, that we're done. But the words hide deep in my throat, unable to expose themselves.

"Yeah, I guess I am," is all I say, as he helps me hop the fence.

Almost two hours later, we're perched at the top of a high plateau overlooking the entire Iao Valley. The hike was exhausting and treacherous, made worse by recent heavy rains in the region. I'm grateful I thought to wear my hiking boots, because the muddy, unmarked trails were steep and impossibly difficult to navigate in parts. I had to keep gripping on to rocks and vegetation for leverage, as my feet kept slipping down the muddy slopes. However, the views along the way were breathtaking.

Kai pointed out wild coffee berries along our route, and we caught the intoxicating scent of eucalyptus trees as we ascended. Wild ginger, guavas and cannas abounded, with an ever-abundant supply of flowers and ferns to make for a spectacular backdrop. And now, up on the peak, mountains tower all around us and numerous waterfalls dot our view. Seeing the town of Wailuku as a small village far below makes me realize the steepness of our climb. I feel like the entire island is at our disposal, like we are sacred witnesses to the land's magic.

"This is spectacular."

"It really is. This is why I love this island. This—" Kai stretches his arms out to the magnificent view around us. Then he turns to me. "I'm so glad you see it as I do, that you're able to call this place home too. I'm so glad you've come into my life." He reaches over to cup my face in his hands and kisses me softly on the lips. The heat grows between us and our kiss becomes deeper, more wanting. As much as I want this moment to linger into a thousand tomorrows, I've got to break it off now before we get to a place of no return.

I pull back.

"What's the matter, Jess? Is something wrong?" He holds his gaze steady on me. "Something's up. You've been quiet all day. It's not just your dad, is it?"

My face gives it away before my mouth has a chance to explain.

"Kai, we're being forced to move. The deal my dad lost—the deal we prevented my dad from making— was apparently the entire reason we came here. CanStar is pretty pissed, and they can't afford to keep my dad on here anymore. They're taking away his temporary green card and sending us back to Canada."

"What? No way! How can they do that? They can't just force you to move? What about school? You still have to finish your senior year!"

"They can force us out, and they are. The whole reason we're here is them. They pay for that massive home, they provide my dad with a car, his salary, my entrance into Maui Gardens even. Legally, we can't stay without a green card. So, now we have to move back." Tears sting my eyes and I use the damp sleeve of my T-shirt to wipe them clean.

"Jess, you can't leave. We've just gotten things started…" He trails off. "God, this is all my fault. If you weren't trying to protect the farm and my family, you'd be able to stay."

"Kai, if we didn't do what we did, you're the one who would be forced from your home. So, that would have been worse." I take a deep breath, trying to quiet the sobs welling up in me. "It's just the way it is, and it sucks. It sucks shit and it makes me feel like I want to scream. I love this place. I love being in this place with *you*." I'm not going to jump off the cliff entirely by using the L-word on him, but I figure using it twice in one sentence while I refer to him probably sends him the message.

"I've loved being here with you, too." he replies, then wraps me up in a hug that I wish would last for an eternity.

Chapter Thirty-One

It's the day of the move and I'm surprised at how little we actually have, considering the opulence we've lived in. Two suitcases full of clothes and personal items sit at the front door, and one crate of extraneous items, like artwork we've purchased and office documents, was shipped out yesterday. Everything else really, our entire existence here, has belonged to CanStar—as if they've owned this dream of ours all along.

Dad agreed to let Kai and me say our goodbyes on a last walk down the beach. I suppose he wasn't ignorant to the fact that Kai and I had stayed together this whole time, even after he'd prohibited it. But he must have known our relationship had an expiration date and perhaps wanted to smooth the prickly vibes between the two of us, so he just let it go. Regardless, I'm appreciative that I've had the last few glorious weeks with Kai, despite the fact that it'll make today's goodbye that much more difficult.

It's almost sunset and boats bob along the rippling water, capturing the last moments the day has to offer. We take off our shoes and wade among the lapping surf, me trying to soak up the feel of the sand between my toes and the sun's kiss upon my neck. I'm heading back to Canada at the precipice between autumn and winter, a time where warm summer days are a lingering memory and dark days full of snow and ice are a harsh reality. I don't know the next time I'll be back to this island, if ever, and feelings of wistfulness overtake me.

Of course, Kai tries to cheer us both up with plans for our next reunion — he could save up his money and come to visit in the summer, or Maggie and I could come back for a post-graduation holiday — but in reality, these are just words we both try to use as a salve for a burn. They make us feel better in the moment but don't actually cure the injury. No, in reality, I can't come up with a single way I'll be able to make it back to this place I love, make it back to him. It's as if the past several months have just been a vivid daydream I've imagined, in order to break the dismal reality of my otherwise-pathetic life.

Maggie was ecstatic when I told her about the move, so that's something. The tension of Marcus is long over, and apparently, she has a new love to introduce me to when I return. She assures me that the swim team is on an epic losing streak because it's missing its best swimmer, but that only conjures up images of me struggling to keep up with Callie and Em in the pool.

The one thing that does have me feeling excited is the arrival of my new baby sister. Yes, *sister*. Mom and Robert found out a few days ago and I can't stop thinking about her ever since. They texted me a picture of her ultrasound, and in an instant, she became real — not the illicit lovechild of a disgusting affair or the wrecking-ball destruction site that has become my life, but the beautiful, perfect baby sister I've always dreamed of. Mine. Someone who will walk side by side with me in this crazy family life we've been dropped into, someone who will always be on my team.

Mom's due in just a few weeks and I'm overjoyed. I'll have the entire Christmas break to do nothing but get my snuggles on, and I feel like her presence will be a welcome distraction from thoughts of Kai that will undoubtedly fill my brain.

Kai — this strong and passionate, funny and gentle surfer-boy who laughs at my jokes, pushes me to take risks and holds my hair when I puke — holds my hand as we look over at the horizon, enjoying our last Maui sunset together.

"You know that I'll always think of you during sunset now, right?" he asks, taking my hand in his.

"You know I'll always think of you as I scrape ice off my car in the dark, frigid December mornings in Canada, right?"

"Yeah, I'm not gonna lie. That shit is crazy. No one should live in a place that's colder than my deepfreeze." He laughs. "But, you know, you always have snowboarding."

"Yeah, I'm thinking I just might make that my sport of choice this winter." I give him an easy smile then interlace my fingers with his. "Thanks for taking me surfing. Thanks for letting me meet your family. Thanks for the endless dates and hikes and food trucks and beach walks. This has been magical, and it's all because of you."

I immediately regret saying all of this because it makes his eyes water, and he looks away. He's trying not to show me how much my leaving destroys him, and I love that about him.

"Okay, well, my dad's probably eager to get going, so we better head back."

He tugs my hand, so I walk in step with him. He wraps his arm around me so that my head can rest on his shoulder as we walk. I catch the last of the sun dipping below the horizon and the final glimmer of light dances across the waves. Something flickers just beyond my periphery, and I turn my head to see what is. There, floating on the water's surface, are the delicate petals of a plumeria blossom. The waves roll under the bloom, shifting it this way and that, pulling it out into sea, only to rush it back toward shore again. It dances on the waves, not knowing where it'll finally rest.

Chapter Thirty-Two

Two weeks after we're settled back in Canada, the crate arrives that we've shipped from Maui. Dad and I are busy moving into our new house, only three blocks from our old one, with cardboard boxes stacked along walls and furniture movers constantly streaming through the front door.

I take a box cutter to open the crate, sweat beading from my forehead. It's been a very long, tiring day, and having to deal with one more box of items I need to find a place for is not what I want to be doing. Mom called three hours ago to tell us she's in labor, and I received a text twenty minutes ago to let me know that she's on her way to the hospital. I wanted to just get the majority of stuff unpacked so I can enjoy the next few days with my new baby sister. I'll tackle this last crate, this one last box, then I'll go.

I gingerly take out the expensive pieces of art dad has wrapped in bubble wrap and an old blanket. There are also a few pairs of shoes and stuff from my room that I couldn't fit in my suitcase. A large box filled with Dad's office stuff sits in the middle of the crate, and a file folder full of papers rests on top of it. As I slide the box out, the file folder drops onto the hardwood floor and random papers fan out everywhere.

"Dad," I call, "what are all these papers? Where do you want me to put them?"

Dad calls down from his bedroom upstairs. "Oh, that's just the last of the mail we got in Maui. I forwarded the rest to our new address. I just didn't have a chance to go through it all before we left."

I start picking up the papers — a slew of grocery store flyers, fast-food advertisements and island real estate property announcements. Then I finger a thick, white envelope with my name on it. I hadn't received any mail while we were in Maui, so I'm not sure of the contents. I open it gingerly, careful not to tear the stack of papers inside.

Dear Jessica Kennedy,

We are pleased to announce that we have approved your application into the University of Hawaii, Maui College, and look forward to your admittance next September. Please browse the enclosed information and pamphlets. We are sure you will be as excited as we are that you are going to embark on a new adventure on our beautiful campus on the Valley Isle. As we often say in Hawaii, "Be the aloha you wish to see in the world."

We hope that at Maui College we can help you to be the best you can be.

Aloha, and see you soon!

I tuck the papers into my purse with a smile on my face and head off to meet my baby sister for the first time. It looks like I'm going to have to enjoy every moment with her now, as I'll be off again, riding the waves, sooner than I'd expected.

Want to see more from this author? Here's a taster for you to enjoy!

Within the Folds of a Swan's Wing
Jennifer Walker

Excerpt

The whispers are like waves rippling through a mountain stream. They start out at the far side of the room then cascade into a waterfall of stolen glances and hushed tones. Their eyes briefly meet mine, then quickly look away as if caught in a trap. The rumor continues like a string of dominoes that has just been flicked, until it's made its way through the entire class and everyone is left looking straight at me.

Again.

For the zillionth time during my painfully wretched start to high school.

What now? I think to myself. *What could I have possibly done this time to deserve all this glorious attention?*

"Hey, Jodie, what's the target for? You trying to attract a bull with that red splotch? I heard they really like the smell of blood. You really should have remembered your diaper today, girl."

Sean Fedun. Ridiculously handsome Sean Fedun, with his side-swept surfer hair, his fresh, sun-kissed skin that always holds a golden glow, even in the depths of winter... Sean Fedun, who, on top of being handsome, smart and popular, is also the biggest jerk in the school and the bane of my existence.

Of course, it is Sean who notices things first, and he's the one who so callously starts the tidal wave that threatens to further drown me. I hear the gasps and murmurs before I see them, although it isn't until the wave of whispers reaches its crescendo at the other side of the room that I recognize exactly what they're all laughing about.

And that's when I feel it, damp and sticky between my legs. My face immediately flushes bright red as the moment of realization hits.

My.

Worst.

Nightmare.

Ever.

As if I'm not already teetering on the periphery of high school's social order, now my body has failed me in the most brutal way. And I know... Immediately I know and I'm hit with a panic and shock so intense that I lose my breath. I have no reaction, no solution. I know right here and now that this is the one thing — literally *the one thing* — that if it were to happen, would ruin me forever. I am forever ruined. No one will forget this. *Ever.* There is no coverup possible. There is no recovery. Slowly, as if time is suddenly filtered through an impossibly small hourglass, I turn my gaze downward to the red bullseye everyone is pointing at — the one quickly seeping through the crotch of my otherwise-white jeans.

In another reality, it could be Kerri Parker sitting across from me. Sweet Kerri Parker, who would quietly come over to me and whisper in my ear, "Jodie, I think you should excuse yourself and go to the bathroom." I would be able to slink out of the classroom without anyone even realizing I had been there in the first place.

Or it could be Maela Xing. She barely speaks English at all and would sit quietly with my secret for the entire year.

Or it could even be one of the robotics nerds. Most of them are so wrapped up in the games on their cell phones that the entire incident would go unnoticed completely.

But it's not. It's Sean Fedun. And like a zillion times before, Sean Fedun finds a way to ruin me.

It's the week right after spring break, and the entire ninth-grade class has just gathered in the auditorium to hear about the parts for the upcoming freshman spring musical. As usual, Miss Pennefore flits around like a sparrow, sorting out music sheets and audition papers, and is barely aware the class has even come in and settled down. Earlier in the afternoon, she had arranged the choir risers into something of a semicircle so that the stage would hold all one hundred and ninety-six of us a little more easily. Yes, almost two hundred ninth-grade witnesses to what is undoubtedly the most humiliating moment of my life.

Most of the kids are sitting and chatting in small groups, excited about the prospect of being one of the leads in this year's freshman production of *Annie*. As if I care one ounce about being in this play... In fact, I wouldn't be here at all except that it was mandatory. Yep, every single one of us is going to be given a part to try out for, even if we have no interest in the stupid play! An apparent attempt at letting every student feel like a *star*. *Yeah, great idea.* Make us all sing the chorus of *It's a Hard Knock Life* to the rest of the class, only to be humiliated and sent to the back row of the choir anyway. None of these kids even know what a 'hard knock life' means. It's clear by the way they've been belting it out in the hallway all week long, ever since we found out that *Annie* was the musical of choice this year. The fevered smiles plastered on their faces, raising their arms to the sky as they attempt to hold the final note in a fake vibrato...

I'm sorry, but if you actually *do* have a hard knock life, you don't go around singing about it in the middle of a suburban high-school auditorium. No, you'd be sitting in the gutter somewhere wondering why your life is a pile of garbage—which is sort of how I'm feeling now to tell the truth.

But, as it turns out, I'm a rule follower. So, despite my better judgment, I had silently trudged to music class today to get my assigned role, and I'd attempted to shrink into oblivion behind the frizzy shield of my hair. I'd even purposely sat down in the front row, the lowest riser, with the hope that no one would attempt a conversation with me. I shouldn't have worried, because, to be honest, no one typically even notices I'm around—except for today of all days, when we sit facing each other in a stupid semicircle of trust, and Sean Fedun happens to be the person sitting exactly opposite me.

Whoosh...thunk.

I feel it before I see it...the first one, at least. A slight tap on my left shoulder, as if someone is trying to get my attention, then it drops softly at my feet. And before I know it, there are dozens hurling past me, zooming past my face and knocking against my body. Before I recognize exactly what it is that they are throwing at me, another tampon bounces sharply against my chest, resting squarely in my lap. I survey the situation— tampons, pantyliners, maxi-pads and even a used tissue, all being thrown at me, all collecting at my feet like a pile of dead moths, attracted to the bug-zapper in my backyard.

And amid the snickers and belly laughs, I can make out Sean Fedun's cocky voice. "Jodie McGavin… Such a disgusting pig. What a waste of a life."

And I decide I'm not going to take it any longer. I can't. I fumble with my books when I try to stand up, spilling the entire contents of my science binder on the floor. As I reach down to pick everything up, I can't help but bend over with my rear end sticking out into the middle of the semicircle of laughing students, giving them an even better look at the bloodstained splotch than they'd had before. And what's even worse, some of the papers that have strewn all over have landed on the spots of blood I've unwittingly left on the carpeted riser. As I pick them up and try to stack them in order, bright red droplets of blood seep from one to the other, like my own personal seal. The burn in my face grows unimaginable, and it takes every ounce of strength in me not to let my humiliation spill over into a heap of tears. I will not let them see me cry. I will *not* give them that satisfaction.

I hastily grab the last of my belongings and bolt from the room as the class erupts into full-blown hysteria. I can just barely hear Miss Pennefore's shrill attempt at maintaining order as she tries to make out what has just transpired behind her back.

The *incident*.

I know this will remain a black splotch on my memory of high school. And as I run from the laughter and the mocking, all I can envision is the spreading red stain of me that will remain in the room long after I leave.

About the Author

Jennifer Walker is a teacher and writer from Edmonton, Alberta, Canada. She lives with her husband Ian, her two children Everett and Kennedy, and her impossibly sweet Bernedoodle puppy Leo. When she's not teaching, writing, or reading, you can most likely find her in a yoga studio, in the kitchen baking muffins, or running off the calories of the muffins she's just baked. She's famous for publicly embarrassing her family by singing terrible show-tunes and practicing 90's dance moves, and if this whole writing thing doesn't work out, she's pretty sure she could make it as the fifth Wiggle.

Jennifer loves to hear from readers. You can find her contact information, website details and author profile page at https://www.finch-books.com

FINCH
B O O K S

Sign up for our newsletter and find out about all our romance book releases, eBook sales and promotions, sneak peeks and FREE romance books!